CARLA NEGGERS

JUST BEFORE SUNRISE

POCKET BOOKS

New York   London   Toronto   Sydney   Singapore

"I'll tell you the truth. All right? If it'll—"

Garvin pivoted to her, touched a finger to her mouth. "No. Don't. Don't say a word."

His voice was raw from exhaustion, tension. He'd been out on the water all night, most of the day. Thinking, Annie expected. Debating what to do. Remembering. She thought she understood. When she'd bid against him for Sarah Linwood's painting, she'd shattered whatever life he'd fashioned for himself in the past five years, whatever shaky peace with his fate.

She had no idea what he meant to do. Ask her to leave? Fetch a tape recorder to make sure she couldn't take back what she was going to tell him?

Instead he drew his finger along her lower lip. Hundreds, thousands of sensations spilled through her, softening any resistance, overcoming any reserve. Yesterday, tomorrow, suddenly made no difference.

"Annie, Annie."

His voice was just as raw, just as exhausted, but without the edge. He took her face in his hands and kissed her gently, softly, letting his palms skim down her shoulders, down her back. She should be all right, she thought faintly. It wasn't the sort of raging, rough kiss as the other night. There was control behind it. Intention. Really, she should be all right. She wouldn't lose herself.

But she was wrong.

Critical Acclaim for Carla Neggers' Wonderful Romances

A RARE CHANCE

"With each subsequent book, Carla Neggers keeps getting better.... She is now one of the superstars of tomorrow. *A Rare Chance* is...an exciting tale of romantic suspense."

—Harriet Klausner, *Affaire de Coeur*

"Wow! *A Rare Chance* was a dynamite read! A crackerjack story—great characters.... One of those books that keeps you turning the pages. I enjoyed it so much I didn't want it to end."

—Kay Bendall, The Book Rack

"Each page is a treasure chest of romance and intrigue. *A Rare Chance* is a must-read for anyone who enjoys mysteries. Great book."

—Margaret Stilson, Paperback Exchange

"The right blend of love and sex, mystery and mayhem, fun and fright. Light humor and a touch of serious family psychology that feels real."

—Janet Coombs, Annie's Book Stop

"An incredible story. Ms. Neggers has become one of my favorite authors because she delivers a wonderful story line, characters, and lots of suspense."

—Pamela Frango, The Book Rack

FINDING YOU

"*Finding You* is a rare find.... Carla Neggers is one of the most distinctive writers in our genre."

—Debbie Macomber

"Carla Neggers at her warmest, wittiest, and down-home hilarious best.... Ms. Neggers has earned her place in the spotlight alongside such notables as Nora Roberts and Jayne Ann Krentz."

—Harriet Klausner, *Affaire de Coeur*

"*Finding You* showcases the award-winning Ms. Neggers' own unique blend of quirky humor, sizzling romance, and engrossing suspense, which combine to produce irresistibly entertaining novels. Perfect reading for those long winter nights."

—Jill M. Smith, *Romantic Times*

TEMPTING FATE

"If you love good, funny, suspenseful contemporary romance, you have got to read this book. It's in the Jayne Ann Krentz/Nora Roberts mode; well-written, fast-paced, and tightly plotted. It is also funny, very funny, on every level. The dialogue crackles, the characters are priceless...."

—*Heart to Heart*

"Talented author Carla Neggers once again demonstrates her extraordinary skill and mastery of the romantic suspense genre. *Tempting Fate* is chock-full of action, suspense, dark secrets, and dangerous romance. A terrific read."

—*Rave Reviews*

"All the characters are fully developed and individually inspired, the mystery keeps the tension and pace at a high, and the romance between Dani and Zeke is passionate and caring. *Tempting Fate* is multilayered and is a fascinating reading experience."

—*Rendezvous*

Books by Carla Neggers

Published by POCKET BOOKS

CARLA NEGGERS

JUST BEFORE SUNRISE

POCKET BOOKS

New York   London   Toronto   Sydney   Singapore

An *Original* Publication of POCKET BOOKS

POCKET BOOKS, a division of Simon & Schuster, Inc.
1230 Avenue of the Americas, New York, NY 10020

ISBN: 978-1-5011-0436-7

POCKET and colophon are registered trademarks of Simon & Schuster, Inc.

Visit us on the World Wide Web:
http://www.SimonSays.com

To my San Francisco friends,
Neff and Paul Rotter
and Catherine Coulter—
thanks for everything!

Prologue

Annie Payne crossed the square of gravel where her cottage had been and stood on the rocks above the bay, listening to the tide coming in and the November breeze rustling in the hemlock and pine. It was just before sunrise, her favorite time of day, and the eastern horizon had taken on a deep lavender cast. Before long, the spectacular colors of dawn would spill across the sky and glisten on the quiet water. But she would be on her way by then, Annie thought. Out of Maine altogether by noon.

Otto, unaware of their impending departure from the only home either of them had ever known, bounded down onto the rocks. He was a muscular rottweiler, undaunted by Maine's treacherous coastline, but Annie knew he wouldn't get too close to the incoming tide. He hadn't been much interested in water since she'd plucked him from the bay as a puppy, the victim of some-body's sick idea of dealing with an unwanted litter. He was about fifteen weeks old, gangly, friendly, not a rottweiler of stereotype and, therefore, probably not easy to sell. The vet had said it was a miracle he'd survived. Annie chalked it up to his intrepid soul. Three years later, Otto was as big and muscular and fierce-looking as any rottweiler she'd encountered, but he had a gentle, slightly goofy temperament. He seemed to understand how close he'd come to death and took each day as a gift.

Annie was trying to adopt that attitude herself. She'd gotten out of her cottage before the nameless October storm had swept it into the bay five weeks ago. She'd managed to save Otto, two photo albums, the framed picture of her parents on their wedding day, and Gran's painting. Nothing else. No clothes, no furniture, no mementos of her trip to the British Isles or anyplace else. None of her plants. Not a piece of jewelry. All of it went.

"Come on, Otto. We have to go."

He stopped on a boulder and angled his massive head back toward her, his brown eyes soft and confused. Annie felt the tears brimming. She'd promised herself she wouldn't cry. She had no real family left in Maine since Gran had died a year ago. Her job as the director of a small maritime museum had long since failed to engage her. Her friends would stay her friends, no matter where she lived. With her cottage gone, there was nothing to keep her on her little Maine peninsula, nothing to keep her anywhere.

Turning away from the bay, she walked over to the gravel driveway where she'd parked her rusting station wagon. It was packed with her few surviving treasures and the clothes and essentials her friends had given her in a post-storm party. She'd left just enough room for Otto. Her friends weren't worried about the two of them heading cross-country together. One, Otto was a deterrent to anyone who might have ideas about her or her meager possessions. Two, most figured she'd turn back before she hit the Mississippi. A few thought pure stubbornness would propel her all the way to San Francisco and a taste of life there, but when reality caught up with fantasy, she'd head back home. They gave her three months, tops.

Annie squinted back at the water. "Otto. Come, boy."

He stood atop a massive granite boulder and watched her with the lavender sky at his back. She wondered if he sensed her ambivalence. San Francisco and an unknown life lay ahead. She had plans, dreams. Maybe they'd work out, maybe they wouldn't. Maybe she was being a little crazy and impulsive. She'd banked her insurance settlement instead of rebuilding, and ten days ago she'd found a buyer for her coveted property with its picturesque views and privacy. She had enough money for her new life. But she wasn't sure about anything except that her father had died when she was a baby, her mother when she was sixteen, and now Gran was dead and her cottage was gone—and if she didn't do something, maybe she'd be next. She'd latched onto the idea of San Francisco and opening her own gallery, starting over, and now she was going.

She opened the back liftgate, hoping that would coax Otto up off the rocks. He loved to ride. But if Otto didn't want to do something, she couldn't force him. He weighed five pounds more than she did.

"Come on, buddy. This'll be an adventure. You and me driving west. Over hill and dale, from sea to shining sea, amber waves of grain, purple mountains. We'll see it all."

Otto plopped down on his rock, tongue wagging. He loved autumn in New England, even chilly November mornings with fallen leaves coloring the ground gold and rust and the taste of winter in the air. Annie frowned, trying to push back any doubts. What if he didn't like California? What if, on some instinctive dog level, Otto already knew this entire adventure of hers was lunacy?

But she had made up her mind. "You'll love San Francisco, Otto. You'll see." The wind was coming in off the water now, catching the ends of her hair, biting into her cheeks. She shivered in her fleece jacket. "Otto. Come."

Otto stayed where he was.

Deliberately leaving her driver's door open, Annie climbed behind the wheel and started the engine. "Fine. I'll go without you."

She wouldn't, of course. She *couldn't.* But the threat was enough to get her recalcitrant dog moving. Brow furrowed, he bounded over to the car and jumped in back, where he just fit amidst the boxes and Gran's crated painting of the cottage on a bright summer morning, window boxes overflowing with pink petunias. Some would dismiss it as tourist art, sentimental and nostalgic. Yet somehow it captured everything that Annie's life in her cottage by the bay had been.

Before Otto could change his mind, she quickly jumped out and shut the liftgate.

Before she could change hers, she backed out of her driveway without even a parting glance at the bay and the picturesque spot where she had lived her whole life. Here today, gone tomorrow. She'd learned the hard way that was what life was.

It was a lesson she was determined never to forget.

Chapter One

Circumstances compelled Annie to take Otto with her to her first big San Francisco auction almost three months after rolling into town. She would have left him at her gallery, up and running for six weeks now, but the woman she'd hired to cover for her today was afraid of any and all rottweilers. She would have left him at her apartment, but her landlord, who didn't have "rottweiler" in mind when he'd agreed to let Annie have a dog, was coming over to fix what passed for heat in San Francisco, and he was still afraid of Otto.

Back in Maine, no one was afraid of Otto. The whole town knew he was a big galoot.

Annie parked in the shade on the wide, picturesque Pacific Heights street and left the windows of her station wagon cracked and Otto sprawled in back. She'd let down the backseat not for his sake but because of the auction. She had one item to buy, and she meant to buy it.

"I'll be back as soon as I can," she told Otto, as if he understood.

It was a dreary day even by San Francisco dreary-day standards. Low clouds, intermittent drizzle, lapping fog, temperature in the upper fifties. Since arriving in the Bay Area, Annie had developed an impressive collection of cheap umbrellas and always kept several in her car and one tucked in the tapestry tote she carried everywhere. She estimated she'd lost at least a half dozen since Thanksgiving. It wasn't that it rained all that much in San Francisco, she'd decided, but that it didn't snow. So it seemed that it rained more than in Maine. She had tried to explain this deduction to Zoe Summer, who ran the aromatherapy shop next to Annie's Gallery, but Zoe, a native of Seattle, said Annie didn't know rain.

She felt a rare tug of trepidation as she approached the imposing, ornate Linwood house, an elaborate Victorian mansion in lemon yellow. It was one of the most famous in San Francisco. Lush green grass carpeted a regal front yard, and beautifully maintained shrubs softened tall, elegantly draped windows that were so spotless they sparkled even in the gloom. The Linwoods were up there with the Vanderbilts, Rockefellers, and Hearsts, not the usual sort Annie was used to hanging out with on her Maine peninsula.

A uniformed guard was posted at the end of the brick walk that led to the front entrance. Annie handed him her ticket to the private auction. She had attended a few of Ernie's Saturday night auctions on the Hathaway farm, inland up toward the lakes. She had once almost talked Gran into letting her buy a lamb.

A different time, a different life.

The guard scrutinized her ticket first, then her. She told herself he probably did that to everybody, not just her. She couldn't look that different from the dealers and collectors at the auction. Although her wardrobe was still limited, she had on a perfectly respectable outfit: a silk sweater over a calf-length skirt in a dusky blue, with silver earrings and her good black leather ankle boots. She'd pulled her hair up into a passable twist and, given the uncertain weather, had brought along Gran's Portuguese shawl, which had spent the nameless, devastating storm at her office at the museum. It was black wool with bright crewel embroidered flowers and exotic birds, and Annie suspected it really was a piano cover rather than a shawl. But it was beautiful and rather Victorian-looking, perfect, she thought, for her first San Francisco auction.

"Use the front entrance, Ms. Payne. A guard will direct you to the ballroom."

The guard handed her back her ticket in a way that made Annie wonder if she had dog slobber on her sweater. Or maybe she was just a tad paranoid because of the strange circumstances that had brought her here today.

With a hasty parting smile, she proceeded up the walk. The cool, rainy winter weather brought out the scent of flowers and grass and earth and reminded her of early spring mornings in Maine. It was the dead of winter there now. She sucked in a quick breath at the sudden stab of nostalgia, the unbidden image of her and Gran watching the fog swirling over the bay from their old wooden Adirondack chairs on the cottage porch. She tucked a drifting strand of hair back into its pin, steadying herself. She was in San Francisco at an auction that would require her to keep her wits about her. She wouldn't—she *couldn't*—indulge in daydreaming about a life that was no more. She planned to enjoy herself even as she completed her rather peculiar mission on Pacific Heights.

"I have to have that painting," the woman whom Annie knew only as Sarah had told her.

After checking with the second guard at the front door, she ventured down the center hall of the cool, beautiful mansion, peeking into elegant rooms that were blocked off to the public with velvet ropes, absorbing every detail of architecture, design, and decor. Although the house had been unoccupied for several years, it was gleaming, spotless, without a single sign of neglect or disrepair. The Linwoods had put it up for sale. Hence, the auction of much of its contents. From what Annie gathered, necessity—banks, debts, the IRS—hadn't played a role in the decision to sell. But she really hadn't done much investigating. She was too busy with her gallery and settling into her new life—and even with her odd mission, there was no need for details. Her role at the auction was simple and clear, and, she had to admit, had an intriguing element of excitement and mystery. She had never represented an anonymous buyer at an auction.

A smartly dressed woman behind a table at the ballroom entrance checked Annie's identification and took a letter from her bank as assurance that any check she wrote wouldn't bounce. It was all brisk, formal, and routine, but Annie noticed that her palms had gone clammy. Wishing to remain completely anonymous, Sarah had deposited ten thousand dollars into Annie's checking account on Thursday morning. It was all perfectly legal, just unusual. What was to keep Annie from ducking the auction and blowing the money herself? But Sarah seemed to trust her.

The woman at the table presented Annie with a white card with the number 112 in large, legible, black print. Suppressing a twinge of nervousness, Annie managed a quick smile before proceeding into the ornate ballroom. Scores of buyers were settling into rows of mundane folding chairs set up against a backdrop of glittering crystal chandeliers, lavish murals of pre-1906 San Francisco and breathtaking views of the bay. Annie found a vacant chair well into a middle row and sat down, tucking her tapestry bag at her feet, suddenly feeling ridiculously tense.

What if someone else bid on the painting? What if she didn't get it?

The rest of the chairs soon filled up, an announcement was made that the proceeds from the auction would go to the Haley Linwood Foundation, and, finally, things got under way. The auctioneer was thin, white-haired and regal, a far cry, Annie thought, from Ernie Hathaway.

The first items went fast, with only token competition. There was no yelling, no complaining, no hooting. This was San Francisco. This was Pacific Heights. Even Gran, a pragmatic woman who didn't stand on ceremony, had considered Ernie's auctions a spectacle.

After forty minutes, the painting came up. Annie held her breath as it was brought out and set on an easel, then gasped in shock the moment it was uncovered. The buyers seated near her glanced at her in surprise. She tried to control herself. She was totally unprepared for this one: the painting was Sarah's work. There was no question.

Clutching her shawl in her lap, Annie forced herself not to speculate on how a painting by a reclusive, eccentric artist had ended up in a Linwood auction.

She'd first met Sarah last week when she'd made a brief, uneventful visit to Annie's Gallery. She was an eccentric woman with lank, graying hair, plain features, and a wardrobe of thrift-store clothes. A debilitating condition necessitated the use of a cane. She hadn't bought anything or asked any questions, and Annie only remembered her because of her unusual appearance— and because she didn't have that many customers. Then, two days later, Sarah called and invited Annie to tea.

With nothing better to do, Annie had accepted, venturing up to Sarah's tiny house on a hill overlooking the city. The strange woman was again dressed in thrift-store clothes but was using a walker to get around instead of her cane. Annie might have dismissed her as a lunatic and politely excused herself but for the canvases haphazardly stacked throughout Sarah's small house.

With a grandmother artist, artist friends, and her own experience setting up art displays at the maritime museum where she'd served as director, Annie had developed an eye for art. She'd learned to recognize the real thing when she saw it. And that was what Sarah's canvases were, without doubt: the real thing.

In her excitement over her discovery of an amazing new artistic talent, Annie had perhaps acted in haste in agreeing to represent Sarah at today's auction. She hadn't pressed for any details of who Sarah was or why she wanted the painting or why she just didn't go buy it herself. All that, Annie had thought, could come later.

Now she had her first hint of why Sarah wanted this particular painting. It was her work, undoubtedly an early piece. The technique was awkward in places, unsure of itself, lacking the boldness and confidence of the canvases Annie had seen over tea. But the essential ingredients of what made the reclusive, eccentric woman in mismatched socks and tattered Keds such a compelling artist were there.

The subject was a red-haired girl of fifteen or sixteen with pale ivory skin and warm blue eyes. She wore just a denim shirt and jeans, her long hair pulled back, her casual manner in contrast to the formal, traditional sitting room background. Even in this early work, Annie could see Sarah's hand in the unabashed nostalgic mood of the painting, its subtle use of color, its determination to capture the spirit of its subject and get at who she was, what she wanted to become.

Sarah, Annie thought, could have dispatched her to buy the portrait in an effort to get any strays back under her control before going public with her art. It would be a smart move. But Annie tried not to get ahead of herself in case she was wrong, and this brilliant, unknown artist had no intention of letting Annie's Gallery represent her work.

The auctioneer announced he had a sealed bid for five hundred dollars. Did anyone want to bid higher? His tone suggested he expected no one would.

Jerked out of her stupor, Annie jumped forward in her seat. A sealed bid? From whom? Someone else was bidding on the painting? She whipped around, searching for the culprit. The serious buyers, she'd already figured out, stood at the edges of the ballroom and slipped to the back when something came up that interested them. But she hadn't expected any competition.

Did someone else know about Sarah? To Annie's eye, her talent was apparent in the portrait up on the easel, but it was only a spark, a hint of the explosive work the artist might eventually produce.

"Five hundred. Do I have a bid for five hundred and fifty?"

Annie thrust her hand high up into the air. She didn't care if that wasn't how the professional buyers did it. She wanted to make sure the auctioneer saw her.

"Five hundred and fifty," he said in acknowledgment of her bid. "Do I have six hundred?"

In a half second, he said he did. Annie still had no idea who in the crowd was bidding against her. She raised her hand for six fifty. Sarah had anticipated that Annie would be the only bidder and would get the painting for a few hundred dollars, but, unwilling to chance missing this opportunity, she'd insisted on making the ten thousand dollars available. Annie had dismissed the gesture as overly dramatic.

It was a long way from six hundred fifty to ten thousand, she thought, calming herself. She wouldn't run out of money. She wouldn't fail. "Bid the entire ten thousand if you must. I don't care," Sarah, the mysterious artist, had told her. Annie desperately wanted to succeed, more so than she would willingly admit. Sarah's work was so incredible—Annie knew it was—that it could be the catalyst she needed for her struggling new life.

The auctioneer looked at her. The bidding was up to eight hundred. Annie pulled her lower lip in between her teeth and nodded.

A murmur of excitement ran through the crowd. Even the bland auctioneer seemed to get his blood up. Annie followed his gaze to the back of the ballroom as he asked for nine hundred.

Before she could pick out who he was looking at, he said he had nine hundred and turned his attention back to her. He asked for a thousand. He was going up by hundreds now. Annie hadn't noticed any of the fifteen or twenty well-dressed men and women standing in back make a move. She could feel her stomach churning. Relax, it's not your money. They wouldn't go higher than ten thousand. That would be lunacy. The artist was an unknown, the girl was an unknown. There was no *point*. Later, when Sarah was introduced to the art world and acknowledged as a major new talent, maybe there would be. But not now.

Annie nodded at the auctioneer.

Her opponent immediately went up to eleven hundred.

She whipped around and glared, and her eyes made contact with a man in a dark suit. And she knew. This was her opponent. This was the man who wanted the painting of the red-haired girl.

Her mouth went dry. His eyes bored into her. Annie inhaled sharply, certain she wasn't sparring with a dealer. There was nothing sporting about his expression, nothing of the dealer who took competition and defeat in stride. He wanted the painting, and he had expected to get it for five hundred dollars.

He hadn't, it seemed, expected Annie Payne.

The auctioneer called for twelve hundred. With her gaze still pinned on her opponent, Annie nodded. She wasn't going to back down. She wasn't going to let him unnerve her. She didn't care who he was or why he wanted the painting.

His expression remained grim and determined, giving no indication he was having any fun at all. He had angular, riveting features and very dark hair, but for some reason she couldn't even imagine, Annie guessed his eyes were lighter: gray or green or even blue. She tried to picture him somewhere besides a tense auction room. Where might he smile? Where might he not look so humorless and intense? Roaming the Marin hills, perhaps. Rock climbing. Horseback riding across a meadow. Anywhere, possibly, but a Pacific Heights auction.

He wasn't here for the thrill of an auction, she thought with a sinking feeling.

He was here for the painting.

Annie turned back around and concentrated on her task. Would he let the bidding go over ten thousand?

In another two minutes, it was up to three thousand. Perspiration trickled down the small of her back. She had her shawl clutched tightly in her hands. She was shaking. She resisted the impulse to spin around in her seat and have another look at her opponent. She didn't want him thinking she was desperate, intimidated, terrified that he would outbid her. She couldn't afford to goad him.

She had to win.

An old woman three rows in front turned around and frowned at her. Let the man have the painting, girlie, her expression said. Who do you think you are?

But Annie bid thirty-one hundred. And her dark-haired, dark-suited opponent bid thirty-two, and she could hear the murmurs of sympathy for him even as she bid thirty-three.

Then he went to four. Annie didn't know how he did it. He hadn't uttered a sound. She whipped around.

His eyes were already on her. Steady, confident. Daring her.

Biting on one corner of her mouth, Annie noticed that everyone else's eyes were on her, too. The auctioneer waited for her response. She put up all five fingers, hoping he would understand her bid.

He did. "The bid is at five thousand."

She thought she heard somebody mutter, "Who is she? Why doesn't she let him have it? Doesn't she know who he is?"

No, she didn't. And what difference did it make who he was? She had as much right to that painting as anyone else in the room. More, perhaps, since she was representing the artist who'd painted it.

Her heart pounding, she waited for him to answer her bid. Five thousand was a ridiculous amount to pay for such a painting. People would think she was crazy—until they saw Sarah's subsequent work. Then they would know and understand.

If she had to use Sarah's entire ten thousand, Annie thought, she would.

But the man in the dark suit passed. Stunned, Annie glanced back at him. He gave her a mock salute with one finger and retreated through double doors into an adjoining room that she was quite sure was one of the ones blocked off to the public.

The painting was hers.

"Well," the old woman a few rows up snapped, "I hope she's happy."

She is, Annie thought, her relief making her feel limp and a little like crying. She's very happy.

Now that the thrill of the battle was over, she became acutely aware of a current of hostility directed at her. It wasn't just that people had sympathized with her opponent, they were *annoyed* with her for outbidding him. And it wasn't just a few people. No wonder Sarah hadn't wanted to come to the auction herself.

Nice, Annie thought. Maybe I can get out of here before anybody finds out who I am.

She pulled her tapestry bag onto her lap, prepared to make a run for it in case someone tried to drag her off to the lions. Why wasn't she garnering any sympathy? She wasn't some tall, rich guy standing in the back of the room. She hadn't tried to burn holes through him with her eyes. What happened to rooting for the underdog?

Mercifully, the runners brought out a magnificent set of rare Austrian china. The auction resumed. Annie got to her feet. She felt jittery and self-conscious, her hands and knees trembling. Excusing herself to each person whose feet she had to climb over, she stumbled back out to the aisle.

A portly middle-aged man on the end said, "You must have wanted that painting very much to go up against Garvin MacCrae."

"Who's Garvin MacCrae?"

"You don't know? I wondered. He's the husband of the girl in the painting."

"*What?*"

But he was trying to see around her, and someone in back hissed for her to move out of the way, and so she did, tightening her grip on her bag and shawl to keep her hands from shaking visibly. She burst out into the aisle.

Her opponent was the husband of the girl in the painting. Well, how was she supposed to have known? Probably he'd intended to buy it for an anniversary or a birthday present. *Here, honey. Remember that crazy woman who painted you when you were sixteen?* Was his wife a Linwood? How had she known lank-haired, odd Sarah? How had Sarah come to paint her as a teenager?

It doesn't matter, Annie told herself. You have the painting. It's yours to return to the woman who had painted it. Garvin MacCrae will just have to find something else to give his wife.

Garvin MacCrae unhitched the thick velvet rope that blocked off the drawing room and stepped into the center hall. Several people taking a break from the auction gave him pained, sympathetic looks. They would know who he was. It seemed everyone at the auction did. The experience had been far more of an ordeal than he'd expected.

He hadn't anticipated Number 112.

She had put up a determined battle, and she'd won, if only because Garvin had no interest in driving up the bidding even further, never mind that the money would go to the foundation he'd established in his wife's memory. He had expected to get the portrait of Haley for the five hundred he'd bid in advance and in secrecy. He had expected to remain anonymous, hidden amidst the professionals in the back of the packed ballroom.

He could have asked John or Cynthia Linwood simply to give him the painting, but he hadn't. He was part of the Linwood past not its future. Whoever had murdered his wife five years ago had seen to that.

He saw John Linwood coming up the hall and knew there was no way to avoid him. "Garvin—my heavens, I had no idea you would be here today. It's so good to see you."

In spite of his friendly words, John looked tense and awkward. Garvin understood. His former father-in-law had a smart, attractive new wife and was shedding himself of all reminders of his murdered daughter and father. Garvin was one of those reminders.

"It's good to see you, too, John." They shook hands, but Garvin couldn't bring himself to smile. It had been a difficult morning, more so than he'd expected. He wasn't in a light mood.

"I'm sorry about the painting—"

"It's all right. Forget it."

"I had no idea you'd want it. I can't—well, I can hardly bear to look at it."

Garvin nodded. He couldn't explain why he'd wanted it himself. There were so many tragic memories associated with it. It had hung in the Linwood library, where Haley and her grandfather were murdered five years ago on two separate nights. And it had been painted by Sarah Linwood, Haley's aunt, John's sister and the woman many believed had contributed to the murders of her own niece and father—or even actually pulled the trigger.

But something about Sarah's portrait of Haley at sixteen had captured her spirit, her soul, and gave Garvin solace that the woman he'd lost to the violent hand of another wasn't going through eternity with bitterness or regret. He couldn't explain what it was. Had Number 112 seen it too?

"I thought it had been destroyed," John went on. "I had it taken down, but I couldn't—well, I couldn't burn it myself. I guess no one else could, either."

"So you decided to sell it?"

"Actually, that was Cynthia's decision." John had lost his wife four years before the murders and had finally decided to remarry a year ago; Garvin hadn't attended his wedding. Cynthia was seventeen years her husband's junior and had operated in the upper echelons of Bay Area real estate, hovering in the background of the Linwood family for years. Now she was a part of it. "She arranged the entire auction. I didn't know until this morning. I might have done things differently had I known—which is probably why she didn't tell me." He attempted a smile, but gave up on it. "But I know she did what she thought was best for all of us. Perhaps it's just as well a stranger has the painting now."

"Perhaps," Garvin said, telling himself he believed it. What would he have done with the portrait anyway? Once he'd heard it was for sale, he'd only known he'd wanted it. The last gasp of his old life, he supposed.

John clapped his hands together, as if dismissing any insidious sense of melancholy. "We've a buyer for the house. Did you hear? A couple from Chicago. Cynthia found them." He glanced around the elegant entry of his longtime family home. "It'll be good to have people living here again."

Garvin swallowed, tried not to remember the terrible night he'd found his wife lying dead just down the hall. "Yes."

John seemed to sense what he was thinking. His face clouded, and he gave up on any semblance of normality. "I didn't expect today to be as difficult as it has been. The memories—well, I suppose this day is long overdue. I'll just be glad when it's over."

"I understand. I certainly didn't mean to make it any harder on you."

"You haven't. Well, Garvin, I hope we'll see each other again soon."

"I hope so, too."

John Linwood withdrew into an adjoining room, and Garvin sighed heavily, cursing himself for having come today. Neither he nor his father-in-law, he noted, had mentioned the name of the artist. Sarah Linwood's family and friends hadn't heard from her since the murders. Five years. Now no one knew if she was alive or dead.

Instead of heading directly out as he'd intended, Garvin abruptly about-faced and made his way down the hall to the table at the entrance to the ballroom. The woman who kept track of the buyers and what items they bought regarded him with sympathy. "I'm sorry things didn't go your way, Mr. MacCrae. A lot of people were rooting for you."

"Thanks. Who's the lady who beat me out?"

"I'm not supposed to say—"

"It's okay. I don't want to put you on the spot." In spite of his tensed jaw, Garvin produced a smile. "If you speak to her, tell her I hope she enjoys the painting."

The woman chewed on one corner of her mouth and glanced into the ballroom. More frenzied bidding was going on. Garvin paid no attention. A runner—a panting college kid—burst up to the table with the tag from a sold item. It would be matched to the number of the buyer, in order to bring item, buyer, and money together at the right time.

As she took the tag, the woman subtly tilted her clipboard toward Garvin. He scanned down to Number 112.

His opponent's name was Annie Payne of Annie's Gallery on Union Street.

A dealer.

Garvin gritted his teeth. A damned dealer! She'd paid five thousand dollars for a painting by an unknown, a painting that, as far as he could see, wasn't worth even the five hundred he'd meant to pay for it. Given the painful memories associated with it, even Haley's family didn't want it.

Maybe Annie Payne was compulsive about bidding and had gotten in way, way over her head when he'd bid against her, ending up with a painting she didn't really want at such a price. Once the adrenaline rush passed and she realized what she'd done, she might have regrets.

Of course, Annie Payne could also be scamming him. She could have known who he was and planned to sell the painting back to him for a tidy profit, assuming he'd play her game her way, which was a hell of an assumption.

Maybe she had another buyer already in mind?

Who?

Garvin swore to himself. It was just a painting. Never mind that Sarah, for all her recklessness and self-absorption, had captured the very essence of Haley's nature. His wife was gone, and Garvin had slowly come to accept life without her, even if he couldn't forgive himself for not loving her enough to have saved her. If only she'd come to him with whatever she'd learned about Sarah's finances, her gambling debts—whatever it was that had compelled her to go back to the Linwood house that night. But she hadn't. And she'd died.

He slipped out the front door, relieved to have the Linwood house at his back. It had been madness to come today. He should have known it wouldn't end up as he'd planned. At the very least, he should have known there'd be no avoiding the past he had worked so desperately to put behind him, if not forget.

He trotted down the steps and out to the street, barely aware that the rain had stopped for the moment. The sky was still gray, the air damp and chilly. Halfway down the block, he recognized Annie Payne wrestling with her new purchase at the rear of a small, rusting station wagon.

He slowed his pace, studying her. She didn't look like a crafty dealer who'd deliberately outsmarted and outmaneuvered him. Most of her blond hair had come loose from its pins and sticks, dropping down her forehead and temples in pale wisps. A brightly embroidered shawl hung off one arm, its fringe tickling the street. One wrong step and she'd trip over it. Garvin felt his curiosity piqued by her. Why on earth had she paid such an exorbitant amount for Sarah Linwood's painting of her niece?

"Otto," Annie Payne said firmly, apparently unaware of Garvin's presence, "you have to move. Now, I warned you I'd have a painting when I got back. So there's no excuse for being stubborn." She glared into the back of her car. "Otto, I mean it. *Move.*"

Glancing into the station wagon, Garvin was surprised to find an enormous rottweiler sprawled in back. Otto, presumably. His massive head was twisted around at her, his big brown eyes studying her without apparent concern or intention of doing as she said.

No, indeed. Annie Payne wasn't what he'd expected at all.

"Otto. You're not keeping your end of the deal."

As if she'd had every expectation that he would. Up close, Garvin noticed she was slender and fit and probably weighed less than her dog. He said, "I see you have a problem."

"Yes, Otto's being stubborn." She looked around at him as she spoke, then took a quick breath, obviously taken aback. "You're the man from the auction."

The man from the auction? Then she didn't know who he was. Or was adept at pretending not to. "Yes," he said. "My name's Garvin MacCrae."

She didn't blush or go pale; she simply pushed a strand of hair from her eyes. "Hi—Annie Payne. I hope there are no hard feelings."

He smiled a little. "Not many."

She smiled back, a glint coming into her eyes. They were pale blue, almost gray. "I thought the crowd was going to eat me alive there for a minute. Someone mentioned the girl in the painting's your wife. I hope she won't be too disappointed. Was it going to be a present?"

Garvin's throat tightened, and he managed to shake his head. A present for Haley. Annie Payne didn't know his wife was dead.

Who the hell *was* she?

She frowned, a touch of color appearing high in her cheeks. "I can see you're still upset. I'm sorry. It was nothing personal. To be honest, I didn't expect anyone else to bid."

"Neither did I." His voice was less strangled than he'd expected.

"That's an auction for you. I'm not much on auctions myself. When I want something, I just like to pay my money and take it home. I don't like this win-lose stuff."

So much for his compulsive auction-goer theory. Annie Payne turned her attention back to her dog, running one hand through her hair in frustration. She caught an ebony hair stick and dragged it out, shoving it into the depths of some skirt pocket. Her movements were unselfconscious, without any indication that she knew he was watching her as closely as he was. He hadn't expected to find the woman who'd beaten him out to be so matter-of-fact, so guileless—so attractive. He noticed the soft rise of her breasts, the slim curve of her hips, the creamy skin at her throat.

Not good, he thought.

She gave an exaggerated sigh. "I might not get the painting home if this dog doesn't move. He has to be the stupidest animal in the entire universe." She leaned forward, hands on hips. "Otto. Otto, I said move."

Otto didn't move.

"I thought rottweilers were smart," Garvin said.

"Not Otto. I think he fell on the rocks one too many times as a puppy."

Without warning, she balanced the painting against the bumper and climbed up into the back after Otto. Garvin grabbed her shawl just before it hit the wet pavement. Annie Payne seemed oblivious to anything but getting her dog to move. She went in on her hands and knees, leaving Garvin with a view of her shapely behind.

Grumbling and cursing, she pushed the huge dog's paws in an apparent attempt to get him to flop over onto his other side. He didn't budge, just kept staring at her with those enormous brown eyes.

"I'm taking you to dog obedience school," she warned him.

Otto seemed unimpressed. He opened his mouth—one designed for crushing—and yawned, frothy white slobber creeping over his jowls.

"There'll be no treat for you tonight, bub, if you don't move."

Garvin wondered what a dog as big as Otto would consider a treat. He folded the large, beautiful, but rather unusual, shawl. It, too, didn't fit his mental image of an ultrasophisticated, wily gallery owner.

Annie Payne, it seemed, had her own way of doing things.

Her tone changed as she tried cajoling, talking to her dog as if he were a recalcitrant toddler. "Roll over, Otto. Come on, buddy. Yes, roll over. Otto." Her tone sharpened, her patience unquestionably exhausted. "Otto. *Roll over.*"

Otto ignored her.

She backed out, ducking her head to keep from banging it on the liftgate as she dropped back onto the pavement. Garvin handed her the shawl. She sighed, defeated. "He's paying me back for not taking him to the auction. I'll just have to wait him out." She squinted up at the gray sky. "I hope the rain holds off."

"What if you let him out of the car instead of trying to get him to shift position? Then you could slide the painting in and let him in again."

She shook her head. "He's not moving."

"Isn't it worth a shot?"

"I suppose." But she clearly didn't think anything would work. She turned back to her dog, patting her hip with one hand in an attempt to coax him. "Come on, Otto. Want to go for a walk? Here, boy. Come."

The big dog blinked at her, then stretched out his long legs, if possible taking up even more of the back of the little station wagon.

Annie Payne regarded Garvin without surprise. "You see? He's stubborn *and* stupid."

In spite of her disgust, Garvin had no doubt of her affection for her rottweiler and knew better than to agree with her assessment. This, he thought, was not his fight. She'd bought herself a painting for five thousand dollars. She could get it home on her own. "Well, I hope things work out."

"Oh, they will. Otto knows sooner or later I always get my way."

She smiled, a dimple appearing in her left cheek, giving her expression an irreverent, sexy touch that suggested that maybe Annie Payne wasn't as innocent as she looked. Garvin found himself intrigued and just a little suspicious. Given his experience with her so far, he wouldn't be surprised if she did always get her way.

She certainly had today.

"Good luck," he told her. "By the way, if you decide you don't want the painting after all, give me a call. I'm over in Marin. My number's in the book."

"All right. I'll do that. But don't get your hopes up. I doubt I'll change my mind."

Garvin narrowed his eyes on her, unable to dismiss the sudden impression that Annie Payne was hiding something. He thought he saw her squirm, just for the flash of a second, under his scrutiny. Definitely, he decided, she was hiding something.

But he needed to regroup, rethink his strategy, before pouncing on her.

The sexual connotation of the image hit him hard, shot urges through him that had nothing to do with paintings or suspicions. He could feel his throat tighten, his body tense. Well, what the hell did he expect? An undertone of sex was the raw, inevitable result of their sparring in the auction room.

He wondered how shocked Annie Payne would be if she knew what he was thinking. Even if he wouldn't act on such an impulse under the circumstances, the thought of going to bed with her seemed perfectly natural.

Also bloody dumb, he added silently.

"Enjoy the painting, then," he said, his throat still tight.

She smiled brightly, oblivious to his tortured state. "I will. Oh, and give my best to your wife. I'm sure you'll find another present for her."

That brought him spinning back to reality. But he'd turned away from her and thus was spared from answering, from having to explain that his wife was dead.

"Hell," he breathed, and kept walking.

Ten paces up the sidewalk, he heard Annie Payne laugh in unbridled delight. Garvin glanced back. Otto had decided to move. Seizing the moment, his master shoved the painting in back, shut the liftgate, and skipped up to the driver's seat with her shawl over her head as the heavens opened up.

Ignoring the downpour, Garvin stood on the sidewalk and watched her old station wagon cough and choke out onto the street.

The woman didn't even have a decent car. How could she have afforded to pay five thousand dollars for a painting he doubted was worth even five hundred?

It was a question, he knew, that needed an answer.

Chapter Two

Annie drove across Divisadero to upper Market Street and found her way to the tangle of streets where the reclusive painter she knew only as Sarah lived. She grabbed a parking space on a narrow street below the little hilltop bungalow. To get to it, she had to take a set of stone stairs that ran up the steep hill between two pale-colored stucco houses. She was still getting used to how San Francisco, built on forty-odd hills between ocean and bay and crunched for space, piled houses on top of each other and tucked them into every possible nook and cranny.

Having become adept at parallel parking in her three months in the city, Annie got her car into the small space on the first try. She laid down the law to Otto and, taking no chances with Sarah's painting in back, locked all her doors. She didn't bother with her shawl or an umbrella. The rain had stopped, and the sun seemed to want to come out. It might decide yes; it might decide no. She'd given up trying to predict San Francisco weather.

She took the stone stairs two at a time, arriving at a little cul-de-sac—a turnaround, really—with several small houses built around it. A street curved sharply, and almost vertically, down the other side of the hill, but Annie hadn't quite figured out how to get to it from the bottom. Even her map of San Francisco hadn't really helped. Back in her part of Maine, there wasn't a road she didn't know.

Perched on the edge of the hill, Sarah's pale pink clapboard bungalow would have been a mundane house but for its sweeping views of the city and the bay, stretching not quite from the Golden Gate Bridge east to the Oakland Bay Bridge. Even now, her heart still pounding from the Linwood auction and her encounter with Garvin MacCrae, Annie took a moment to appreciate the picturesque San Francisco skyline, the tufts of fog clinging to dips and valleys, the impressive expanse of the Bay Bridge, the bay gleaming in the distance. Nothing, she thought, seemed to detract from the beauty of her adopted city.

The little house had no yard, not even a scrap of grass, nor was there a front porch or front steps. Only a sloping square of concrete marked the entrance. Pots of hydrangea on either side of the white-painted front door would be a nice touch, Annie thought. Gran had always hated a bare entrance. Anyone, she'd maintained, could manage to grow something with a packet of seeds and a few cheap pots of dirt.

But Gran had never met Sarah. Not only was she possibly incapable of such endeavors, she seemed thoroughly disinterested in her surroundings.

Annie rapped on the front door. "Sarah? It's me, Annie Payne."

"Door's open."

Given the dampness, the door stuck. Annie had to push on it with her shoulder.

She found Sarah sitting in her rattan chair to the right of the front door, from which she could take in the impressive views of the city and still see who came into her house. How, Annie wondered again, had this woman ended up painting such an intimate portrait of a Linwood? With her fair skin and horsey jaw, her faint eyelashes and eyebrows, she had none of the wealth and sophistication of the Linwoods. Her reddish, softly curling hair was erratically chopped, probably by her own hand, and going gray ungracefully. But her eyes were a vivid, penetrating blue, her best, and most revealing, feature.

She studied Annie without moving from her chair. Today she wore navy stretch pants and an oversize white polyester pullover with a fuzzy, bright yellow sunflower stamped on the front. She was a tall woman, at least five ten, but whatever condition she suffered from had left her stooped and gnarled. Despite her swollen, twisted joints, she continued to work, which Annie found nothing short of amazing. Her bungalow seemed as suited to her lifestyle as her functional attire. It was set up less for living than for working. Every available space—shelves, counters, cupboards, walls —in both the kitchen to the left of the front door and the living room to the right was crammed with canvases, paints, brushes, supplies, paper, drawings, books. Yet Annie detected nothing deliberate or affected about how Sarah lived. She wasn't playing to anyone's idea of who she was or how she should live but her own.

"Did you get the painting?" she asked without preamble.

Annie nodded. "I had to pay more than I thought I would."

"Over ten thousand?"

"No. Five on the nose."

"Then there's not a problem. Where is it?"

"Down in my car. I thought I should make sure you were here before I brought it up."

"Where else would I be? Go get it, please." Her thin mouth twitched into the self-deprecating smile of a woman who had no illusions about who she was. "I'll wait right here."

Annie retreated and raced down the stone steps back down to the street, her pulse racing. Her first two visits to the pink cottage, peculiar as they were, hadn't given her a false reading of the reclusive artist's talent. Even one quick glance at Sarah's work had reassured her that she was right. Here was a stunning artistic discovery.

Otto gave her no trouble when she removed the painting. Indeed, he seemed glad to be rid of it and immediately reclaimed the entire back of the station wagon. "Behave," Annie warned him, and started back up the steps. She was slightly winded from excitement and exertion. The painting, at least, wasn't heavy, just awkward. She wondered if the girl who'd sat for Sarah had framed it herself, if she'd ever even owned it herself. *Would* she be disappointed now, as an adult, when her husband reported that he'd tried to buy it and failed?

All was fair at an auction, Annie reminded herself. If Garvin MacCrae had wanted to pay ten thousand and ten dollars, he'd have gotten the painting. She needn't feel guilty. But as she labored up the stone steps, breathing in the damp smells of the northern California winter, she remembered his expression at her mention of his wife and felt a pang of regret. Still, the painting was Sarah's work. She had a right to it, and she'd paid for it, fair and square.

"Set it over in the corner," Sarah said when Annie, slightly winded, came through the door.

She leaned the painting against a kitchen counter. Seeing it amidst other examples of Sarah's work, Annie was even more confident of her assessment. This was the artist early in her development. Her style wasn't set, wasn't polished, but it was very much *there.*

Using her walker, Sarah pulled herself slowly to her feet. She seemed to be in more pain today; perhaps the dampness made her stiffer. She struggled over to the counter where Annie had set the painting. "She was a lovely child." Her eyes misted unexpectedly. "I didn't do her justice."

"Then it is your work," Annie said, her excitement subdued by Sarah's unexpectedly somber mood.

"Yes." Her voice was barely audible. She tried to straighten but winced in pain, her spine remaining stooped. She turned to Annie, her vivid eyes shining with tears. "Thank you. I knew I hadn't made a mistake when I chose you."

"Why did you? Choose me, I mean. I haven't quite figured that one out."

Sarah shrugged, then said simply, "I've been to your gallery."

"I know, but that doesn't explain—"

"Yes, it does."

"I don't understand."

Sarah smiled, her tears subsiding, and for a moment she might have been a gentle, maternal older woman instead of an eccentric recluse. "It was the painting behind your register that convinced me you were who I wanted."

Gran's painting. "It's a watercolor my grandmother did of our cottage in Maine. Most people dismiss it as tourist art."

"So?"

"Exactly what I say. Gran managed to make a decent living as a painter, and she just loved it. She did our cottage, the rocky shoreline, wild roses, lobster boats, lighthouses, you name it. They're all skillfully done, unpretentious, openly sentimental— just what people want to take home with them from vacation."

"Is the painting in your gallery the only one of hers you have?"

Annie nodded. "Gran died about a year and a half ago. Our cottage was lost in a coastal storm last fall."

"A hurricane?"

She shook her head, remembering the relatively innocuous weather reports, a storm coming at high tide, the potential for some coastal flooding, then, seemingly out of nowhere, the surging ocean, the wind, the panicked fire chief racing down her isolated peninsula, yelling for her to get out. "It was just one of those nasty, unnamed New England autumn storms that got out of hand. I escaped just before it washed my cottage into the bay." She cleared her throat, fighting back the memory of that terrible moment when she'd realized with utter finality that Gran was gone, her cottage was gone, and no matter what she did, her life in Maine could never be put back together again. "There was hardly a stick of the place left. The painting and Otto were about all I had left. I decided I needed a new start."

"So you came west," Sarah said.

"I guess I'm hardly the first. I didn't agonize that much over leaving Maine. I pretty much woke up one morning and decided it was what I wanted to do." She smiled. "I've lasted out here longer than any of my friends thought I would. Anyway, it's refreshing to find someone who appreciates Gran's work. I'm glad I could help you, Sarah. I can write you a check for the balance of your ten thousand—"

"Keep five hundred for yourself."

"We agreed on one hundred, but I don't really want any payment. It was fun." For the most part, she thought, remembering Garvin MacCrae's eyes boring into her from the back of the Linwood ballroom.

"I put you in an awkward position. You had to go up to five thousand—it must have been far more of an ordeal than you expected. Please. Take five hundred out for yourself." Sarah started back toward her chair on her walker, but paused to glance back, her vivid eyes warm and far too knowing. "Who bid against you, do you know?"

"A man named Garvin MacCrae. He's—"

"Haley's husband."

Standing in the middle of her tiny house, Sarah gazed back at the portrait she had dispatched Annie to buy on her behalf, then proceeded slowly to her chair. The name Haley struck a chord with Annie. Haley MacCrae. No, she couldn't place it, but there was something hovering in the back of her mind, out of reach.

"Then you know him?" she asked Sarah.

"Oh, yes. I know Garvin, John Linwood, Cynthia." She staggered back to her chair, sank into the soft cushions, cast her walker aside. A sheen of perspiration had formed on her upper lip. She brushed one large, paint-stained hand through her hair. She seemed suddenly exhausted, overcome. "I know them all."

"Because of the painting? This Haley—she's a Linwood?"

Sarah's eyes seemed focused elsewhere, another time, another place. "I painted Haley a long time ago, before Garvin or Cynthia were in the picture—before I even knew what I was doing with a paintbrush. I was taking a painting class. The portrait was an assignment." She sank her head back into a tattered cushion. "Haley was my niece."

Annie could barely contain her shock. "You were married to a Linwood?"

Sarah glanced at her and, momentarily, looked amused. "Why do you think that?"

Annie flushed. "Well, if Haley Linwood was your niece and isn't now, I assume you must be divorced—"

Her face clouded and went pale. "No, no, Annie, that's not what I mean—" She faltered. "I used the past tense because Haley's dead."

Dead? Annie felt her knees go out from under her. The red-haired girl in the painting was dead. That explained Garvin MacCrae's pained look at Annie's innocent, idiotic mention of his wife. The painting hadn't been a present for her. His wife was dead. No wonder the crowd had been rooting for him. They must all have known that was Haley Linwood MacCrae in the painting, and they'd thought the man who'd loved and married and lost her should have it.

Sarah, clearly, hadn't troubled herself to give Annie a wide range of pertinent details before letting her walk into that auction room.

"She and my father were murdered five years ago," Sarah went on softly. "Haley's father, John Linwood, arranged the auction today. He's my older brother. I'm Sarah Linwood."

She paused, eyeing Annie as her words sank in. "A Linwood—you're a Linwood?"

"Yes."

"So that's how you could afford the ten thousand dollars you put into my account. But I don't understand—" Annie took a step into the living area, toward Sarah. "You don't live like a Linwood."

The older woman smiled thinly. "Nor do I look like one, at least not anymore. Annie, I'm sorry. I knew you didn't realize who I was the other day, but I thought—I assumed you knew about the murders."

The Linwood murders. Yes, Annie thought, feeling sick to her stomach. Now she remembered. Not everything—not the details— but enough to understand that sense that she'd been overlooking something she knew, missing something. "I suppose I did know. But I didn't—I just didn't make the connection between the auction today and a sensational case I read in the papers five years ago."

"It's my fault. I should have explained. I've struggled to maintain my privacy—to go on with my life—and perhaps was more secretive than I should have been, in fairness to you. I hope you don't feel used."

Annie stared out the windows overlooking San Francisco, noticing that the sun was shining through the clouds, scraps of blue sky visible, giving the city a sun-washed look. It was so damned pretty. She hadn't headed west to escape life's ugliness; she wasn't naive that way. But she hadn't expected it to catch up with her so soon, so terribly. She'd bought a painting of a murdered girl out from under the man who'd married and lost her. She was standing here, talking to a misshapen woman—a Linwood —whose father and niece had been murdered, who was obviously trying to keep her location secret from her wealthy, prominent family.

"I just thought," Sarah went on tiredly, "that it would be simpler and easier if you didn't know who I was. You wouldn't be tempted to tell anyone, you'd have nothing to hide. Believe me, if Garvin MacCrae sensed you were trying to hide something from him, there'd be no peace."

"Why? Does he think you had anything to do with the murders?"

Her shoulders slumped. "I don't know what Garvin thinks. That I didn't tell the police everything I know, that I led them to the real killer, that I helped him get away. I just don't know. I haven't seen him in so long..." Her voice trailed off; the faded pink of the chintz cushions behind her made her face seem even grayer. "Maybe I should have stayed away."

"Why did you leave? If it made people suspicious—"

Her vivid eyes focused on Annie. "I left because I had to. I didn't think much about the consequences. I just knew I had to leave."

"But now you've come back."

"To San Francisco, yes."

But not to her family, Annie thought. The Linwoods—and her niece's husband—didn't know she was in town. "Did you come back because you'd heard your family home was being sold?"

"That's one reason. The catalyst, I suppose. I read about it in the papers, and I knew I had to come home. Again, it was impulsive, with the same certainty I felt when I knew I had to leave."

"Then why not go buy the painting yourself? It would have been a way to let your family know you're back."

She shook her head. "I couldn't. I—I'm not ready."

"But you were willing to go to all the trouble of finding me, hiring me—"

"That wasn't just because of the painting." She sat forward, just a little. "I want you to represent my work, Annie. When I'm ready." She looked toward the painting Annie had just delivered, the strawberry-haired girl smiling, innocent. "Soon."

Annie didn't feel the thrill she'd expected to feel; it would have seemed greedy, selfish, given the circumstances. She'd never met anyone as strange and as compelling as this plain, soft-spoken woman. "When you're ready, I'd be honored. The painting—did you want it so much because it's your work?"

"I'd thought my brother had destroyed it."

"What? How could he—"

"I'd painted it. It was of his only child whom he'd lost in such a horrible way. It had hung in the room where she and Father were killed. It was too painful to keep—but also apparently too painful for him to destroy." She inhaled through her nose, plainly holding back tears. "It's all I have of Haley. I wanted it for myself, Annie. There's no other reason."

26

Annie nodded thoughtfully. "I think I understand. You were able to capture something—"

"Not capture. When Haley sat for me, she gave me her spirit. She gave me everything she was. I suppose"—she bit her lower lip and sighed heavily—"I suppose I wanted some of her back."

"Sarah—"

She waved a hand, dismissing Annie's concern. "Now. About our deal. Can you keep my secret?"

"Does anyone else know you're in San Francisco?"

"No. Only you, at least for now."

Annie glanced at the recent canvases, at the framed portrait of the strawberry-haired girl. Could she have guessed, then, that her life would be a short one?

"I won't be committing a crime?"

Sarah smiled sadly and shook her head.

Annie glanced at the tattered furnishings in Sarah's tiny house, the decades-old appliances. A Linwood didn't have to live this way. "Yes," she said, "I can keep your secret."

Sarah, spent, had closed her eyes. "We'll speak again, Annie. Soon."

Seeing that the reclusive artist had nothing left in her, Annie quietly retreated. It wasn't until she was halfway down the stone steps, hanging onto the rickety handrail to keep from tripping on the ends of her skirt on the steep terrain, from going too fast, from utterly losing control, that she thought, once more, of Garvin MacCrae. As mortified as she was at her assumptions about his wife, he would have to know she hadn't deliberately bid against him knowing he'd merely wanted a profoundly moving painting of his murdered wife.

"Look before you leap next time," Annie muttered to herself as she stumbled to her car. She suspected her reputation in San Francisco would take a hit until people realized she hadn't known the background of the man bidding against her. But she was in no mood to cut herself any slack, never mind ask anyone else in town to. She should have done her research before she'd walked into that auction room.

Groaning, she climbed into her car and stuck the key in the ignition. The sun, she noticed, had given up and decided not to stay out. The skies were gloomy again, threatening rain. She glanced back up the steep hill, toward the little pink bungalow. It had been five years since the Linwood murders. Maybe, she thought, no one really cared whether or not Sarah Linwood was back in town.

Chapter Three

Annie had her gallery swept, dusted, and straightened by the time Zoe Summer arrived with the Sunday paper, two large gourmet coffees, and two fat, warm wild blueberry scones an hour before their noon opening. "Sorry, Otto," Zoe said, lifting the scones from their bag. "None for you."

"Don't let him fool you," Annie said. "He just had a treat. We went for a run on the beach first thing this morning."

"I'll bet no one bothered you with a rottweiler at your side."

"Not a soul."

Zoe laid out the scones on paper napkins on the chest-high half-moon desk in the far left corner of Annie's Gallery, then uncapped the coffees. She was in her late thirties—tall, angular, dark, thin—and had two children in junior high and a doctor husband who tolerated, if not endorsed, her passion for aromatherapy. Her inexhaustible wardrobe was in just two colors: black and ivory. Today she wore black knit pants and an ivory sweater and looked sleek and sophisticated. Annie, having had to rebuild her wardrobe from scratch, was enjoying the freedom of dressing for herself. She still tended to scope out the sales and stick to neutrals, preferring to keep her expenses down until she was better established in San Francisco. Given her morning of cleaning, she'd opted for a chamois-colored jacket over slim jeans, with her ankle boots, good watch, and silver earrings.

"I see you made the Sunday paper," Zoe said.

Annie sat on the edge of one of her two tall swivel chairs. "I did?"

"Yep. You hit the local gossip column. That'll teach you to buy a painting out from under Garvin MacCrae. What were you thinking, m'girl?" Zoe whipped out the paper and thrust a long, unpolished fingernail at the paragraph in question. "There. 'Annie Payne, owner of the new Annie's Gallery on Union Street, shocked the two hundred gathered for the Linwood auction on Saturday when she outbid Garvin MacCrae for an amateur painting of his murdered wife.' "

Blood draining from her face, Annie snatched the paper. "Let me see."

Going on in the same snide tone, the columnist related how MacCrae had "thrown in the towel" at five thousand dollars and Annie had "gleefully picked up her prize before the crowd could hiss her out of the elegant ballroom, just down the hall from where Haley Linwood MacCrae lost her life."

"Did they really hiss?" Zoe asked, biting into her scone.

Annie winced, remembering the hostility directed toward her after she'd bought the painting. "Pretty close to it. Oh. Did you see this? It says Garvin MacCrae looked 'fit to be tied' and had 'vengeance in his eyes when he stormed out of the Linwood house.' Actually, I saw him afterward. He didn't seem to have any hard feelings. He even tried to help me get the painting into my car. Otto was being a pain and—"

"Well, that explains it. I'd pretend I had no hard feelings with Otto around, too." Hearing his name, Otto stirred under the desk. Zoe, who loved dogs, scratched him with her toe. "You scared that mean old Garvin MacCrae, didn't you, buddy?" She sipped her cappuccino, eyeing Annie. "So. What *do* you want with that painting?"

Annie had anticipated Zoe's question and was therefore prepared. "I was asked to buy it for someone who wishes to remain anonymous."

"No kidding. You can't tell me?"

"That was the deal I made."

"Puts you in an awkward position, doesn't it? Well, I'm not going to ask you to break a confidence—not that you would."

"I can tell you this much—I had no idea the painting was of a murder victim, or even of a Linwood."

Zoe made a face. "Then you stumbled into this thing blind? Eeekk. Five grand's a lot to pay for a painting by an unknown artist. Your anonymous buyer must have wanted it badly." She eyed Annie hopefully. "Not going to budge, are you? Your integrity is to be admired. I hope you got a decent commission for putting up with the insult."

Annie frowned. "I hope this doesn't hurt my reputation that much. I really didn't know who Garvin MacCrae was—"

"Not to worry, Annie. The publicity'll bring in the window-shoppers, you wait." She slid off her chair. Naturally, Zoe being Zoe, she had a tiny vial of something she wanted Annie to sniff. She opened it up and stuck it under Annie's nose. "First reaction. That's all I want."

"I'm going to sneeze."

Zoe snatched the vial away and screwed the cap back on. "That's what you always say."

"All right, all right. I smelled coconut."

"Coconut?"

Obviously the wrong answer. Annie smiled. "Almonds?"

Zoe sighed. "Never mind. Tell me how you felt when you first smelled it." She gave her friend a warning look. "Besides wanting to sneeze."

"I felt…I don't know, it's a soothing smell, I guess. Nostalgic. Made me think of foggy nights in Maine, right before winter sets in. You know, when you're looking forward to eating pot roast and stew instead of grilled chicken and corn on the cob."

"Easterners," Zoe muttered.

"Wrong answer again?"

"There is no wrong answer, but only someone from New England would get nostalgic about eating pot roast." She headed for the front door. "Better get ready for the onslaught. Maybe some of it will spill over onto me. My kids are coming down to 'help.' Better busy than bored, I always say."

She whisked out into the small brick courtyard they shared behind a Victorian house on Union that had been converted into shops. Their building, a former stable, was accessed via a narrow brick walk that ran from the street back to the courtyard, in the shadow of the Victorian and the larger building next to it. In exchange for a break in her rent, Annie had talked her landlord into letting her plant a border of impatiens and ivy along the walk and tend the courtyard, keeping it swept and making it more enticing with pots of flowers. She'd already put out pansies, cyclamen, lobelia, impatiens, ivy, letting them soak in the after-noon sun.

Just as Zoe had predicted, within thirty minutes of opening its doors, Annie's Gallery had more browsers than in the entire past week. Her gallery, Annie knew, reflected her disinterest in snob appeal and her dislike of pretentiousness. She offered a range of artwork and services: high-quality prints, signed lithographs, original oil and watercolor paintings, original graphics, some pottery and glasswork, framing, and advice on displaying art. She'd relied on Maine artists, friends of hers not that well known on the West Coast, for much of the original work she offered. That would change, she thought, when she introduced and represented Sarah Linwood.

Two teenaged browsers grinned at the print of Spiderman adorning the wall just inside the open doorway of her workroom at the back of her gallery. "Where's Batman?" one asked.

"In my apartment," Annie said, straight-faced.

They laughed and bought a couple of comic-book prints for themselves.

Three different browsers during the course of the afternoon outright asked to see the painting she'd bought at the Linwood auction. Annie explained it wasn't on view. One man asked if it was for sale. She said no. *Keep it simple.* Part of her wanted to drive out to Marin County, find Garvin MacCrae, and apologize to him for her insensitivity, however unintentional. But what good would that do? She couldn't sell him the painting. It wasn't hers and never had been. And she couldn't explain. She'd given her word to Sarah.

No, she had to put the humiliation of the column and the awkwardness of her encounter with Garvin MacCrae out of her mind.

When her last customer left just before five, Annie noticed a few drops of rain on her window and started bringing in the pots from the courtyard, taking in the heaviest ones first. While she worked, Otto crept out from behind the half-moon desk, where he'd been conked out most of the day. He stretched and yawned. She liked to give him jobs when she could think of something he wouldn't destroy—he was fond of picking up trash in the court-yard—but right now she couldn't think of anything. Not that he seemed that interested.

"San Francisco's spoiling you," she told him as she set down three little pots of yellow pansies just inside the door. "You need about a week in the wilds of downeast Maine to get you back into shape."

He gave a low growl way back in his throat.

Annie raised her brow, mock insulted. "The nerve. Who feeds you? Who brushes you? Who saved your life?"

But his ears went back, his brow wrinkled, and he actually barked.

Annie straightened. Otto seldom barked. "Otto?"

He barked again, growling. His attention was directed at the open door of her workroom. It was possible, Annie thought, that upon awakening from his nap, her not-always-brilliant dog had mistaken her poster of Spiderman for a stranger. His powerful, well-muscled body was tensed in anticipation of a challenge. It was an impressive sight. He wouldn't attack unless attacked, at which point she had no illusions that his rottweiler genes would kick into full gear.

"Otto, that's Spiderman. He's one of the good guys."

He barked three times in succession, possibly a record.

Just as she was realizing something might be up, a man walked in front of the Spiderman poster. He hadn't made a sound. Annie jumped back in surprise. Otto lunged toward him.

"Otto!"

"Hey, poochie," the man said nervously, taking a step back.

He looked to be in his mid-fifties, with a stocky, muscular build, thick, wavy iron gray hair, and a prominent aquiline nose. He wore a white turtleneck that hugged his trim torso, close-fitting black jeans, and black running shoes. Annie hadn't noticed him in her gallery today.

His dark eyes stayed on Otto even as he addressed her. "He friendly?"

"Depends." Annie remained close to the front door, just in case her surprise visitor proved to be a threat. If necessary, she was fairly certain Otto would give her time to get out. Not intentionally, of course. Just by virtue of being a rottweiler. "Who are you?"

The dark eyes still didn't leave Otto. "The dog."

"He won't attack you unless you attack him."

A near smirk. "Why would I do that?"

"Yes. Why would you?"

He seemed to relax slightly but didn't move from the back room doorway. To do so would involve making peace with Otto, who was still agitated, if no closer to biting than he ever was. "You're Annie Payne, right?"

She nodded.

"Nice place you got here."

"Thank you."

If she didn't remember him from today's customers, did that mean he'd snuck in while she wasn't looking? She didn't think she'd been so busy she wouldn't have noticed him, but maybe it was possible. Could he have broken in through the back door in her workroom?

"I don't know much about art myself," he said conversationally, Otto pacing uneasily in front of him. "I kind of like Norman Rockwell, though."

"Many people do. His romantic view of American life has an undeniable appeal."

"It's a lot of bullshit, I know that. I mean, my life was never all that apple pie and stories by the fireside crap. I don't know anybody's whose was. You?"

"Not really." If she could keep him talking, respond to him normally, she thought, maybe she could buy herself some time to figure out what to do—and whether he was dangerous. "I've always thought that's why he's so popular. He appeals to the memories we wish we had, not to the ones we do have. He creates a nostalgia for a nonexistent past, speaks to our yearnings."

"Yeah, well. I like the one in the barbershop."

Annie licked her lips. Otto had settled down a bit, but his forehead was still wrinkled in suspicion. Ordinarily, by now he'd be licking a stranger's hand. "I have a print of it if you'd like to see it. I was just about to close up, but I don't mind—"

"I'm not here about Norman Rockwell."

She hadn't expected he was. "Is there something else I can help you with?"

The stranger's dark eyes leveled on her, almost as if Otto weren't there between them. "Sarah Linwood."

Annie looked down at the flowers spread out at her feet, their array of colors, and pushed a pot of yellow pansies with her toe. A nice, comfortable new life in San Francisco. Attractive surroundings, a successful gallery, a chance to prove to herself she could live away from her peninsula in Maine, to put a few of her dreams to the test. That was all she'd wanted. Now, it seemed, she'd gotten herself mixed up in the problems of a prominent, wealthy, troubled family.

She licked her lips, glanced back at her visitor. "Who?"

His gaze remained steady. "Sarah Linwood," he repeated. "She painted that portrait you bought yesterday. She gave you the five grand to buy it. She back in town?"

"I'm afraid you have me at a loss, Mr.—"

"Sarah's good at getting people to do her dirty work for her."

He spoke calmly, even matter-of-factly, but the undertone of bitterness was unmistakable. Whoever he was, he clearly had a bone to pick with Sarah Linwood. Annie just hoped it had nothing to do with the murders of Sarah's father and niece.

She took a breath, glad for every stereotype of the fierceness and unpredictability of rottweilers, and wondered if hers could sense her growing uneasiness. "My purchase of the painting yesterday is a private matter. I'm sure you understand. Now if you'll excuse me, I need to finish closing up. A friend's meeting me here in a few minutes." She made a show of glancing at her watch. "In fact, he should be here now."

The intruder grinned. "Is that a fact?"

"I have nothing to tell you. Please leave."

His grin faded. "If you made a deal with Sarah Linwood, kid, you're in way over your head."

"You're upsetting my dog," Annie said.

"Yeah, well, your dog's upsetting me."

But he sighed, plainly frustrated with his situation. He wanted answers about Sarah Linwood, but Annie wasn't cooperating and Otto wasn't going to let him pry them out of her. She tried to look as if she had nothing to hide.

"Okay, I'll leave," he said finally. "But you can tell Sarah that me and her still have unfinished business. I'm going to find her. One way or the other. I'm not giving up."

His voice was low, calm, virtually without emotion. Annie felt a chill that had nothing to do with the damp weather. She managed to speak, her jaw muscles aching with tension. "Who *are* you?"

Otto gave a deep, low growl, almost a purring sound. It surprised Annie as well as her intruder.

"I think he senses my tension," she said.

The man grunted. "I hate dogs."

She didn't think Otto would bite or rip off a leg or anything, but he could knock the man down and keep him down while she went for help. But she didn't know if the man was armed, if he'd shoot Otto or knife him if he felt threatened, if the police would end up arresting *her* and demanding her dog be put to sleep for attacking innocent people.

"It's okay, Otto," she said soothingly. She raised her eyes to the gray-haired man. "I really don't know anything about Sarah Linwood."

He smirked in disbelief. "Sure, kid."

But without another word, he withdrew into her workroom, pulling the door shut tight behind him.

Otto shot to the closed door and barked loudly, growling as if he had delusions of being a proper watchdog. Annie waited until she heard the back door, which led out to the alley behind her building, shut before she moved.

She put her ear to the workroom door, heard nothing, and finally pushed it open, motioning to Otto. "Go ahead, Otto. You go first."

Eager to do so, he bounded into her workroom and sniffed a trail to the outer door while Annie checked to see if anything had been disturbed. But the shelving unit where she kept her framing and office supplies was intact, the sawhorse table she used for framing, her tools, the two projects she had waiting for her. Nothing seemed to be missing or out of place. She peeked into her small half bath, smelled the goat's milk soap she'd bought from Zoe. All was well there, too.

The metal back door showed no sign of a break-in. She pushed the deadbolt back in and made a mental note to speak to her landlord about an alarm system, never mind that her peculiar visitor must just have slipped in back when she and Otto weren't paying attention.

"Well, Otto." She was trembling, teeth chattering now that the immediate crisis was over. "I suppose this is a case of all's well that ends well. We'll have to keep a closer eye on our customers." She exhaled, trying to calm herself. "Who *was* that guy?"

Not a customer, obviously. He'd deliberately hidden in her workroom and waited until everyone had left in order to interrogate her about Sarah Linwood.

Why?

Otto seemed to have forgotten him altogether. He pushed his head into the trash can to get at the remains of her and Zoe's wild blueberry scones.

Annie scowled at him. "Otto, get out of there."

He looked up at her, drool dripping off his massive chin.

She sighed. "You don't know what's wrong with me, do you, buddy? So what do I do now? Call the police? The guy didn't steal anything. He didn't even break in. If I call the cops, they're going to want to know if I have been in touch with Sarah, and things could get messy real quick."

Talking to herself. Not a good sign.

What she would do, she decided, was tell Sarah Linwood about the gray-haired man and see what she had to say.

"A pity there's no scone left for me, huh, Otto? I could use a bite to eat. Come on," she said, encouraging him to abandon the trash can, "we might as well finish closing up shop."

The afternoon sun had given way to a light, steady rain as Garvin made his way down the narrow brick walkway off Union Street, emerging into the small courtyard where Annie's Gallery was located. He noticed the simple sign, the half-opened door, a few pots of pansies out front. This was not one of Union Street's distinguished, expensive galleries. He pushed the door open and peeked inside, even a quick glance confirming his impression of eclecticism and unpretentiousness. More pots of flowers, he noted, were on the floor just inside the door. He must be catching Annie Payne closing up shop. But as he stepped inside, he saw no sign of her.

A dog growled, and the big rottweiler of yesterday padded out of a back room. Garvin took an involuntary, automatic step back. "Whoa, boy. It's Otto, right? Yeah. Nice dog."

He plopped down onto Garvin's feet, drool dripping from his massive jaw.

"Otto, it's okay," came his owner's voice. "You remember Garvin MacCrae from yesterday, right?"

Garvin glanced up from the dog, and immediately went still, his eyes narrowed on Annie Payne. She was pale and obviously shaken, not just surprised to see him but unnerved. He'd come straight from the marina he'd bought a couple of years after Haley's death. He hadn't bothered changing from his sweater and torn, stained jeans. He knew he looked very different from yesterday at the auction, but that didn't explain her reaction.

"Oh," she said, clearing her throat, "hello."

She was visibly trembling, with none of yesterday's easy manner and cheerfulness. He supposed she'd learned about Haley. "Are you all right?"

"Yes, I'm fine." She gave him a quick, phony smile. "It's been a busy day."

"Because of that stupid piece in the paper this morning?"

"It did bring out the browsers. I—one of them—he just—" She inhaled, breaking off. "It's just been a weird day."

"Ms. Payne?"

Her slate eyes fastened on him abruptly, and she seemed steadier. "It's Annie. And I'm okay. I just had an unsettling experience with a man who hid in my workroom. He's gone now. He slipped out through the back—"

Garvin didn't wait for her to finish. With Otto on his heels, he ducked into the workroom. It was small and tidy, used for storage and a modest framing operation. He checked the back alley but saw no one. On his way back into the gallery, he noticed the print of Spiderman. It wasn't the sort of thing he'd have found at any of the galleries Haley had dragged him to during their brief time together.

Some color had returned to Annie's cheeks, but she was still clearly shaken. "Did this guy threaten you?" Garvin asked.

She shook her head. "Not really."

"What do you mean, 'not really'? What exactly did he say?"

She shut her eyes and ran a hand through her hair, and Garvin was again struck with the gut feeling that Annie Payne was hiding something. Otto yawned and flopped down between them.

"It was about the painting," she said finally. "The one I bought yesterday. I had no idea—" Her gaze, direct and pained, focused on him. "I didn't know about your wife."

"I know you didn't."

"I'm sorry."

He gave a curt nod in acknowledgment of her words.

She took a breath. "The man just now—he said the painting was done by your wife's aunt, Sarah Linwood. He thinks—he accused me of buying it on her behalf. He said they have unfinished business. I don't…" She paused, averting her eyes. "I don't have any idea who he is."

"Vic Denardo," Garvin said, his body rigid, his mind reeling.

Annie Payne frowned. "Who?"

She didn't know. She'd paid five thousand dollars for Sarah's painting of Haley and yet knew nothing about the murders, the scandal, that had shattered the Linwood family.

It didn't, Garvin thought, add up.

"This man," he said. "Describe him."

She licked her lips, no color left in her face. "He was probably in his mid-to-late fifties. Stocky, maybe five nine. Thick, wavy gray hair. Dark eyes."

Garvin clenched his hands into fists. "That's Vic."

"Look, Mr. MacCrae, I don't—"

"Garvin." He forced himself to glance around the gallery, assess the situation. "You're closing up, right?"

"Yes, but—"

"Good. I'll buy you coffee. There's a shop around the corner. Otto will be okay here for a bit?"

Annie Payne stared at him.

"We need to talk," he said softly.

He watched her swallow. "I don't have anything to tell you."

"Well, I have a few things to tell you."

"This man—Vic Denardo—who is he?"

Garvin didn't mince words. "Vic Denardo is the chief suspect in the murders of my wife and her grandfather five years ago."

She started to sway, her knees going out from under her, but Garvin grabbed her arm. She steadied herself. He could feel the warmth of her skin through her jacket. She gave him a feeble smile. "Maybe coffee would be a good idea."

Union Street was crowded even early on a drizzly Sunday winter evening, helping Annie to feel a little less uneasy about going for coffee with Garvin MacCrae. Possibly, she thought, she'd told him too much about her intruder. She was shaken by the idea he could be a suspect in two murders, not to mention on Sarah Linwood's trail, but maybe Garvin had gotten it wrong. Annie glanced at him. He seemed taller than yesterday, more powerfully built. It could just be his casual clothes or even her own sense of vulnerability after what he'd told her about the man who'd hidden in her workroom. Vic Denardo. The name meant nothing to her.

As they crossed Union, she could see the drizzle glistening on her companion's dark hair. His eyes were an unusually deep, earthy shade of green. She hadn't really noticed yesterday. He pulled open the door to the coffee shop, and she ducked in ahead of him, welcoming the warmth, the smell of coffee and sweets, the chatter and laughter of the crowd.

Garvin offered to get their order while she slid off toward the back of the shop to find a table. She settled into a wooden chair at a two-person round table amidst bookcases, brass lamps, wood-paneled walls with old photographs. The shop resembled a Victorian library, and it was packed with people of every age in every manner of dress. Annie watched Garvin MacCrae weave through people and tables with his tray. He was a good-looking man, at ease, it seemed, wherever he found himself. But she sensed that he was a man with a mission, and she doubted that an item in a local gossip column was sufficient reason for him to have tracked her down.

He set the tray on the small table and lifted off her frothy cappuccino and chocolate-dipped biscotti and sat down with a black coffee for himself. "You're new in town, aren't you?" he asked.

Annie nodded. "I'm from Maine. I came out here in November and opened my gallery just before Christmas."

He studied her with a disturbing, penetrating intensity. "Why San Francisco?"

"It seemed like a good idea at the time. I'd visited twice before and liked it, and I had this fantasy of opening my own gallery. Then my cottage was swept out to sea in a storm. I'd lived there my whole life. My father died when I was a baby, and for a long time it was just my mother, grandmother, and me. Then my mother died when I was sixteen, and Gran died the summer before last." Annie used a tiny spoon to skim cinnamon-sprinkled foam off her cappuccino. "So when my cottage was lost, it seemed like an opportune moment to leave."

"Any regrets?"

"No, not really. I love Maine—it's home. But I'm enjoying San Francisco, and I love running a gallery. I thought about opening one in Maine, but I don't know if I could have brought myself to quit my job there. I was director of a small maritime museum. It's hard to give up that kind of security. But if I headed west"—she shrugged—"then I'd have no choice."

Garvin settled back in his chair, but Annie had no illusions that he wasn't watching, listening to everything. "How does the painting you bought yesterday fit in with your gallery?"

"I'm not sure," she said quickly, hoping she didn't look as if she'd been caught unaware.

"It just struck your fancy and you paid five thousand dollars for it?"

His tone was nonconfrontational, without even a hint of disbelief or sarcasm. Very slick, Annie thought. But she wasn't fooled. Garvin MacCrae no more believed she'd bought that painting for her gallery than the man in her workroom a half hour ago did. She tried her cappuccino. "Pretty much."

He opened his mouth, then shut it again and drank some of his coffee. Finally, he said, "When you're ready, I'd appreciate it if you would tell me exactly what this man who hid in your workroom said to you."

Annie dipped her biscotti into her cappuccino and bit off the end, welcoming the rush of sugar and chocolate. She could feel

Garvin's eyes on her. In spite of his patient words, he looked cold, hard, tight, as if he were steeling himself against giving a damn about anything she might say or do. Yet he was having a curious effect on her. With the sleeves of his sweater pushed up, she could see the cords of muscles in his tanned forearms and found herself wondering what he did for a living, who he was, how he'd ended up married to a Linwood. She caught herself looking at the calluses on his hands—she hadn't noticed them yesterday—and suddenly imagining them on her. She tore her gaze away, her face hot.

As succinctly and accurately as she could, she related her encounter with the man in her workroom. She admitted nothing more about Sarah Linwood and the painting than she'd admitted to the gray-haired man.

"This Vic Denardo," she said finally. "If he's the police's chief suspect, why hasn't he been arrested?"

Garvin sat forward. "He disappeared after the murders."

Blood pounded in Annie's ears. Vic Denardo had disappeared too? "I had no idea. None of this—I just didn't know." She drank more of her cappuccino, willing herself not to blurt out everything about Sarah. She'd made a promise, and she meant to keep it until and unless she had no choice. "Why would he risk being recognized just because he thinks I can lead him to Sarah Linwood?"

"I don't know. I can only speculate. Annie, is he right? *Can* you lead him to Sarah?" Garvin's voice was deep, persuasive, undemanding. "Did she get you to buy that painting for her?"

Annie shifted uncomfortably in her seat. "I'm afraid I'm not at liberty to discuss any details of my purchase of the painting."

"Ah." He dropped his empty cup onto the tray, crumpled up his napkin, and tossed it there too. "Well, Annie Payne, allow me to explain to you just what kind of pile of muck you're sinking into. I met Vic Denardo about a year before my wife was murdered. He was a merchant marine, a colorful character. One day he showed up at the marina where I kept my boat, and we got to talking. Next thing, he was crewing for me on a regular basis. He didn't mind rough, cold conditions. Sometimes it was just the two of us. Other times I'd have Haley with me, her father, her grandfather, Linwood friends, members of their staff or mine. He got along with everyone."

"Did Sarah Linwood sail?"

"No, and Haley only when conditions were ideal. Do you sail?"

The question caught Annie off guard. She nodded. "I grew up on the water—my father was a seaman. I don't remember him, but I guess one of the ways I felt I could get close to him was by going out on the water." She managed a smile. "And I'm from Maine—if I waited for perfect conditions, I'd never leave land."

Garvin surprised her by smiling back. "Understood."

"Please," Annie said softly, "go on."

"One day Sarah came out to the marina to pick Haley up, and she met Vic. Pretty soon he was showing up less and less. I assumed he'd gone back to sea or found other things to amuse himself. I literally didn't think a thing of it." His tone was steady, clinical; it was as if he were struggling not to engage his emotions as he related the events that led to two murders five years ago. "A few months later, I found out he and Sarah were having an affair."

Annie held back a gasp of pure shock. The woman in the little pink house and the man in her workroom? It seemed an impossible combination. "Was it a secret?" she asked.

"Oh, yes. Sarah's father—Thomas Linwood—was a difficult man, especially harsh with her. She knew he wouldn't approve. To make matters worse, Vic introduced her to gambling. For years Sarah lived the life her father expected her to live. She was well-mannered, dutiful, absolutely devoted to her family. She occupied herself with good works and polite hobbies. When it all came apart, it came apart in a big way. She took up gambling like there was no tomorrow. Cards, horses, slot machines. She loved them all. She lost thousands of dollars before anyone found out."

"Was she an addict?" Annie asked, feeling herself go pale.

If Garvin noticed, he didn't say. "I'd say yes, definitely. Once he found out, Thomas did what he could to cut off her funds and get her away from Denardo. But she went up against him in a way she probably should have at fourteen. Refused to budge. Smug as hell. She was the center of attention maybe for the first time in her life, and I think she liked it."

"How sad."

"It was a sad year. Thomas and Haley were killed about a week later. From what we've been able to piece together, Sarah decided she didn't want Linwood money. She had Vic get her money from a couple of loan sharks so she could support her gambling habit. She refused to pay up. She believed her jackpot was around the corner. But Vic got impatient or his loan sharks did, and finally he went to see Thomas."

"Without Sarah's knowledge?"

"That's what she told the police."

Annie's eyes narrowed. "You have doubts?"

"Let's just say I've tried to keep an open mind. Thomas and Vic met in the library one evening. A housekeeper heard them arguing. A little while later, Vic stormed out. The housekeeper left not long after. About a half hour after that, Haley stopped in. Her grandfather was dead."

"She found him?" Annie shuddered, trying not to imagine the grisly scene. "How awful. And then she—"

"Yes," Garvin said. "And then she was killed."

"You don't have to tell me," Annie said quietly.

He shook his head. "I think you need to know everything, Annie. The police wanted to talk to Vic. Sarah claimed she hadn't seen him that day and didn't know where he was. Before the police could track him down, Haley was killed in the same room where Thomas was killed. No one was in the house at the time."

"But it must have been a crime scene still. What was she doing there?"

"I don't know for sure. She'd been doing some investigating on her own, looking into Sarah's finances, trying to get a lead on the loan sharks, I think. She was very devoted to Sarah and wanted to help her."

"Who—how was she found?"

"I found her."

Annie swallowed, twisted her fingers together. She'd seen death before. She'd been with her mother when she'd died, then, years later, with Gran. But they hadn't been snatched from her by the violent hand of another. They hadn't been murdered.

"There were no witnesses," Garvin MacCrae went on in a level, almost clinical, voice. "Ballistics tests showed she and Thomas were killed with the same gun. The police questioned Sarah. Again, she claimed ignorance."

"And Vic Denardo?"

"Nobody has seen or heard from Vic since the night he stormed out of the Linwood house. Sarah took off without a word to anyone two days after Haley's death." He paused, studying Annie. "She hasn't been heard from since. There's been a lot of speculation about what happened to her, how much she knew about the murders, how much she was involved."

Annie's head shot up. "Involved?"

"Some people think she could have put Vic Denardo up to killing her father."

"But that's horrible!"

"It's all horrible, Annie. Whether she was involved or not, whether she helped Vic get away or not, whether she was just as shocked and horrified as the rest of us, two people are dead."

"I'm sorry," Annie mumbled. "But all I did was buy a painting."

Garvin grabbed up the tray, got to his feet. He stared down at her. "No, I don't think that's all you did. In fact, I'm pretty sure Denardo's right and Sarah got you to buy that painting yesterday."

"I told you I can't discuss the details—"

"Right. Look, if you've made promises you're trying to keep, I understand. But now you have the facts. If that man was Vic Denardo today and he has unfinished business with Sarah and thinks you can lead him to her, he'll be back."

"Maybe I should just tell the police about him."

"Maybe you should. But they'll want to know why you paid five thousand dollars for that painting yesterday, and if you're in touch with Sarah—all of it. You'd better get your loyalties and promises straightened out before you start withholding information from the police."

"I never said—"

He ignored her. "Maybe you were just trying to do a good deed yesterday. But two people are dead, and their murderer is still at large. I'm not trying to be hard on you, Annie, but I wouldn't forget that if I were you."

Without waiting for her to respond, he started across the crowded shop. Cursing silently, Annie followed him out to the street, where a light, steady rain was softening the hard edges of the evening. She whipped an umbrella out from her tapestry bag and unfurled it without inviting Garvin MacCrae under its bright yellow canopy.

He didn't seem to mind. The rain, in fact, seemed to have a calming effect on him. Or perhaps it was this sudden conviction of his that she was in cahoots with Sarah Linwood—which she was. Annie gritted her teeth, leading him across Union. How could she have been such an idiot as to walk into the Linwood mansion yesterday without any facts, any background—without even the last name of the woman she was representing?

"Sarah must be pretty persuasive," Garvin MacCrae said calmly, "for you to have gone blindly into that ballroom yesterday morning."

Annie refused to answer.

"A little pissed at her for not giving you the facts, are you?"

"You're so sure you're right, aren't you?"

"Tell me I'm not."

"Why? You wouldn't believe me."

He gave her a half smile, a glimpse into a man she suddenly knew could be warm, understanding, a trustworthy ally. But she wasn't destined to experience that side of Garvin MacCrae when he thought—when he knew—she was withholding information from him. "You got that right, Annie Payne."

"Well, I don't believe that man today was this Vic Denardo character," she said huffily. "I think he's someone you dispatched to throw me off guard. Then you could swoop in, play the good guy, and try to get me to confirm this theory of yours that—"

"No, Annie." His voice was deadly serious. "That's not what happened."

Her heart pounded, and she knew it wasn't, knew before she'd even made her lame accusation. She turned down the narrow walk that led between the two upscale converted Victorian houses to her courtyard. Garvin, she noted, stayed with her. He seemed unaffected by the rain, the chilly temperature, the dark. She found his presence oddly reassuring, despite his doubts about her. She closed up her umbrella and leaned it against her storefront while she unlocked the door. Otto was pacing inside, impatient with being thrown off his routines. Not many men, Annie thought, spirited her off for coffee.

She glanced back at the man who had. He was standing in the doorway, watching her. "Thank you for coffee." Her voice was steady, formal. "If that man comes back—whoever he is—I'll let you know."

"For your sake, I hope he doesn't."

She acknowledged his words with a nod before retreating into her workroom for Otto's leash. When she returned, Garvin MacCrae was still standing in her doorway.

"Can I give you a ride home?" he asked.

She shook her head. "I'll be fine. I don't live all that far away. Otto could use the walk." She swallowed, smiled. "Me too."

Garvin walked briskly to her half-moon desk, whipped a page off a notepad, grabbed a pen, and jotted something down. "Here's my home number and address," he said, "and the number and address of my marina." He walked over to her and tucked the sheet into her tapestry bag. "Call me anytime."

"Thank you."

He remained close to her, close enough that she could smell the dampness of his thick dark navy sweater. "And when you see her next," he said softly, "ask Sarah about what I've told you."

Annie started to speak, but he touched one finger to her mouth and shook his head, and a moment later, he was out the door.

Chapter Four

Later than usual on Monday morning, Garvin took the winding road down from his hillside house in Belvedere and headed toward the water. The winter rains had turned the usually golden Marin hills across the Golden Gate from San Francisco a lush spring green, and the bay sparkled in the morning sun. He had grown up in San Francisco, made his mark there, found love, endured loss. His parents, his two sisters, his brother all lived in the city. He had traveled extensively but had never lived anywhere else. He thought of Annie Payne packing up a rusting station wagon and a rottweiler and heading clear across the country to open an art gallery. Was she running away from her losses—or toward a new life?

He'd been tempted to run after Haley's death. In a way, maybe he had. He'd moved out of the city, abandoned the financial district. If Haley came back to life tonight, she'd find him a different man from the one she'd married. She might not like what he'd become. She might not even recognize him.

He seized his steering wheel and forced himself to concentrate on his driving. The bay sparkled in the late morning sun. It was winter, and not many boats were out. He rolled down his window, inhaling the cool air, tasting the salt on the breeze. But he remained tense, distracted by the certainty that Annie Payne was way, way over her head in Linwood troubles.

He gritted his teeth, annoyed with himself. Any urge he had to protect Annie Payne was ridiculous, unasked for, and totally beside the point. She had crossed the country on her own. She'd set up a gallery on her own. She'd come to the auction Saturday on her own. She was *not* helpless.

He swerved off onto a narrow road, veering down to a strip of land along the water where he owned a struggling marina. It had become his focus, his anchor, in the years since the murders. No one would mistake it for a posh San Francisco Bay yacht club. It was a working marina, with a boatyard, sheds, a marine supply store, a machine shop, and docks for those who didn't care about amenities.

He found Ethan Conninger waiting for him out on the dock. He was dressed for his job as the Linwoods' personal financial manager, his deep blue eyes behind studious round glasses. He was a tall, well-built, good-looking man, as smart about money as Garvin, just never as ambitious in his career.

"Morning," Ethan said. "Thought you'd be up with the seagulls."

"Not today." Not, Garvin thought, after a night of tossing and turning over the plight of Annie Payne, of thinking about her troubled slate eyes and how she'd licked biscotti crumbs from her lower lip.

Ethan glanced around at the marina. "Bare-bones operation, huh? You always did go for the basics when it came to sailing."

Garvin shrugged. "Not everyone likes a fancy yacht club. Anyway, you didn't come for a tour dressed like that. What's up?"

Ethan's expression changed almost imperceptibly, a seriousness coming over him. "I'm here about the auction on Saturday. You and this Annie Payne character really have people stirred up over your fight over that painting. You saw the piece in yesterday's paper?"

"Just gossip." Dangerous gossip, Garvin thought, if it had brought Vic Denardo out of the woodwork.

"Maybe, but you know John and Cynthia when it comes to gossip. They've both had enough of it. I've tried to talk her out of it, but Cynthia's decided to look into why a new gallery owner in town would pay so much for such a painting. She thinks there might be more to it than just fancy." Ethan grinned suddenly, some of his usual irreverence creeping in, but the seriousness stayed in his eyes. "Though God knows, Garvin, you could drive a saint into a bidding frenzy."

Garvin shifted his gaze out to the water, boats bobbing in the waves. A day of hard work. That was what he'd promised himself after yesterday's jaunt to Union Street. He'd considered going to the police, but what would he tell them besides that Annie Payne had been pale and scared yesterday and had described a man who fit Vic Denardo's description? What could they do that they hadn't already done in the past five years?

But early this morning, in the milkiness of dawn, half awake, he'd felt the curling, snaking doubt. What if he hadn't gone to the police because he was afraid they'd scare Vic away?

"Garvin?"

"What? Sorry. I was just thinking about the auction. What does Cynthia plan to do?"

"Just check this woman out, I guess. She's asked me to keep my eyes open."

"What about John?"

"He hasn't said anything to me. If I had to make a guess, I'd say Cynthia's trying to keep him from getting hurt, in case this Annie Payne's up to something."

Garvin turned his attention back to Ethan. "Such as?"

Ethan shrugged, awkward. "I don't know."

But he did. Garvin could see it in his discomfort, the way he pushed up his glasses and gave a little laugh, never one to appreciate anything that might interfere with his good humor. Ethan Conninger preferred to avoid confrontation, to enjoy life. It made him fun to be around, if not a good shoulder to cry on. He didn't like to dwell on his own problems, never mind anybody else's. He'd never had Garvin's drive and ambition, but seemed content working for the Linwoods, operating in their social circle, but not really being a part of it, wanting nothing more than what he had.

"I've thought—" He breathed out, hunched his shoulders against a gust off the water. "Well, I suppose it's possible Annie Payne's in cahoots with Sarah somehow, although how and why I can't imagine. If Sarah wanted the painting, she had every right to it. She didn't have to send someone to buy it for her."

"What if she didn't want anyone to know she's back in town?"

"That's what Cynthia said." Ethan bit off a sigh. "It's all speculation. For all I know, Annie Payne doesn't even know who Sarah Linwood is and she's just some Linwood groupie."

"Is there something you wanted from me?" Garvin asked.

"I was just hoping you'd heard something that could put Cynthia's mind at ease or if you're suspicious yourself."

Oh, he was suspicious. Even before his visit to Annie's Gallery late yesterday, he'd had reason to doubt Annie Payne's story. But he saw no reason, at this point, to inform Ethan or the Linwoods of what he knew and suspected. "Sorry, I can't help you. If and when I can, I'll let you know."

Ethan's dark eyes narrowed on him. "You're pursuing this thing?"

Garvin tucked a toe between cracks in the weather-grayed boards of the dock and peered back at his friend. "I don't know yet. I'll put in a full day's work here, then decide."

Ethan grinned irreverently, handsomely. "Never thought I'd see Garvin MacCrae gassing up boats for a living. Well, it's not like you'll starve."

That was true. Although he had refused to take one penny of Linwood money when his wife had died, Garvin had made enough money from his previous work to keep him going for as long as he needed.

"Take care, Ethan," he said.

"Yeah, I'll keep you posted on any developments. We should go out on the water sometime."

Garvin smiled. "We should."

But he suspected they both knew it wouldn't happen. They hadn't been sailing together in five years, since a merchant marine named Vic Denardo had wormed his way into their trust and betrayed it in the worst manner possible.

After Ethan had left, Michael Yuma joined Garvin out on the dock. He was about five seven, all sinewy muscle and black eyes and black hair, a smart, driven mix of Chinese, Mexican, Irish, and probably a few other things. Garvin had taught him to sail in a program for troubled inner-city kids and agreed to take him on at his marina. True to his word, Yuma was a twenty-four-year-old workhorse.

"Hey, MacCrae, you look like you're ready to pitch someone into the drink. Maybe I shouldn't stand too close, huh?" Yuma laughed. He had on jeans, a ratty gray sweatshirt and boat shoes he'd adopted after a year in lost-and-found, a contrast to the very correct gear of most of the marina's clients. "I remember the first time you dunked me. I thought I was seal meat for sure. Water was so cold—man, I'd rather jump into a tub of ice cubes."

He could have used more colorful language. Michael Yuma knew every raunchy metaphor and crude word there was. But in cleaning himself up, he'd cleaned up his language. Garvin had never met anyone with more grit and determination.

He thought of Annie Payne, wondered at what measure of grit and determination had brought her across the country.

Garvin clamped his jaw shut. "Hell."

His young partner was still grinning. "Woman trouble, Mac-Crae?"

"Yuma—"

"I read about the auction in the paper. I know you don't like to show it now that you're mellowing out under my supervision, but, man, you do hate to lose. You check out this lady who beat you?"

Garvin's gaze fell on him. "Don't you have any work to do?"

He flashed a cheeky smile. "Lots. So do you."

"Then let's get to it."

"Yep, I'm right," Yuma muttered as they started up to the supply store, where there'd be coffee, sailing talk, work. "Woman trouble."

Annie felt as if she were trapped in an old rerun of *The Streets of San Francisco* as she drove up to Sarah's pretty, out-of-the-way neighborhood. She kept checking in her rearview mirror for any sign she was being followed. She hadn't formed any strong opinions about the man in her workroom, but she figured Garvin MacCrae for one relentless man. He would stoop to following her. No doubt in her mind.

She had to hunt for a parking space, found one two blocks up from the stone steps, but it was a glorious sunny afternoon. Her shop was closed on Mondays, and she had spent most of the day cleaning her apartment and thinking. She had on black leggings, her oversize Mt. Desert Island sweatshirt, and sneakers.

As tempted as she was to take Otto with her on such a beautiful day, she didn't think that would be a smart idea. Visions of bulls in china shops came to mind, not to mention Sarah's disability.

"I won't be long," she told him. "You be a good boy."

Her good boy was flopped on his back, paws in the air, before she'd gotten the doors locked.

She enjoyed her walk to the stone steps, reveled in the crisp, clean smells, the bright red leaves that had fallen on the sidewalk. When she reached the little cul-de-sac at the top of the hill, it occurred to her that for all she knew, Sarah Linwood could have packed up and gone.

But she hadn't. As usual, she'd left her door unlocked, and Annie walked right in.

Sarah was standing at the ancient stove in her cluttered kitchen. A teakettle whistled, and she motioned for Annie to sit at the rickety table just inside the front door. An extra cup and saucer were already set out with a plate of simple baking powder biscuits, small dishes of strawberry jam and soft butter, and cream and sugar. As at their previous tea together, Sarah had laid out her good china, in a delicate pattern of tiny pink rosebuds.

Annie gave her hostess a questioning look. "You knew I was coming?"

Sarah smiled. "I always put out two cups for tea, just in case I have company. Not that I ever do, of course, but I can always hope someone drops in at just the right moment. Is Irish Breakfast all right with you?"

"It's perfect."

Balancing herself with one hand on the stove, Sarah filled a rosebud teapot with the boiling water. Today she wore cheap elastic-waist jeans and a turquoise button-front top in a pilled polyester knit with her white Keds and mismatched socks, one white, one pink. Her graying strawberry hair was clean and neatly brushed, without any clear style.

"How do you manage groceries?" Annie asked, resisting the urge to start firing questions at her about her dangerous and secret affair with Vic Denardo, about her compulsive gambling.

"A little at a time. I have a string bag I carry. I don't have a car, but I use public transportation when I can, a cab when I must. It's a chore. I try to go on days when I can manage with just the cane. Sometimes I can even get along without it, but I always take it with me." She shrugged. "I don't get out much."

She took her cane from where she'd leaned it against the counter, then picked up the teapot. Annie started to volunteer to help but saw there was no need. Accustomed to the challenges of her physical condition, Sarah had everything well in hand. She made her way to the table, moving slowly but not clumsily, and set the pot on the table. "It'll need a couple minutes to steep." She eased down onto her chair, her expression registering just the barest flash of pain. "You can tell me why you look so troubled."

Annie took a biscuit from the plate, realized she was hungry after her long day pulling her head together after her twin encounters with the man in her workroom and Garvin MacCrae. "A man came to my gallery yesterday afternoon looking for you."

Sarah frowned. "Who?"

"He didn't tell me his name." Annie decided to give her the description she'd given Garvin MacCrae. "He was stocky, muscular, in his mid-to-late fifties. He had thick, wavy gray hair and very dark eyes."

"Vic," Sarah breathed, without hesitation.

Annie took a breath, trying to stay composed. "Then Garvin MacCrae didn't lie to me."

"Garvin?"

"He stopped by yesterday too."

Despite her shaken look, Sarah managed a sardonic smile. "Quite the day you had."

"Yes."

She poured a small amount of tea into her saucer, nodded in satisfaction at its color and filled Annie's cup, then her own. She set the pot down, her hands steady. She was an artist, Annie remembered, and a Linwood. She would know how to keep her emotions in check. "I let you walk into a potentially dangerous situation without all the facts," she said simply. "I'm sorry."

"Water over the dam now."

"I never thought—" Sarah inhaled, as if breathing in the steam from her tea. "I never thought Vic Denardo would dare show his face in San Francisco. Tell me everything, Annie. Please."

Annie sighed, watching Sarah take a biscuit and carefully cut it in half, then spread it with butter and jam. Her movements were precise and finishing-school delicate, even with her swollen, twisted joints. Would any of her family and friends believe this was the same woman who had taken up gambling and had a scandalous affair with a merchant marine? Would anyone recognize her? Had there been any signs of the disease that now swelled and twisted her joints? Had she worn mismatched socks and Keds? Annie couldn't imagine what Sarah Linwood had been like five years ago. She only saw her as she was now.

Finally, she simply did as requested and told Sarah everything, leaving out only her complicated emotional and physical reaction to Garvin MacCrae.

When she finished, Annie could feel her pulse racing. "Sarah, do you—do you believe Vic Denardo killed your father and your niece?"

Sarah suddenly looked very gray and tired; she reached for another biscuit, a slight tremble to her hand. "I don't know."

Not the words Annie had hoped to hear, had told herself last night and all day that she *would* hear. She wanted Sarah to tell her that the man who'd hidden in her workroom—if Vic Denardo— was, without doubt, innocent. "Do you have any idea what he meant when he said you and he have unfinished business?"

"He thinks I framed him."

"*What?*"

Sarah's vivid, striking eyes filled with tears as she fought back a sob, visibly struggling to compose herself. The murders of Thomas Linwood and Haley Linwood MacCrae weren't an intellectual exercise, Annie realized. The pain of them lingered, even after five years. The unanswered questions. The horror.

"Vic thinks I framed him. He thinks I…" Sarah broke off, her voice croaking and ancient-sounding, barely audible. A thin stream of tears worked its way down one cheek into the lines around her mouth. "He thinks I killed my father and—" She gulped, breathed out, made herself say it. "My father and Haley."

Annie had gone still. She noticed the picturesque, sun-washed city sprawled along the hills and valleys below the little pink house, noticed the hum of the refrigerator, the occasional sound of traffic outside in the distance.

She could be sitting here having tea, Annie thought, with a murderer.

Which was a loony idea. Truly loony. She glanced over at a canvas tucked up against the wall by the front door. A rose garden in the sun. It compelled the viewer into the world Sarah had created. Pink roses, yellow roses, warmth, beauty. Annie was *there*. She could feel the sun on her cheeks, smell the roses.

She forced herself to turn back to her hostess. "If he thinks you're guilty, then that must mean he's innocent."

"No." She shook her head, cleared her throat, but left her tears to dry on their own. "No, it doesn't. It could just mean he's trying to avoid responsibility for what he's done by blaming me."

"But it's been five years. He's avoided the police all this time. Why risk exposing himself?"

"Because that's Vic," she said firmly.

Annie gave her a faltering smile. "Maybe I'll be lucky and the man yesterday wasn't Denardo. That piece I told you about in the paper brought out all kinds. What about Garvin MacCrae? I don't suppose there's any hope he'll back off?"

"Not if he thinks you can lead him to Vic. Or to me."

A man with a mission, Annie thought. His apparent concern for her yesterday—the cappuccino, the biscotti, the effort to be patient—didn't mean Garvin MacCrae didn't have his own agenda. Annie pushed the unsettling thought aside. Her attraction to him was probably only transitory anyway, a not unexpected product of the tension and surprises of her weekend, her isolation in California.

"That must mean he thinks you might have some information that could help settle things. He told me he's trying to keep an open mind—"

Sarah scoffed. "Oh, it sounds it."

"I know," Annie said dryly. "If it's any consolation, I don't think he believed a word I said."

"Did you lie to him?"

"Not exactly. I just was careful in my choice of words and didn't tell him everything."

Sighing, Sarah reached across the table, took Annie's hand into hers. Her skin was warm, softer than Annie would have expected. "Listen to me, Annie. Garvin MacCrae is one of the most tenacious men I've ever met. He'll want to see whoever killed my father and Haley brought to justice. If he sees you as a means to that end, he won't back off. He'll use you, Annie, in any way he feels he must. And I can't say in his place I wouldn't do the same."

Before she could control it, dispel it, Annie was taken aback by the image—clear, detailed—of him studying her from across the table. His deep, earthy eyes, his blade of a nose, his thick brows. His mouth, sensual, compelling. Even his callused hands as he'd held his mug of black coffee. Her throat went dry, her mouth tingled. So much for a transitory attraction, she thought.

Sarah released her hand and sat back, suddenly looking exhausted. "He and Haley were so different. For a while I thought some of his strength and drive would rub off on her, some of her softness and joy in living on him. But I don't know. They'd only known each other a year before they married, and then a year later Haley was killed."

Two years total. Not long at all. "How sad."

"Yes," Sarah said. She grabbed her cane, leaning on it without making a move to rise. "Yes, how very sad. Haley was always so optimistic, so determined to enjoy life and see the good in others. She was charming, totally without pretense." Sarah's shoulders sagged; she seemed almost to sink into her chair. "I can't imagine how losing her the way he did affected Garvin."

Annie thought of him walking down Union Street with the drizzle collecting on his dark hair and his face grim, uncompromising. He had looked determined, but not haunted, as if he'd gone on with his life with the understanding that he would never be the same again.

"Dear God," Sarah mumbled, her voice strangled, "we lost her too soon."

Supporting herself heavily on her cane, she got slowly to her feet. A quiet melancholy had settled over her. She'd been in such a pleasant, homey mood when Annie had arrived. She felt a pang of guilt at having inflicted herself on this pain-racked, isolated woman. What if that hadn't been Vic Denardo yesterday? What if Garvin MacCrae had latched onto him and the painting in his desperate desire to find his wife's killer, and Sarah out of guilt and regret over her past association with him?

"I'm sorry, Annie. I can hardly warn you against Garvin when I've used you myself. I should have told you everything before I sent you to the auction. The painting—can you understand why I wanted it?"

It was all that remained of her early work, and it was a portrait of a niece she'd lost to murder. "Yes. I understand."

Sarah made her way to her rattan chair in the living room and, thrusting her cane onto the floor, dropped down into the faded chintz cushions. Feeling awkward, concerned, even a little scared for Sarah, Annie collected her walker from the kitchen counter and brought it to her, setting it against the wall near her chair.

"I haven't gambled since the murders," Sarah blurted, her eyes suddenly fierce on Annie. Then her face crumpled, and she covered her mouth with a big, paint-stained, gnarled hand and choked back a sob.

"I'll go now," Annie said quietly.

"The police—you can call them if you want. It won't do any good. They haven't found Vic in five years. They won't now. But you can call them. I can't hold you to your promise."

"Sarah, I haven't figured out what I should do or—"

"I *won't* hold you to it." Her voice was little more than a murmur. She sank back against her chair, staring up at the ceiling. "I'm getting all muddled. I need to think. I—" She sighed, breaking off. "Perhaps it wasn't wise to try and come home after all."

"I'll leave," Annie said. "We can talk later."

Sarah didn't answer, just lifted a hand in a feeble wave, and Annie withdrew without another word. As she started down the stone steps, she glanced back. Through the curtainless windows she could see Sarah Linwood, one-time heiress and mercurial recluse, back on her feet, edging her way to the easel she had set up in corner of her cottage, all of San Francisco spread out before her.

When her doorbell rang at six-thirty, Annie expected it was her landlord coming to tell her he'd changed his mind about Otto after all. She had a tiny ground-floor apartment behind a building on Russian Hill. It had its own entrance via a brick wall overgrown with the kind of greenery that didn't grow in Maine even in the summer. The three floors of the main building were reserved for larger, more elegant, far more expensive apartments.

Her doorbell rang again.

She smelled faintly of bleach. She had resumed her cleaning spree after tea with Sarah Linwood. Her little apartment fairly gleamed. She knew she was playing ostrich, avoiding facing up to the consequences of walking into that auction room on Saturday.

She stopped just in front of her door, Otto at her side.

What if it was the stocky, gray-haired man from yesterday?

"Hello," she said through the door, "who is it?"

"Garvin MacCrae."

She felt an unexpected surge of excitement mixed with a flicker of trepidation. She'd been rattled all day, especially since her visit with Sarah Linwood. Her resistance was down. What if she said something she shouldn't say? She still hadn't figured out what to do. Call the police, not call the police, trust Sarah, not trust Sarah. It was as if she were paralyzed by the shock of what she'd learned in the past two days.

"May I come in?" he asked.

His voice was deep, persuasive. Annie felt a slight tremble in her hand. This is absurd, she thought, and pulled open the door.

Her breath caught at the sight of Garvin MacCrae on her threshold. Tonight he wore a tuxedo, and he looked as comfortable in it as he had in his torn jeans yesterday, his business suit on Saturday. He was elegant, rugged, mercurial. The light struck his eyes, then his mouth, as he tilted his head back and smiled at her. "Evening."

Otto returned to his spot in front of her couch, apparently having dismissed Garvin as a possible intruder. Annie fingered a lock of hair that had escaped the rolled-up bandanna she used as a headband while cleaning. "Hello. Um—this is a surprise. How did you find me?"

"I pried your address out of Saturday's auctioneers."

"I see. Well, come in."

She backed out of the way, and he strolled into the small main room of her apartment, looking for all the world as if he belonged there just because he *was* there. He gave the place a quick once-over. At least she didn't have to worry about it not being clean.

Her kitchen sparkled, her two-person oak table gleamed, the cushions on her simple couch were plumped and vacuumed, and there wasn't a dog hair in the place not attached to Otto.

"I could have rented a whole house in Maine for what this place is costing me," she said.

Garvin glanced around at her. "San Francisco's rents are high." He eyed her posters of Yoda and the Hulk, her museum-mounted print of Winslow Homer's *The Fishwives.* "Your taste in artwork isn't easy to categorize, is it?"

She shrugged. "I just like what I like. You'll notice I have followed all the earthquake guidelines to the letter. I didn't hang anything that could fall on my head and kill me, should the Big One hit."

Amusement flashed in his eyes, his quick smile. "That's sensible, I suppose."

"You'll find I have no illusions about natural disasters."

"No, I wouldn't think so."

Otto sighed heavily, dropping off to sleep. Annie had taken him for a good, long walk at midday, hoping to clear her head. It hadn't worked. Neither had cleaning her apartment top to bottom.

"Can I get you something to drink?" she offered.

"No, thanks. I can't stay. I'm on my way to an opening at the Winslow Gallery."

"The Sauveur opening?"

His eyes narrowed on her, missing nothing. She didn't bother trying to hide her interest. For a moment she thought Garvin MacCrae could see her heart skipping at the prospect of attending a Winslow Gallery opening. "Are you going?"

"Me? No, but I've heard about it. I gather the Winslow Gallery's known for its Monday night openings."

"T. J. Winslow likes to go against the grain."

"Well, he has a wonderful gallery. I've been through it several times. And Sauveur—I know his work. He's from the Canadian Maritimes. He does sort of a takeoff on the Hudson River School of the nineteenth century, but with his own twist. He paints huge, dramatic landscapes—"

Garvin held up a hand, silencing her. "Get dressed. You can come with me."

She raised her eyebrows at the unexpected invitation. "Are you serious?"

"Sure."

"But that's not why you came here, is it?"

He sighed. "Annie, if you want to come with me, get dressed and let's go. If not, just say so." He bit off each word as if he'd invited her on impulse and wasn't sure he shouldn't have kept his mouth shut, but then he sighed, and his expression softened. "Look, I didn't come here to harass you. I just stopped by to make sure Vic Denardo hadn't been back."

"He doesn't know where I live."

The deep green eyes darkened. "He can find out."

Annie ignored the shiver that ran right up her back. "Well, I'm not convinced the man yesterday wasn't just some crazy pretending to be Vic Denardo."

"That's wishful thinking."

"Maybe." She eyed him. "If I go with you tonight, are you going to keep at me?"

He sighed. "Would it do any good if I did?"

She smiled brightly. "None whatsoever. I've handled crusty lobstermen and stingy museum trustees, and Gran—my grandmother could be downright crotchety. I think I can tolerate your suspicions for one evening, if," she added, "your invitation still stands."

"It does," he said, watching her closely.

"Give me ten minutes to change."

"Take twenty. I'm in no hurry." His shoulders relaxed, and he folded his arms on his chest, again baffling, intriguing Annie with his easy mix of elegance and ruggedness. "Mind if I take a look at Sarah's painting while I wait?"

Annie swallowed hard. She'd been an idiot to let him manipulate her. He hadn't ventured to her apartment because he was worried about her having to face Vic Denardo again; he'd wanted to catch her in a lie about Sarah's painting.

But she held her ground, squaring her shoulders and meeting his eye. "It's not here."

A gleam of victory flashed back at her. "Then where is it?"

"At a friend's house. I didn't want to leave it here after the trouble at the gallery yesterday. Plus with all the publicity—" She dragged her rolled-up bandanna from her hair and ignored the rush of adrenaline at telling Garvin MacCrae what amounted to a boldfaced lie. "I just thought it'd be smart not to keep it here."

"I thought you were new to San Francisco."

She frowned. What did that have to do with anything? "I am—"

"But you've made a friend you'd trust with a fivethousand-dollar painting."

"You got it," she said stubbornly, and ducked into her bedroom.

She shut the door firmly behind her. Her bedroom was just big enough for her double bed and skinny dresser, but she'd cozied it up with a basket of Zoe's potpourri, lots of bright, inexpensive pillows, and a framed photograph of a Maine sunrise. She paused at a photograph of Gran and her mother on her dresser, felt their presence, let it help anchor her. An evening out with Garvin MacCrae, who didn't for a single, solitary second believe she'd bought that painting for herself or anyone but Sarah Linwood. Well, it would be her first big San Francisco opening, and she meant to enjoy herself.

She stripped off her cleaning clothes and grabbed a dress from her tiny closet. If Garvin were truly devious, he would search the premises, find her checkbook, discover her neatly noted deposit of ten thousand dollars on Thursday, and know she was lying through her teeth.

"Not that he doesn't know that already," she muttered, slipping into her versatile black knit dress; it hugged her torso but gave her legs room to move. With a silk scarf, it could do a gallery opening. With her ankle boots and a sweater, it could do a chilly walk on the water with Otto. With Gran's crewelwork shawl, it could do anything.

She skipped the scarf and opted for the shawl. It would give her confidence a boost.

She added black stockings and her dressy black flats and scooted into the bathroom, ignoring Garvin on the couch and Otto, with one paw on his lap, getting himself scratched on the neck, maybe preventing her guest from searching the place.

Her bathroom had a shower and a pint-size sink; no tub; no linen closet. She kept her change of linens on a wicker shelf above the toilet. A basket of Zoe's potpourri gave off a cheery citrus scent. Annie used spray-on gel to revive her hair, then dusted on translucent powder, a smudge of a neutral eyeshadow, one coat of mascara, and two coats of the darkest berry lipstick she could find.

"Hey, not bad," she said aloud to her reflection, pleased with herself.

Except her hands were shaking just enough to remind her she wasn't going out with Zoe and her husband or having yet another tête-à-tête with her richer fellow tenants about Otto being at least as friendly as their Lhasa apsos and cocker spaniels. No. She was going to a gallery opening with a man who thought she could lead him to his wife's killer. That he was attractive, compelling, and intriguing didn't change that basic fact.

A spray of cologne, and she was off.

Garvin dumped Otto's paw off his lap and rose, his eyes impenetrable, not a spot of drool or a single dog hair on him. "Ready?"

"I think so. I don't smell like bleach, do I? I disinfected Otto's dish before supper."

He'd moved close to her, close enough to make her pulse race. "You don't smell like bleach."

His eyes glinted with sudden humor, suggesting there were layers and layers to Garvin MacCrae, things to intrigue and catch a person defenseless. Annie quickly pulled her shawl onto her shoulders and fetched a fat rawhide bone for Otto, then she stood in the middle of her hardwood floor and looked around for his favorite toy.

"Can I help you find something?" Garvin asked.

"Otto's bowling ball—oh, there it is."

She spotted it in the corner next to the couch, rolled it out with her toe, and nudged it toward Otto, who was busy with his rawhide bone. "He's not used to having me go out at night, and I don't want him chewing my new furniture because he's bored or annoyed with me."

"I expect," he said wryly, "that Otto fit in better in Maine than he does in San Francisco."

"In some ways, yes, but I think city life appeals to him on a certain level. He really likes people."

"A good thing."

She grinned. "Isn't it, though?"

With Otto settled down with his bowling ball and rawhide bone, Annie followed Garvin MacCrae outside into the cool night air.

Chapter Five

Both floors of the Winslow Gallery were brightly lit and packed with well-dressed people from all over the Bay Area, some of whom Annie recognized from the newspaper and television news. She noticed that Garvin stayed close to her as they made their way into the crowd.

"I'll bet T. J. Winslow doesn't have to put out flowerpots and sweep up cigarette butts and dead leaves to offset his rent," she muttered.

He glanced at her. "You want to be a T. J. Winslow?"

She shook her head, not feeling even a flicker of envy. "No, but I'm not going to pretend I don't want my gallery to succeed. I do, but on its own terms. I can't do this." She took in the ultrasophisticated gallery with a wave of the hand. "I can only do what I do."

A current of excitement ran through her at the thought of the canvases in Sarah Linwood's studio. Others would experience the same thrill that she did, the same mix of awe and nostalgia and pain and hope. Sarah Linwood was that mesmerizing an artist.

Half convinced Garvin would guess what she was thinking, Annie focused on her plush surroundings even as she remained very aware of the hard-to-figure man at her side. Despite the scores of people to meet, the paintings that drew her attention, she kept catching herself staring at him, noticing his straight back, the breadth of his shoulders, the quick smiles that never quite reached his eyes. Definitely a hard man to figure. And an impossible one to ignore.

The occasional raised eyebrow told her who knew about the weekend auction and who didn't. No one said what a heartless thing she'd been to buy the painting of Haley Linwood right out from under her widowed husband. Everyone—eyebrow raisers or not—managed to convey a certain curiosity about her and why she was there with Garvin MacCrae. His behavior toward her must only have fueled more questions. He would touch her elbow, her shoulder, whisper names to her. As wary as she tried to remain,

Annie found herself relaxing in his company, wanting to trust him, and, even more dangerous, wanting him to trust her.

When he was waylaid by two men and whisked into a conversation that clearly didn't concern her, she seized the moment and snaked through the elegantly dressed crowd to the gallery where Sauveur's work was actually on display. His huge canvases of the stark, familiar North Atlantic coast immediately assaulted her senses, playing on her memories. If Sarah Linwood's work was focused on the essence, the soul, of what she painted—people, objects, landscapes—Sauveur's landscapes were focused on the rawness and possibility of North America, even at the turn of the millennium. His subject was the continent's easternmost fringe of rock, sea, and sky.

After a while—she couldn't say how long—Annie became aware of Garvin's presence beside her.

"This landscape reminds me of Thomas Cole's *The Oxbow*," she said without looking at him. "It's called *Grand Manan*. Grand Manan's a Canadian island in the Bay of Fundy."

"You've been there?"

"Yes." She gestured at the cliffs depicted in the painting. "I've stood right on that ledge, watching the tide crash in. The Bay of Fundy has the most extreme tides in the world. They're incredible to watch. Grand Manan's further down east than where I used to live."

Garvin, she noticed, was studying her, not the painting. "You miss Maine," he said.

"Yep. I don't deny it. But I figure I need to miss it."

"Why?"

He seemed interested, but it wasn't a subject she wanted to delve into right now. "So I know I can live without it, I guess. That my life isn't a place." But the thought of her old job, her old life, only made her feel more isolated. Not out of place, she thought. Just alone. She directed her attention back to the landscape. "There's a tension between the real and the ideal in Sauveur's work. It's almost palpable, isn't it?"

Out of the corner of her eye she caught Garvin's wry smile. "I was just thinking the painting's too big, it won't fit over a sofa."

She laughed but eyed him sardonically. "Now, why do I have the feeling you're being disingenuous? I think you've heard of the Hudson River School and maybe even Thomas Cole. I don't pretend to be an art historian myself, but"—she caught herself and smiled—"but don't get me started."

Something crept into his eyes; she couldn't define it but knew only that it made her throat catch. "Another time, perhaps. Look, there's someone I need to see." He touched her shoulder, leaning in toward her, his mouth so close to hers she could feel his breath. "Excuse me for two minutes, okay?"

"Sure. Take your time. I'm sure I can amuse myself."

He made his way through the crowd, and Annie, breathing out in a long sigh, swept a glass of champagne from a passing tray. She was far, far too aware of every nuance of Garvin MacCrae, noticing the length of his fingers, imagining the taste and feel of his mouth. Such an attraction would only distract her from the business at hand. That business, she reminded herself, wasn't falling in any way, shape, or form for a man as unpredictable and driven as Garvin MacCrae. And what he wanted from her, she had to remember, were answers to his wife's death.

An attractive, slim woman joined her in front of a huge painting of the windswept coast of Nova Scotia. She was perhaps in her late thirties, with dark Jacqueline Kennedy hair. She wore a classic, understated black dress and simple diamond earrings and carried a light scent of an expensive perfume. She smiled. "Excuse me, you're Annie Payne, aren't you? I'm Cynthia Linwood. I saw you at the auction on Saturday. I would have said hello then, but I must have missed you."

"It's a pleasure to meet you. I left right after I bought the painting."

"That's what I understood." With her sharp features, small bones, and dark coloring, Cynthia Linwood didn't look like either Sarah or her older brother, John, whom Annie had only seen from afar in the Linwood ballroom. Maybe she'd married a Linwood? Did Haley have a brother? Were they cousins? "The decision to sell that particular painting wasn't an easy one. My husband…" Her gracious smile faltered. "I'm sure you can imagine."

"Your husband?"

"Oh, I'm sorry. I assumed you knew. My husband's John Linwood."

As in Sarah's older brother. There had to be close to a twenty-year difference in John and Cynthia Linwood's ages. Annie smiled through her awkwardness. "I didn't realize. I'm new in town—I'm afraid I don't know a lot of people in San Francisco."

"I understand you're from Maine."

Annie nodded, relieved to move off the shifting ground of relationships among the Linwoods. "I moved here just before Thanksgiving."

"Alone?"

"Yes. Well, I have a dog."

Cynthia smiled. "I love dogs. What kind?"

"Rottweiler. He's—he doesn't fit the stereotype. He's getting used to life in the city. So am I."

"Did you know anyone in San Francisco before you moved here?"

Annie shook her head.

Cynthia Linwood's beautifully groomed eyebrows shot up. "Really? I would think that would be—I don't know, scary. Moving to a new city, opening a gallery. You've started over, in essence."

"That was the point," Annie said softly, remembering how quiet the bay had been the morning she'd left, how alone and yet hopeful she'd felt. If she'd stayed in Maine, she'd have had to start over there too. Not in all the same ways, perhaps, but in all the ones that were important.

Before her mind drifted off to nostalgic memories, she smiled and tuned back into her surroundings. "San Francisco's a beautiful city. I love the history, the architecture, the views. The Golden Gate Bridge is everything I imagined. It's expensive here, but I'm enjoying myself. And my gallery's holding its own."

"Wonderful. I'd love to see it. I'm afraid I'm hardly an expert on art, but I'm learning. My husband's far more knowledgeable."

Her comment seemed intended to be neither effusive toward her husband nor defensive toward herself, simply a statement of the facts. Annie found herself liking the woman.

"Here's John now," Cynthia said, smiling broadly as her husband swept up to her. He was energetic, lean, fit—and, Annie thought, appeared far healthier than his younger sister. He had her expressive mouth and fair coloring but none of her plainness, none of her eccentricities. And he had no walker, no shuffling gait, no swollen, twisted joints. His tuxedo was clean, pressed, sophisticated. No doubt his socks matched.

When his wife introduced Annie, he took her hand in a firm grip and greeted her warmly. "Annie Payne. Of course. I just saw Garvin. He said you two had worked things out."

They had? Annie tried to keep her surprise from showing. So far as she could tell, Garvin MacCrae still thought she was a liar. She said diplomatically, "I'm afraid I didn't understand his interest in the painting when I bid on it."

"Yes, he mentioned you were new in town. Welcome."

"Thank you."

His wife hooked her arm into his, leaning close, almost protectively. "Annie was just telling me about her gallery. I plan to stop by one day soon." She smiled at Annie. "You're going to be swamped for the next few days. Everyone's madly curious about you after Saturday."

Including her, her expression suggested. Annie was suddenly grateful for her years of dealing with bluntspoken, tightfisted supporters of her little maritime museum. A smooth, polished Linwood was a breeze in comparison. "Come whenever you can. I'd be happy to show you around."

John Linwood gave a distracted smile, glancing around the crowded room before shifting his vivid blue eyes—his sister's eyes —back to Annie. She wondered if, like his former son-in-law and, possibly, the man wanted for his daughter's murder, he'd contemplated that she might be in touch with Sarah. "If you'll excuse me," he said pleasantly, "I need to tear my wife away for a few moments. Do you mind?"

"Of course not. It was a pleasure to meet you both."

After they'd retreated, Annie checked out a few more Sauveur landscapes, but her attention kept wandering. She couldn't focus on cliffs and waves and dramatic mountain ranges, all, it seemed to her, designed to make her homesick, never mind their gripping mix of romanticism and harsh reality. Out of the corner of her eye she could see Garvin MacCrae laughing with a group of men and women, their gold watches and jeweled necklaces glittering in the careful, expensive lighting. She tugged Gran's shawl around her, no illusions that she was on her home turf.

Garvin caught her eye, smiled, and started toward her. Annie couldn't tear her eyes off him. It wasn't as if he'd changed in the last twenty minutes. He hadn't. His tuxedo, his lean ruggedness, his dark hair and deep dark green eyes were all the same. Yet she couldn't stop herself from staring at him, from feeling a rush of anticipation as he came closer, even as she warned herself that being attracted to Garvin MacCrae would likely get her nowhere but deeper into the morass of Linwood troubles.

"Sorry to abandon you," he said as he eased beside her.

"I didn't feel abandoned."

"No?"

She smiled. "Not my style."

He studied her, seemingly unaware of the powerful paintings in front of him, the crush of San Francisco elite. He had an uncanny ability to make the person he was addressing believe nothing else would or could interfere with their conversation. Annie felt she had his complete attention. It wouldn't be easy to hide anything from him for long, she thought. And probably not smart to try.

He settled in close to her. "Used to getting along on your own, aren't you?"

She gave him an amiable smile. "I expect we both are."

"Yes." His narrowed eyes penetrated her, as if trying to gauge how much he really didn't know about her. She met his gaze dead-on, not afraid of what he might see inside her. He gave her a quick smile, and shifted his gaze, taking in their surroundings. "I noticed you met John and Cynthia Linwood."

"Yes, they seem very nice. You told John Linwood we'd worked things out?"

"Just that we'd reached an understanding. Which we have, after a fashion." His mouth twitched in a wry half smile. "I know you haven't told me everything, and you know I know."

"I do, do I?"

"Without a doubt."

Without giving a reply, she moved on to a final painting, a smallish, for Sauveur, landscape of a Nova Scotia bog enveloped in fog. But Garvin caught her by the elbow and drew her close to him, just a few inches, enough to set her blood boiling but not to attract attention. "So innocent, Annie." His voice was low, deep, probably at least as sexy as he intended, and suddenly she knew he was aware of her attraction to him. "I know damned well you bought that painting for Sarah."

"Garvin—"

He touched a finger to her mouth. "Not now. We'll talk later."

The brief, intimate contact had her reeling. Her shawl slid down her arms and brushed the floor. She scooped it up, wrapped it over her shoulders, and clutched its edges with cold, shaking hands. "Please try to understand—"

"Later, Annie."

His mouth almost touched hers, and his eyes had taken on the color of an evergreen in the Nova Scotia fog of the painting beside them, sending a mix of sparks and chills through her. He didn't back off, paid no attention to the whirl of activity around them.

He hooked her arm into his and drew her back into the crowd before she could come to her senses and march out, get a cab, *walk* home—do anything she had to do to get away from him. But he gave a relaxed smile as he approached two couples in their thirties and introduced her without a trace of suspicion or nastiness.

"People seem surprised to see you here," Annie half whispered as he dragged her off to meet more people.

"They are."

"Why?"

"Because I don't usually come to this sort of thing."

"Then why are you here tonight?"

He didn't answer.

And she knew.

"You didn't come to my apartment to make sure I was all right," she said. "You wanted to sweet-talk me into coming here with you. Why? What's the point? Do you think you'll get your way by preying on my vulnerabilities?"

He regarded her without a hint of apology. "I thought coming here might help you to realize what you're up against."

"I'm up against you!"

"Not me. Two murders that are unsolved. A past that's not going to go away." His tone softened ever so slightly. "Annie, if you're in cahoots with Sarah Linwood, you know she has nothing to fear from these people. They are her family, her friends—"

But she refused to listen to more and pushed through the crowd out to the elegant gallery's main entrance. Tears stung her eyes. She noticed the curious looks and choked on the knowledge of how alone she was. She had let herself believe that Garvin MacCrae had invited her here tonight on the spur of the moment because he knew she was new in town, alone, eager to meet people. He'd capitalized on her eagerness to attend a Winslow Gallery opening. He'd *manipulated* her.

Sarah Linwood. Vic Denardo. They consumed him. They were what he wanted.

Not her, she thought. Not her friendship, not her trust. Just what she knew about his wife's aunt and the man he believed had killed her.

Never mind that she knew more than she'd told him. Never mind that he was absolutely right in thinking she was withholding crucial information from him, even lying.

"Annie," he said, catching up with her.

She jerked around at him, her indignation outstripping any sense of guilt. "I'll find my own way home."

His eyes bored through her, but she detected a flicker of sympathy in them. "You knew you were playing with fire when you showed up for that auction. Don't be surprised you got burnt."

"I just—I just wanted a pleasant evening out. I didn't ask for you to come to my door. I could have stayed home and watched TV with Otto."

His eyes held hers. "Why didn't you?"

"Because I trusted you!"

"No, Annie," he said confidently. "Because you thought you could have your cake and eat it too. You thought you could come here tonight, enjoy yourself, play the San Francisco gallery owner, and not have to account for Saturday. Well, sorry. That's not the way I do things. Trust is a two-way street."

He kept his voice low, but they were out of anyone's earshot. Annie started to defend herself, then clamped her mouth shut and shot out to the street. Garvin swore and came after her. He was a man with a mission, she thought, and she'd allowed herself to be lulled into a false sense of security.

Besides, he had a point about trust being a two-way street.

She shivered out on the sidewalk, more from frustration and humiliation than the cold. It was a long walk back to her apartment, but she could do it.

Garvin touched her shoulder and said softly, "Annie, I'll drive you home."

"No, thank you." Stiff, uncompromising. She wished her knees weren't going jittery at his touch, her resolve melting at the regret she heard in his voice.

"I guess this wasn't a very good way to make my point."

She cast him a cool look, not caring about her brimming tears. "No, it wasn't. I—I'm trying to do the best I can."

He sighed. "Maybe you are, but—"

A movement off toward the gallery stopped him, and Annie spotted Cynthia Linwood bursting from the entrance. "Garvin, I wanted to talk to you before you left." She hurried up to them, no sign she was aware of their altercation. "I wanted to remind you about Friday. It would mean a lot to John if you could make it."

It was as if a mask dropped over Garvin. He stood very still, his expression completely unreadable. "Thank you for the reminder, Cynthia." But there was no gratitude in his tone.

Cynthia Linwood pretended to be oblivious to his manner. "We would all love to see you, Garvin. And, please, bring Annie with you." She turned to Annie. "We would love to have you join us, Annie. I mean that."

Before she could ask what they were talking about, Garvin broke in. "It was good to see you and John tonight, Cynthia. If I can be there Friday, I'll let you know. Good night."

Cynthia nodded, a touch of annoyance cooling her dark eyes. "It was good to see you, too." She gave Annie a formal smile. "A pleasure to meet you, Annie. I look forward to visiting your gallery."

When Cynthia Linwood retreated, Annie let sheer curiosity drag her down the street with Garvin, who marched to his car without a word. "What was that all about?" she asked, finally, when he stopped at his sleek, expensive sports car.

He glanced back at her, his eyes lost in the shadows of the night. "Friday is the annual dinner for the Haley Linwood Foundation. I'd forgotten."

"Oh. I see. I'm sorry."

"Don't be," he said, curt, almost harsh. "I'm not still in love with my wife."

Annie jumped backward at the unexpected ferocity of his words and stumbled on the curb. His hand shot out, steadying her, his touch an electric current. "It's okay," she said. "I can manage."

"That's you, isn't it, Annie?" His voice was ragged, husky. "Always one to manage. Sometimes you can't, you know. Sometimes life just throws too damned much at you."

She nodded dully, weakening at the flash of memory, the gleaming white casket that held her mother's remains, the spray of pink roses, herself at sixteen with no parents, only Gran, only their cottage by the bay. And now not even that.

She heard his sharp intake of breath, felt his hands gentle on her as he drew the folds of Gran's shawl up over her shoulders. His fingers skimmed her throat, melting her resistance. "Come on." His voice was soft now, liquid. "I'll take you home."

Garvin kept his eyes pinned to the road as he negotiated Annie's steep Russian Hill street. She hadn't spoken since leaving Winslow's. Just as well. A tight coil of tension had knotted itself in his gut as he'd watched her tonight. It had nothing to do with Sarah Linwood or Vic Denardo and everything to do with Annie Payne. Her smile, her laugh, her ease with who she was and what she wanted to be. She was a captivating woman.

And a liar, of course.

He double-parked in front of her building. He remembered living on a shoestring, working toward a dream. Not giving a damn about anything else.

She opened her door. "Thank you for the ride."

Her voice was soft, reserved. He narrowed his gaze on her. Her eyes shifted away from his. Guilt, he thought. Annoyance. He studied the shadows on the line of her jaw in the harsh light from the street, watched her throat as she swallowed. "Annie—Sarah Linwood was a troubled woman five years ago, and two people were murdered. I'd keep that in mind if I were you."

Her gaze came back to him. "I will."

The coil in his gut tightened even more.

She started from the car, but he leaned toward her, careful not to grab her arm, to touch her in any way. He'd be lost if he did. He knew it. Sprung loose, all the tension in him would send him spinning out of control.

"Why did you leave Maine?" he asked softly.

Surprise flickered in her face at his question. "What?"

"Maine. Tell me. What were you thinking when you packed up your car, packed up Otto, and headed west? What were you hoping to find out here? What did you dream about on the drive west?"

For a moment he thought she wouldn't answer him. Then she said, "I just wanted—I needed a chance to figure out who I am now that everything that made me who I was is gone. I don't know if that makes any sense to you."

He nodded, if anything the coil of tension tighter. "It does."

"I should go."

"Annie, Sarah can be very persuasive. She knows how to use her Linwood manners and bearing. She can exact promises from people they later regret making." He paused, but Annie Payne didn't jump out of the car and race into her apartment. She kept one hand on the door, listening. "Haley believed in her. She couldn't understand that Sarah was responsible for the choices she made about Vic Denardo and her gambling. Haley kept expecting her to snap out of it, kept believing she would. She saw her aunt as a victim of her father."

Annie frowned. "You mean Sarah's father? But he was killed—"

"Thomas Linwood was a harsh, controlling, difficult man. When Sarah first started painting—not long after Haley sat for her —and he found out, he was furious. He didn't mind her dabbling in art. It was a ladylike enough hobby. But when she started making noises about showing her work in public, he objected. He claimed he was trying to protect her from disappointment and humiliation."

"But you don't believe it," Annie said quietly.

Garvin shook his head. "No, I don't. I think he was a sanctimonious old bastard and a mean one. He couldn't stand Sarah doing something he couldn't control."

"How did she react?"

"She burned her canvases."

"What?" Horror drained the color from Annie's face; her grip on the door faltered. "But that's so self-destructive!"

"Sarah has a self-destructive streak."

"What about the portrait of your wife? How did it survive?"

"Haley had it. She presented it to her grandfather after Sarah had destroyed all her other paintings and insisted he hang it in his library. If he didn't, she vowed never to speak to him again. He doted on her, and he knew she meant what she said." Garvin paused, remembering Haley's laughter the day she'd told him that story. She'd been so damned proud of herself. "So he obliged her."

"She must have been an incredible woman," Annie said softly.

Garvin nodded. "She was. Sarah managed to capture her spirit in her portrait. I can't explain—"

"You don't have to. I saw it, too."

"Annie—" He inhaled, trying to get distance, control, where there was none to be had. "Tell Sarah about me if you haven't already. Ask her to let me see her. I'll go to her or I'll meet her anywhere of her choosing."

"Please, I—"

"I only want the truth, Annie. Nothing more."

She pushed open the door and leaped out of the car.

Garvin sighed. He could go after her. Pin her to the wall and demand she prove to him she wasn't in contact with Sarah. Scare her. Intimidate her. Damn it, *make* her talk.

Or try. There was always Otto.

In spite of himself, he smiled. He stepped out of the car and called to her over the hood. "I'm not giving up on you, Annie."

She didn't even glance back at him.

"If you need me, you can find me at my marina or up at my house. You have the addresses and numbers."

No answer. She opened the high gate to the walk that led back to her apartment.

And before he knew it, Garvin had crossed onto the sidewalk and was standing in back of her, casting a dark shadow over her. The tension had him in its grip. He couldn't get a decent breath. His mind reeled with images of carrying Annie Payne inside to her bed.

She turned to him, her brow furrowed. She didn't take a step back but still she said nothing.

Her eyes, however, never left his.

And he knew.

"Annie."

He pulled her against him, groaned at the feel of her warm, slender body, and fell upon her mouth, tasting her, filling himself with her, desperately trying to release the tension that had built up inside him, forcing that tight coil to spring free.

Yet somewhere from far within the deep recesses of his conscience, caution and control wormed their way forward.

He tore his mouth from hers. Lurched back from her. His breathing was ragged, his body consumed with a hunger that had never been so deep, so insistent. He dragged the back of his hand across his chin, staring at her. He'd only made matters worse for himself, he knew.

Not even a night in bed with Annie would satisfy him.

"I'm sorry," he said curtly.

Her eyebrows quirked up. "You are? I'm not. If I hadn't wanted you to kiss me, Garvin MacCrae, I'd have told you so. And if you hadn't listened, you'd be doubled over right now wishing you had. I've an effective move to the privates." She gestured toward the area in question. "You leave yourself open to such a blow."

"Annie, I swear—"

She curved an arm around his neck and kissed him softly, fervently. He heard her quiet moan deep in the back of her throat. Her mouth opened against his, and he wondered if she knew, if she had any idea what it took for him not to sweep her up and carry her down the walk to her apartment.

But there was Sarah.

There was whatever Annie Payne was hiding from him.

Yet her tongue, the taste of her, left him breathless, aching. When she finished, she searched his eyes, smiling as if she had total control of him and herself. "There. Now you know."

Garvin wasn't sure he knew anything.

"I wanted that kiss as much as you did, Garvin MacCrae. And took from it as much as you."

He smiled back, just a hint of what lay beneath the surface. "So you think."

That stopped her. She drew back, not so smug. Her shawl dusted the ground. "And I know where to find you," she said. "If I need you, I'll be in touch. Good night."

"My best to Otto," he said, and headed for his car before his desire to have Annie Payne in his bed overtook his common sense.

Or hers did.

Chapter Six

Annie sniffed a jar of something that looked like dryer fuzz that Zoe had brought over just before closing late Tuesday afternoon. "I don't smell anything."

"But how do you feel?"

"Harassed, but I felt harassed before you walked in."

Zoe groaned, snatching the jar away. "You're impossible."

"I'm sorry. Let me try again."

"Only if you'll tell me if that was Cynthia Linwood in here after lunch."

Annie gave a mock frown. "Who's doing whom the favor here?"

"It was," Zoe said, thrusting the jar back under Annie's nose. "Garvin MacCrae, Cynthia Linwood. You're certainly getting around, my friend."

"Apple pie."

"What?"

"The smell. It's apple pie."

"No, it's not."

Annie laughed. "Why do you keep having me smell stuff if you're always going to argue with me?"

Zoe screwed the cap back on the jar. "Because I'm ever amazed at what an untrained sense of smell comes up with. Apple pie. Good God."

"Well, what is it?"

"Essential oil of juniper with a touch of vanilla. I drizzled it over raw cotton, just for fun. The vanilla must have triggered your apple pie response. It's the only thing I can figure. But how on earth could apple pie make you feel harassed?"

"It didn't. My day did. And there's no vanilla in apple pie."

"Yes, but it has a similar nostalgic scent." Zoe plopped down on Annie's high swivel chair. Business was slow on Tuesday. "Did she buy anything?"

"Who?" At Zoe's long-suffering sigh, Annie said, "Oh. Cynthia Linwood. No, she just stopped in to see my gallery. I met her at Winslow's last night." She'd already provided Zoe with a detailed account of the opening that morning over corn muffins. Zoe, of course, had accused Annie of willfully leaving out crucial details about her and Garvin MacCrae, which she had. "She seems nice enough. I think she's curious about the painting I bought at the auction."

"Well, who isn't?" But she became serious. "Cynthia Linwood's in a position to really help you, you know. All she has to do is recommend you to her friends, and you won't have to worry about paying the rent. Our miserly landlord might even be forced to hire someone to keep up the courtyard." She leaned forward, peering at Annie. "You have dark circles under your eyes, kid. Up late pondering Garvin MacCrae?"

For sure, Annie thought. "Zoe, last night was not a date."

"Doesn't keep a body from staying up late pondering." She slid off the stool and grabbed up her concoction. "But you're already feeling harassed, so I'll leave you alone. Go home and take a hot orange blossom bath, get some sleep."

"I was going to take Otto for a run on the beach."

Zoe grinned. "That too."

She departed with her dryer fuzz, and Annie called two customers to notify them that their frame orders were ready. She reached answering machines for both and left what she hoped were coherent messages. She hadn't had so much as a browser in the past forty-five minutes. No Winslow Gallery was hers, especially on a Tuesday.

Suddenly, out of nowhere, she could see herself and Gran out on the rocks on a quiet summer afternoon, the only sounds the wind and the gulls and the lapping tide. Gran had never lived in the city, had never wanted to live anywhere but on her bay. She'd seldom even traveled. Everything she needed, everything she wanted, was right there on the peninsula. She didn't miss art galleries, coffee shops, big-screen movie theaters, city lights.

Annie rubbed one foot over Otto's back. Lethargic all day, he was conked out behind her desk. Cynthia Linwood hadn't even noticed him. Probably just as well. How could she explain herself, her life, to someone like Cynthia Linwood?

"I'm homesick, Otto," she said softly.

It was only because she was so damned desperate to have Garvin MacCrae on her side, she decided. An inexplicable bit of insanity on her part. Totally misguided. But there it was, eating away at her, making her squirm. Time to latch onto the woman she'd been before Saturday morning's auction. Before kissing a man who only wanted to use her to get to his wife's murderer.

A man materialized in front of her desk, jerking her from her stupor. She jumped and just managed to keep from falling off her chair and making an ass of herself. "I'm sorry," she said, her heart pounding in classic startle response. "I didn't hear you come in."

He was a dark-haired, good-looking man in his mid-to-late thirties, conservatively dressed in a gray suit and red tie. He wore expensive preppy glasses. Obviously not expecting her extreme reaction, he gave her a tentative smile. "No apology necessary. I didn't mean to startle you. I had no idea you hadn't heard me." His smile reached his dark eyes, helping to calm her. "No one's ever accused me of being light on my feet."

Annie waved a hand, not feeling so embarrassed. "Oh, it's not your fault. My mind was wandering."

Abandoning Otto, who hadn't alerted her to company or even stirred, she went around her half-moon desk. She had on one of her better outfits today, a bisque-colored silk sweater with a slim black skirt and silver hoop earrings. Basic, mix-and-matchable, but attractive.

Her new customer did a quick survey of the gallery, then glanced back at her. "You're Annie Payne, I take it? I'm Ethan Conninger. I work with the Linwoods. I—" He broke off as Otto took it upon himself to emerge from behind the desk and stretch, an impressive sight even for someone accustomed to rottweilers.

"It's okay," Annie said quickly, "he's friendly. His name's Otto."

"After von Bismarck?"

She shook her head. "After this old lobsterman who spotted him in the water. Otto Miller. It's a long story."

Ethan Conninger's easy manner didn't change. "I see. He doesn't deter business?"

"No one's complained yet."

He grinned at her, irreverent. "Who would?" Otto, ever unpredictable, decided to make friends with him. Ethan

Conninger gingerly patted his massive head and stood back from his slobbery mouth. "Hey, fella. You're a big guy, aren't you?" He looked back at Annie as he straightened. "He's a beautiful animal. I've considered getting a rottweiler, but I've never really been around one. How old is he?"

"Three." Having someone to pet him instead of cringe at his presence, Otto flopped happily down at Ethan Conninger's feet. "I rescued him from a bay in Maine when he was just a puppy. He's never been your stereotypical rottweiler."

"I can see that." Since Otto hadn't chomped off a leg or anything, Ethan Conninger seemed more at ease. "Well, I just stopped by to introduce myself while I was in the area. Cynthia Linwood mentioned you were at Winslow's last night. I couldn't make it myself."

"Yes, she stopped by earlier."

"Did she? I knew she was planning to." He grinned easily, self-conscious in a charming way. "Look, to be perfectly honest, we're all curious about you after the auction. The painting you bought—frankly, I thought it had been destroyed years ago. So when you came out of the blue and paid as much as you did—" He shrugged. "Tickles my curiosity bone, anyway."

Annie smiled. "I understand. I didn't expect this reaction on Saturday when I bought the painting. I had no idea of its background."

"It must have come as a shock when you learned." He peered closely at an oil painting of a meadow of lupine that one of her Maine friends had done. "You had us glued to our chairs, I'll say that. Garvin and I have been friends for years—long before either of us got involved with the Linwoods. He's very tenacious. Actually, I was surprised when he stopped at five thousand."

"I'm glad he did." She tried to keep her tone light, that of a woman who had nothing to hide. Garvin wouldn't be fooled, but maybe Ethan Conninger would be. "I don't know if I'd have paid more than five thousand myself."

He cocked his head back at her. "No regrets?"

"I wouldn't say that. If I'd known about—if I'd known why Garvin wanted the painting, I might not have bid at all."

It was the truth, she thought. She hadn't known about the murders. If she had, she might have argued with Sarah and refused to represent her. At least she would have better been able to assess the risks of what she was getting into.

Ethan Conninger moved on to her pottery and glasswork displays, apparently giving them his full attention. "Cynthia mentioned you and Garvin have made peace."

"I didn't know we needed to."

He raised his eyebrows, giving her a rakish grin. "Then you're the only one."

She could feel the blood rising to her cheeks and wondered if he noticed.

"Any plans to put the portrait on display?" he asked casually.

"No, not right now." Maybe, she thought, when Sarah went public with her work. "I certainly didn't mean to stir up bad memories—"

"A lot of memories went on the block this weekend, Annie." Abruptly serious, he moved back toward her, Otto on his heels. "John and Cynthia wanted to do a real housecleaning. The painting wasn't the only hot button that could have been pressed. The house itself—" He broke off, his dark eyes clouded behind his glasses. "It wasn't an easy day for any of us, but at least it was all for a good cause. The Haley Linwood Foundation has become a real force in the community."

"I'm sure it has," Annie mumbled awkwardly. She recalled Garvin's reaction to Cynthia Linwood's reminder of the foundation's annual dinner on Friday. Maybe he'd moved on after his wife's death, but he wasn't over it. On some level, he could hope that finding her killer would give him the closure he needed.

"Look, I've taken up enough of your time," Ethan Conninger said. The earlier casualness and smoothly irreverent manner were back. "You've a nice gallery here, Annie Payne. Good luck to you. I hope it succeeds."

"Thank you."

As he turned to go, Gran's painting caught his eye, and Annie suddenly decided that Ethan Conninger knew a bit about art. "That's an interesting work," he said. "Not so easy to dismiss, is it?

It makes me feel homesick, and I've never even been in a cottage that looks like that."

"My grandmother painted it. She lived in that cottage her entire life."

"Amazing. I suppose it's not for sale, either?"

Annie smiled, shook her head. "Nope."

He laughed. "It's going to be tough to stay in business when you insist on keeping your best stuff for yourself."

"Well, not many would consider Gran's painting or the painting I bought Saturday quality work—"

"But you do."

"They have heart. They're honest. I don't know, they just work for me. I don't pretend I'll ever get the five thousand back for the painting of Haley Linwood MacCrae, and Gran's—" She glanced up at it, immediately comforted. "I wouldn't take a million dollars for it."

Ethan Conninger winked at her. "It'll be interesting to see how you survive in San Francisco with that attitude. But it is refreshing. Glad to have met you, Annie Payne. Next time I'm ready to buy some artwork, I'll be in touch."

"I'd appreciate that."

After he left, Annie spent a restless hour before finally closing up shop for the day. She skipped her run on the beach with Otto and instead walked him up and down a couple of hills, then headed back to her apartment. She grabbed an apple and paced around her small main room. Five minutes later, without thinking too hard about whether she had the time, the energy, or the nerve for it, she decided that objective details on the Linwood murders were long overdue, and she headed to the San Francisco public library.

Garvin headed up the dock, yachts and launches and the sparkling bay behind him, a strip of grass with benches and a parking lot up ahead, and the main buildings and grounds of the marina up to his left. He knew he looked like hell. It was Wednesday afternoon, and he'd spent the last twenty hours out on the water. He'd just anchored his boat. He needed a shower, a meal, someone to handcuff him to his desk to keep him from going back out across the Golden Gate to see Annie Payne.

But Michael Yuma waved to him from the front of their marine supply store, a small white building in need of paint. Typically, Yuma looked as if he'd been scraping barnacles off the bottoms of boats all day. "Hey, MacCrae. You're twenty minutes too late. Your damsel in distress was just here."

"My what? That's a pretty sexist term, you know, Yuma."

Michael squinted at him in the late afternoon sun. "Yeah, well, you didn't hear what she called you. Man, her feet weren't touching the ground, she was so mad."

" 'Damsel in distress' implies troubled—"

"Oh, she's that too. Didn't want to show it, but I could see it. Blond lady. Had a big ugly dog in the car with her."

"That would be Otto," Garvin said dryly.

"Yeah, well, I wasn't going to argue with him in the car. She wouldn't give me any details. She said to tell you she'd hunt you down like a rabid dog."

"Those were her words?"

"Yep. I'm from the city. What do I know about rabid dogs?" He grinned, but the concern hovered in his dark eyes. "I wondered why you headed out to sea. Now I'm getting an idea."

Garvin raked a hand through his hair and glanced back at the water, half wishing he'd stayed out another twenty hours. Yuma was perfectly capable of running the marina without him. He had yesterday, when Garvin had headed across the bay and kept watch on Annie's Gallery, ducking into Union Street shops and restaurants in which he had no interest in a half-hearted effort to keep her from spotting him. Anyone who ventured down the brick walk to her courtyard shop, he saw. Cynthia Linwood, Ethan Conninger. The odd browser. Aromatherapy customers for the shop next door.

But no Vic Denardo. And the only one watching Annie Payne seemed to be him. By dusk he was so disgusted with his own behavior and agitated by the situation that he'd had to get out on the water. He'd stayed out all night and then most of the day.

"You told her where I was?" he asked Yuma.

"Yep. Told her I expected you in before nightfall and offered her coffee and a place to sit inside if she wanted to wait here, gave her directions to your house in case she wanted to wait there. She chose to leave. My bet is, she's up at your place."

"You don't think she went back to San Francisco?"

"Uh-uh. She was after your hide." Yuma clapped him on the shoulder. "Nothing like an angry woman to greet a man just come in off the water. You need me, MacCrae, give a holler."

"Always good to know, Yuma."

The kid was still chuckling as he headed back to work, but Garvin knew that Michael Yuma had meant what he'd said. If Garvin needed him, Yuma would be there. But what could he—or anyone—do about Annie Payne?

He got in his car. He'd go home, see if Annie was there. If she wasn't, he'd head over to San Francisco. One way or another, he'd find her.

Or she'd find him.

If she was mad about what he thought she was mad about, Garvin didn't blame her.

Annie got lost three times on her way to Garvin MacCrae's house in the hills above San Francisco Bay. Michael Yuma's directions were rough at best. Unfamiliar with the narrow, winding roads of exclusive Belvedere, she wasn't surprised she kept taking wrong turns. The streets were a maze, and the expensive houses nestled into the hillside were often not even visible from the road.

Plus she was on edge. She was gripping the wheel too hard, breathing too hard, *thinking* too hard.

But not thinking clearly. Otherwise she'd be on her way back to San Francisco by now, looking after her gallery, checking in with Sarah Linwood, whom she hadn't seen since Sunday. She slowed to a crawl in front of a wood-and-stucco house tucked atop a steep hill overlooking the bay. Although not as remote as her cottage in Maine, it seemed isolated, removed from the rest of the world, with tall oaks and evergreens drenching it in shade and ivy and myrtle and sweet woodruff tangled in its small front yard.

This had to be Garvin's house, Annie decided, pulling over. She left her car idling. The front entrance was clearly on the house's upper level, with more house below, out of view given the near-vertical incline of the hill. It was attractive but not ostentatious, an intriguing contrast to his working marina.

"Well, Otto," Annie said, staring over at the shaded house, "what do you say? Doesn't look as if anybody's home to me."

Otto flopped down on the backseat, never to be convinced he didn't really fit there. On nonauction days, it was often his preferred place to ride. He seemed in no dire need of a walk. The trek across the Golden Gate had amused him. He'd be fine if she decided to venture down Garvin MacCrae's front walk.

Annie climbed out of the car and breathed in the clean, cool air before accepting that she was going to do what she was going to do, and she might as well get on with it. Maybe Garvin was home, after all. Maybe she'd wait for him on his doorstep.

"Maybe you're nuts," she muttered.

She'd spotted him following her last night at the San Francisco public library. She had no idea where—or when—he'd picked up her trail. It was only by chance he hadn't followed her all the way up to Sarah Linwood's little pink house, except she might have been more on her guard if that had been her destination. She'd simply glanced behind her at the right moment, and there he was, watching her from across the lobby. By the time she'd made her way through the crowd to have his head, he'd vanished.

She was fit to be tied. Had he followed her all day? Had he thought kissing her gave him the *right* to follow her? She'd spent a restless day at her gallery before giving up and calling someone to cover for her for the rest of the afternoon while she tracked him down.

Squirrels chattered in the trees, the pungent greenery scented the air. A light breeze rustled as she mounted the two wide, flat stone steps to the front door. She rang the doorbell, just in case a housekeeper or somebody was there.

No one answered.

She sighed, glancing around, noticing the silence.

What if she had to leave before he came back? She'd have missed her chance to get a picture of the man.

Otto, his head stuck out the back window, yawned as he watched her, white slobber oozing out over his jaw. She could leave him stuck in the car for only so long. It wasn't as if she could wait around forever.

With no rail to impede her, she had only to step off the side of the step to reach Garvin's front window and have a peek inside his house.

Without further thought, she did just that. She squeezed behind an overgrown rhododendron, its fat buds and waxy leaves poking into her back as she stood on her tiptoes and pressed her face to the window.

From what she could see, the house was long and narrow, the front door opening into a main room with spare, functional furnishings in neutral colors. There were french doors to a deck, the gleam of San Francisco Bay and San Francisco beyond.

It wasn't easy, Annie thought, to integrate all she'd learned about Garvin MacCrae into one tidy, predictable, or even understandable man. Her library research had only added to her confusion. He had married a Linwood heiress. He had worked for a decade as an ambitious, driven financial wizard. He had refused to take a dime of his wife's money and instead had established a charitable foundation in her name. Five years after her death, he ran a marina.

A car sounded on the street, and she ducked down behind the rhododendron. Peering through the leaves and buds out at the street, she saw Garvin's black sports car ease in behind hers.

She groaned, feeling like a sneak. "Terrific."

Garvin got out of his car, frowning. Otto gave a low bark. It wasn't anything fierce, just a greeting. He and Garvin MacCrae were pals. Garvin eyed her car, he eyed Otto. Even knee-deep in ferns and myrtle and squatted down among rhododendrons, she could tell he was in a raw mood. He wore a black plaid flannel shirt, unbuttoned, over a black polo shirt, a pair of tattered jeans, boat shoes. He looked haggard, hard, sexy, in no mood to catch a woman hiding in his rhododendrons.

But with Otto and her car right there, he'd know she couldn't be far away. Ever one to look reality straight in the eye and do what had to be done, Annie pushed her way through the rhodo-dendrons and tangle of undergrowth out across the small yard.

Garvin started down his walk. He was hyperalert, studying her closely, and she remembered her encounter with Michael Yuma. She hadn't, she recalled, exactly had her temper under tight rein.

"I understand you're looking for me," he said.

She picked a long vine off her ankle and cast it behind her. "Damned right. I'm here to skin you for following me last night."

"I figured as much."

She tripped out to the street. He ground to a stop about a yard from her. She noticed the frayed collar of his polo shirt and the day's growth of beard along his jaw. Everything about him was raw-edged, earthy. "I don't like being followed."

"I don't like being lied to." There wasn't even a hint of guilt in those dark green eyes. "I'm just sorry you ended up at the library instead of Sarah Linwood's doorstep."

Annie snorted, incredulous. "Wait just a minute! You're the one who's done wrong here. I just spent a nice, quiet day running my gallery, experiencing San Francisco—"

It was his turn for an incredulous snort.

She thrust her hands on her hips and glared at him, not nearly, she realized, as furious as she'd expected to be now that they were face-to-face. But she *was* indignant. "All was quiet yesterday. Really. No strange men hiding in my workroom, no suspicious, irritating, stubborn men interrogating me. I did have Cynthia Linwood stop by—"

"And Ethan Conninger."

She frowned, eyeing him suspiciously. He looked smug. Too smug. "How do you know?"

"Because I watched you all day."

She stared at him. "You what?"

He shrugged, matter-of-fact. "I started in the morning and kept at it until you spotted me at the library." He strode past her, unrepentant, and glanced back when he reached his doorstep. "Lucky for you I'm not Vic Denardo."

Speechless, she spat and sputtered while he shoved his key into his front door. He pushed the door open and turned back to her, his eyes lost in the shifting shade. "If it's any consolation," he said mildly, "for the most part I was bored as hell and not exactly thrilled with myself."

"Where were you?"

"At the coffee shop on and off, and that maternity store—"

"You must have fit right in there," Annie said dryly.

Something vaguely like humor flashed in his expression. "It has a good view of your courtyard from the back window. I pretended I was contemplating the perils of fatherhood."

Suddenly—unwillingly—Annie could see him as a father, a dirty-faced toddler on his shoulders. She shook off the image. "Well, I'm glad you suffered."

He laughed. "I'll bet you are." He rubbed a hand across his stubbled jaw, and she could see how tired he was. "You look done in, Annie. Chasing over hill and dale after me doesn't agree with you. Why don't you come inside and have a glass of iced tea?"

"Chasing after you feels just fine," she said airily, then, seeing the amused look on his face, realized what she'd said. She groaned. "I meant—"

"I know what you meant." He grinned and stood to one side, motioning her in. "After you, Annie."

Gathering her remaining shreds of dignity, she breezed up the steps, shot past him, and entered his house. The interior was cool and still and shaded, all wood and neutral colors. Across the main room, the world seemed to drop straight off into the blue waters of the bay, sparkling and glistening in the last of the afternoon sun. In a sitting area off to her right, an Audubon print of a peregrine falcon hung over a huge stone fireplace. Further to her right, on the short wall at the end of the room, nautical maps had been perfunctorily tacked into every inch available. A chest in the corner next to the french doors held a small telescope and a half-dozen pairs of binoculars.

"I'll get the tea," Garvin said, withdrawing through a doorway off the dining end of the room, where a large table of polished, gleaming cherry looked unused.

Still tense, uncertain she shouldn't have just jumped back in her car and gone home, Annie unfisted her hands and shook her fingers, trying to work blood back into them. "You're tense," she muttered to herself. "Tense, tense, tense."

She wandered across the room and examined the wall of maps. The daughter of a seaman and former director of a maritime museum, she could find her way around a nautical map. These, it seemed, were all of San Francisco Bay and the surrounding waters.

Garvin materialized beside her, handing her a tall glass of iced tea. As he took a sip of his own, he reached an arm in front of her and pointed to a spot on one of the maps. "This is where we are." He moved his hand down toward the water; she watched the muscles in his wrist, noted his scars and calluses. "This is my marina."

Annie drank some of her tea, aware of how close he was to her. "I didn't expect a real working marina."

"A lot of people don't."

"Because of your background?"

"And its location. This is a high-income area. But I'm finding a lot of boat people are like myself and don't care about the frills."

"My father was like that. He did a variety of things—fishing, lobstering, crewing—whatever work he could get that was on the water. He died at sea."

"What happened?"

Suddenly it seemed natural to tell him. "He answered a distress call. Some college kids had gone out frostbite sailing and got into trouble. While he was getting the last one aboard, he went into the water himself and was lost. He had hypothermia. He couldn't hang on."

"I'm sorry."

"My mother said he'd never have been able to live with himself if he didn't do what he could to save those kids' lives."

"Did she blame them for what happened?"

Annie shook her head, remembering her mother telling her the story, trying to make the man she'd loved real to his daughter. "They shouldn't have gone out that day. They didn't know how to handle such conditions, but they didn't know what would happen. My father could have waited for the Coast Guard to get there. If he had, all three boys would probably have died of exposure. So he minimized the risks and did what he felt he had to do."

"And your mother understood that," Garvin said quietly.

"Yes."

"The boys?"

"They were from Boston. They're grown men now, of course. Long before I became director of the local maritime museum, they funded a new wing dedicated to my father's memory. They've had to live with the consequences of that day, just as I have."

"You've a forgiving nature, Annie Payne."

"They made a mistake that day, but there are those who said my father made a mistake, too. That he should have remembered he had a wife and infant daughter at home." She drank more of her tea, trying to put into words something she'd never tried to explain to anyone before, not even Gran. "But I think he did remember, and that's why he did what he did."

Garvin stared at her a moment, then nodded slowly. "He owed it to you both to do the right thing."

"If you want right done by you," she said, "you have to do right by others."

He turned to his wall of maps. "It's complicated, knowing what's right."

"Sometimes. Not always."

"Not on that day?"

She glanced at him. "They tell me he never hesitated."

Garvin's gaze seemed focused on some point on one of his maps, his face expressionless, unreadable. Annie thought of the pictures she'd seen of him last night. A different Garvin MacCrae from the one she saw now. He'd had a young wife, a successful career, a future very different from the life he now lived.

Everything—his very soul, it seemed—had changed with the murders of Thomas Linwood and Haley Linwood MacCrae.

"I can understand why you want to catch up with Vic Denardo," Annie said, her voice suddenly shaky. "But we don't even know if that was him on Sunday."

"I know."

"If I could see a picture of him—"

"You could ask Sarah." He drank more of his tea, eyeing her. The dark shadow of beard only added to his air of rough masculinity. "She might have one."

Annie gave him a sideways look. "You don't give up, do you?"

He swore under his breath and surged forward, snapping locks on the french doors, flinging them open, pushing out onto the narrow deck. An icy breeze blew into the house. Annie shivered. The temperature must have dropped. Or maybe she was so overheated, she felt the cold more. She debated walking out the front door and driving off. Garvin could stand out on his deck the rest of the afternoon and the whole damned night with just his bitter suspicions for company.

Of course, his suspicions had merit.

She bit off a curse of her own.

After only a fraction's hesitation, she set her iced tea on the chest with the binoculars and followed him outside. She was no coward, and last night's research in the library had made her realize in a way she hadn't before just what was at stake for Garvin MacCrae. She noticed his broad back as he leaned against the deck rail, the thick, corded muscles that betrayed the kind of work he'd taken up since his wife's death. Kissing him the other night might not have made sense, but Annie couldn't quite make herself regret it.

"It's not any easier for me to trust you than it is for you to trust me," she said quietly.

He didn't glance at her. "I know."

"Since the auction..." She stumbled over words; trying to communicate with this man, to connect with him on some level other than the physical, was a challenge not for the faint of heart. It was also important. It was starting to scare her how important. "None of this is what I expected when Otto and I packed up and headed west."

His gaze shifted to her, probing, unrelenting. "That's not my problem, Annie. I'm sorry, but it just isn't."

She bore down on her lower lip, averted her eyes. She could sense his exasperation with her continued refusal to tell him what he wanted to know. "Look," she said, "I'm trying to do the right thing too."

"Did you tell Sarah about Denardo? She should know. If he decides to follow you—"

"Garvin, please."

He pushed off the rail and muttered a string of curses before swinging back around at her. "If Sarah Linwood didn't kill her father and Haley or conspire in any way to have them killed, she has nothing to fear from me."

Annie's pulse quickened, her breath had gone shallow, shaky. She grabbed hold of the rail with such ferocity, her knuckles immediately turned white. She wasn't afraid of what Garvin would do to her if she refused to talk. She wasn't mad at him for pushing that same button again and again. She simply didn't know what she should do. She had none of her father's clarity that awful day at sea thirty years ago.

She licked her lips, cleared her throat. "For the sake of argument, let's say I do know where Sarah Linwood is."

His smile was thin and unpleasant. "Let's say that."

"Let's also say I have reasons for wanting to protect her. Let's say she—" Annie hesitated, choosing her words carefully. "Let's say she's not the Sarah Linwood you once knew. That she's changed. That she's changed a lot."

"In what way?"

"In every way."

"That's a stretch," Garvin said. "But I'll go along with it."

"And let's say she had no more idea than I did that my purchase of her portrait of Haley would cause such a ruckus." Struck by the beauty of the view before her, Annie leaned against the rail. The water was glass smooth, dotted with boats. She glanced at the man beside her. "Then why would I trust you with her?"

"Sarah's not that fragile, Annie." Some of the edge went off his tone. "No matter what's happened to her in the last five years. Don't let her fool you."

"I'm not as skeptical about everything as you are. I went bounding into this thing with the best of intentions, and next thing, I've got a ballroom full of people hissing at me, a possible killer on my case, Linwoods everywhere, you." She took a breath. "It's more than I bargained for."

"Annie—"

"I'll tell you the truth. All right? If it'll—"

He pivoted to her, touched a finger to her mouth. "No. Don't. Don't say a word."

His voice was raw from exhaustion, tension. He needed rest, a hot bath. He'd been out on the water all night, most of the day. Thinking, Annie expected. Debating what to do. Remembering. She thought she understood. When she'd bid against him for Sarah Linwood's painting, she'd shattered whatever life he'd fashioned for himself in the past five years, whatever shaky peace with his fate.

She had no idea what he meant to do. Ask her to leave? Fetch a tape recorder to make sure she couldn't take back what she was going to tell him?

Instead, he drew his finger along her lower lip. Hundreds, thousands, of sensations spilled through her, softening any resistance, overcoming any reserve. Yesterday, tomorrow, suddenly made no difference.

"Annie, Annie."

His voice was just as raw, just as exhausted, but without the edge. He took her face in his hands and kissed her gently, softly, letting his palms skim down her shoulders, down her back. She should be all right, she thought faintly. It wasn't the sort of raging, rough kiss as the other night. There was control behind it. Intention. Really, she should be all right. She wouldn't lose herself.

But she was wrong.

Her head spun, her blood heated. She savored the taste of him, the feel of his hands on the small of her back. He edged her lips with his tongue, eased in. Control. Oh, yes. He had it. And intention. Indeed. He knew exactly what he was doing. To her. To himself. Somewhere deep within her a moan of pleasure, of sweet torture, formed and then slowly escaped. He responded by pulling her against him, urging his dark, thrusting need against her.

Her head roared. For a wild moment she expected they'd end up tearing off their clothes and making love there on the deck, never mind the hard boards, the cold breeze, the tension between them.

But even as the thought of his body inside hers gripped her, he drew back.

She threw one hand back and braced herself on the rail, gasping for air, staring at him.

He raked a hand through his hair, hissed a curse. "Talk to Sarah, Annie. Tell her what I've said. Then you can talk to me."

He turned back to the bay.

Annie peeled her hand from the balustrade. She started to speak but changed her mind. He'd dismissed her. Summarily. With the taste of him still on her mouth.

Without a word, she walked unsteadily back through the living room and out to her car. She would do well to remember that Garvin MacCrae was a man with a mission. He would roll over her —over anyone—to get what he wanted. Not because he didn't have feelings for her but because finding whoever was responsible for his murderer was the right thing to do.

About that, Annie thought, she could make no mistake.

Chapter Seven

Annie took a circuitous route—no difficult task in San Francisco —up to the tangle of streets where Sarah Linwood had her cottage. She pulled over several times and let cars pass, telling herself she was just being cautious, not paranoid. But damned if she'd let anyone follow her today.

Once she stopped and walked Otto around a little park. Twice she almost turned back and went home. She could just forget about Garvin MacCrae and the Linwoods. Forget about Sarah's paintings. Vic Denardo. Two unsolved five-year-old homicides. She could make her mark in San Francisco without "discovering" Sarah Linwood.

She found her way up to Sarah's cul-de-sac in her car for the first time, thus permitting her to bypass the stone steps. Unbeliev- ably, there was even a parking space. She promised Otto a treat if he hung in there one more time, then ventured to the front door.

Her knocks went unanswered. She frowned, the wind swirling and cold enough that she wished she'd worn her fleece jacket over her sweater. But the brisk air revived her, helped remind her she wasn't the first woman to kiss a man she had no business kissing. Garvin MacCrae just had a way of stirring her up. That stubble of beard, those earthy eyes, his worn, sexy clothes—even his fatigue was sensual, calling up images of taut muscles and sweat as he'd sailed the bay.

Another two knocks, and Sarah still didn't answer her door.

Impatient, Annie pressed her face up to the front window. The little table was immaculate. No sign of her reclusive painter in her kitchen or in what she could see of the rest of the house. Was she asleep? Had she fallen out of sight of the window? Had she gone out?

Where would a woman who could barely walk, who had no apparent means of transportation, no friends, go?

The grocery, you idiot. Annie sighed, very aware that she'd let a simple kiss cloud her thinking. Then she remembered how close she'd been to making love to Garvin MacCrae on his deck.

Well, maybe it hadn't been such a simple kiss.

Sarah could be at the grocery or the pharmacy. She could have a doctor's appointment. She could have decided to have tea at the Japanese Tea Garden in Golden Gate Park. She could even have gone out to Garvin MacCrae's herself. Sarah Linwood was not a helpless woman. She was accustomed to getting along on her own. Whether she ordered in provisions and supplies or fetched them for herself, she did manage to get what she needed.

She could simply have called a taxi, Annie reasoned, and gone out for the afternoon. But she couldn't repress a stab of fear. What if Vic Denardo had found her?

Grumbling and growling at her paranoid state, Annie marched back out to her car, got Otto's big leather leash, attached it to his collar, and walked him around the top of the hill while she considered her options. She was disturbed that chief among them was to call Garvin. It meant she still wasn't thinking clearly.

It must have been the salt air that had her wanting him so badly, she decided. Belvedere was an exclusive little peninsula that jutted out into the bay, and there'd been a stiff breeze off the water.

Of course, she was used to salt air.

"There's no explaining it," she said under her breath. "You cannot rationalize what is on the face of it not rational. Right, Otto?"

Otto sniffed a tree trunk. After ignoring her for a minute or two, he finally acquiesced to her tugs on his leash, and they started back up the hill together. She wondered if he'd like a place like Belvedere or Garvin's marina better than the city.

"Stop!"

Mistaking her command, Otto plopped down on his butt.

Annie laughed, feeling the tension that had gripped her for hours finally ease. "Oh, Otto, not you! Me." She scratched his head. "Poor fella. You don't know I'm a crazy woman, do you? C'mon, let's go see if Sarah's home."

They returned to the little pink house, and Annie knocked on the front door. Again, no answer. She debated walking down the steps to the street below, which had several shops, including a convenience store where she could at least get a candy bar. As tense as she was, she'd hardly eaten all day. Maybe her brain could use a jolt of sugar.

Before she could commit to her next move, a taxi pulled up to the cottage, stopping as close to the front door as possible without landing in the kitchen. Annie backed onto the flat, sloping front step and shortened Otto's leash, commanding him to sit.

The driver came around and stopped abruptly, eyes on Otto.

"He's friendly," Annie said automatically.

Keeping his distance, he opened the rear door of his cab and assisted Sarah Linwood in getting out. He was a good five inches shorter than she was and not any younger, but he took her by the elbow as she leaned onto her cane and struggled to her feet. He kept glancing back at Otto, whose attention seemed to be focused on a trail of ants marching across the step.

Sarah moved slowly, painfully. She was pale, even her vivid eyes watery and fatigued. Fumbling in the pocket of her ratty, frayed red corduroy jacket, she produced a wad of bills and thrust them at the driver.

"You need me to see you in, ma'am?" he asked, not even counting the money. Clearly there was more than enough.

"No. I'll be fine."

He seemed relieved not to have to pass Otto. He eyed Annie. "You got her?"

She nodded. "Thank you."

"No problem, she's a nice lady."

He waved a hand in a quick farewell, scooted around the front of his cab, and climbed in, wasting no time getting out of there. Otto, Annie knew, sometimes had that effect on people.

Sarah scowled after him. The wind caught the ends of her shapeless graying hair. She had traded her Keds for a pair of sturdy men's ankle boots and her usual mismatched socks. Otto, judiciously, left her alone as she hobbled toward her front door, muttering more to herself than to Annie. "I won't be treated like a daft old woman."

Annie couldn't stop a smile from creeping across her mouth. "Well, what do you expect when you dress like a bag lady?"

"Bag ladies should be treated with respect."

"That driver looked like he took pretty good care of you."

She sniffed. "He was patronizing."

"He was solicitous. There's a difference."

"I'm in no mood for seeing the bright side of things," she grumbled, unlocking her door.

"I've been worried about you," Annie said, not sure she was going to be invited in.

"First the cab driver, now you." She shot Annie a sharp look. "I suppose you think I should have left a note?"

Definitely touchy. Annie didn't back down and just managed to hold on to her patience. She'd had a rough day of her own. "Since there's a chance Vic Denardo's on your tail, it would have been nice."

"Vic," she sneered, pushing on inside. "He doesn't worry me."

"Well, he worries me."

Sarah leaned on her cane. "Are you coming in or not?"

Otto lunged forward, eager to get inside. But Annie held him back, although he could have dragged her in if he'd wanted to. "You don't seem in the mood for company."

"I'm not." But she sighed, her expression softening. "It's very sweet of you to fret about me, Annie. I'm afraid I've become an old crank. I'm not used to having anyone worry about me, and I haven't had anyone to worry about in—well, a long time."

At least five years. According to the papers, she and her niece had been close. And there'd been her father. Like him or not, Sarah Linwood had tended to his needs longer than should have been required of any daughter. And, of course, there'd been Vic Denardo, but Annie had yet to sort out Sarah's relationship with him.

"Perhaps I can make you a cup of tea," Annie offered quietly.

"I can make my own tea."

No hint of blue-blooded breeding this afternoon. Gritting her teeth, Annie followed the old crab into her house. "If you're too tired, I can come back tomorrow."

"I'm fine. A glass of water and some crackers will revive me."

"Otto can stay outside—"

"No, let him in. He won't hurt anything."

Annie wasn't worried about him knocking Sarah over; Gran had straightened him out on that score as a puppy. She just didn't want him shredding, slobbering on, or otherwise mucking up any of Sarah's canvases. "Really, it's no problem if—"

"Annie. Please. He won't hurt me. He won't hurt my paintings. Come inside."

It occurred to Annie that Sarah could have some justification for losing patience with her. Holding Otto short on his leash, she went inside. She discouraged her eager dog from sniffing around to familiarize himself with the territory until Sarah barked at her to let the poor animal off his leash.

Annie complied. *Go ahead, Otto. Lift your leg on one of her still lifes and see how she likes it.*

But Otto, obviously in a traitorous mood, immediately plopped down in the middle of Sarah's kitchen floor as if he were back in Maine.

Sarah got her glass of water and handful of saltines, standing at the sink while she ate and drank without comment. Finally, she took a sleeve of crackers and hobbled on her cane back toward her rattan chair with the chintz cushions. Annie remained close to the front door and kept an eye on Otto, just in case he got any ideas.

"I suppose," Sarah said, sinking painfully onto her chair, "you're wondering where I've been."

"You don't owe me an explanation."

She might as well have not spoken. Sarah showed no sign she'd even heard her. "I went out to the house on Pacific Heights. Until five years ago I'd lived there my entire life, you know. I'd expected to die there. I just—I suppose I just wanted to see it before it was emptied of all its furniture, its very soul."

Annie quickly sifted through Sarah's drama to the facts of what she was saying. "You went inside?"

"I still have a key." She glanced up, cracker crumbs on her pale, purplish lips. "My brother didn't change the locks after I left San Francisco."

Or after the murders, Annie thought. But if the killer was Vic Denardo, he hadn't had to break in to do his handiwork. Even if it wasn't Denardo, there'd been no sign of forced entry, at least according to the press accounts she'd read. Security hadn't been the problem that terrible night. "You weren't afraid of being seen?"

Sarah smiled grimly. "Who would recognize me?"

She had a point. The pictures of her in the newspapers at the time of the murders showed a very different woman from the one Annie knew. That Sarah Linwood had worn pearls and cashmere, had been every inch the Linwood heiress. Now, in her red corduroy jacket and pilled polyester flowered top, with her debilitating illness, she wasn't a woman her family would readily recognize as one of their own.

"No one was around," she went on. "My footsteps echoed in a way I've never heard. It was almost as if the walls were trying to tell me something. I don't know how to explain—" She caught herself and glanced up at Annie. "I suppose you think I'm being ridiculous."

"Sarah, it's not my place to judge you. I wouldn't—"

"I kept telling myself it's only a house. I hadn't been there in so long, I thought time would have made it easier. But the memories flooded in, bad right along with the good. The wasted years, the years not knowing who I was, the deaths of two people I loved dearly—" She broke off, tears spilling into her eyes, making their blue even more vivid. "I know a lot of people don't think so, but I did love my father."

"Sarah…"

"Going back there…" Her voice cracked, but she seemed to will her tears not to spill down her cheeks. "It was as if someone had ripped out a piece of my soul." "I think I understand," Annie said quietly.

Sarah's head jerked up, her artist's incisiveness sharpening her gaze, yanking her out of her self-absorption. "Of course. Your grandmother's cottage. It was swept out to sea."

"I know it's not the same—"

"But it gives you a frame of reference, a way into what I'm feeling right now. Walking around those silent rooms…"

She swallowed, choking back any open display of emotion. She was a woman who didn't easily express her feelings except in her work. Annie's gaze drifted to the canvases leaned up against a cheap kitchen cabinet. In her work, Sarah Linwood held nothing back.

When she went on, her voice was calm, quiet, tortured. "I could feel my family in a way I never have before. The empty rooms, the distance of five years. My father, my mother, John. Haley. Even my grandfather, who built the house. I remember he had a great booming laugh. Mother thought him coarse. Father despised him. But they were all there today. I felt them." She swallowed again and fumbled for another cracker, her eyes unfocused. "I'll never go back there."

Annie ventured forward, moving closer to this woman she found so compelling, so solid and strong one moment, so conflicted and sad the next. "Because it's been sold?"

"It wouldn't matter. I know who I am now. I'm not the woman who lived in that house, who once belonged there and nowhere else. Who knew her place. But I—" She shut her eyes, squeezing back tears; in spite of her best efforts, a trickle found its way down her pallid cheeks. She looked homely and pathetic, no longer at peace with herself or her life. "Dear God, I wish I could have found out who I am without having abused the people I care about in the process. I brought tragedy and terror into their lives."

"But if you didn't kill anyone—"

Sarah's eyes opened, clear and focused. "I didn't."

Annie nodded. "I know. Then the murders aren't your fault."

"Vic. I brought Vic Denardo into their lives."

"Actually," Annie said carefully, "from what I understand, you didn't. Garvin did. He invited him to crew for him. Vic Denardo had already sailed with Garvin, Ethan Conninger, your brother—even your father—before you met him."

Sarah frowned. "I never thought of it that way."

"Which isn't to blame them, either. If Denardo did commit the murders—if he was determined from the start to wreak havoc on your lives—he'd have found another way into your circle."

"Perhaps."

"I'm not saying that's the case. I have no idea. I wasn't there."

Calmer now, Sarah studied her guest a moment. "I've been blathering. You came here for a reason, didn't you, Annie? What is it?"

"There's no need to trouble you right now—"

"It's Vic?"

Annie shook her head.

"Garvin," Sarah said with certainty. She folded the ends of her sleeve of crackers, her movements neat and precise, her cashmere-and-pearls self perhaps not as dead as she believed. "Sit down. We'll order in Chinese and talk."

"Sarah, I don't want to inflict myself on you if you're tired—"

Sarah shook off her protest. "You're a charming and insightful young woman, Annie. I *need* your company. I don't want to become a morose old crone. And I know I can't run from my problems. The past has its obligations—and a hellishly long reach into the future. Now. Order dinner." Her smile was soft, almost beautiful; the demons were at bay. "Then let's talk about Garvin MacCrae and why he thinks I might have talked Vic Denardo into killing my own father and niece."

"So she in trouble or what?" Michael Yuma asked.

"I don't know if she is or not," Garvin said.

Yuma had spent most of the last twenty minutes grilling Garvin on Annie Payne with limited success. Garvin was helping him work on his much-patched, much-abused launch, which had started taking on water again late yesterday, probably while Garvin was out on his deck kissing Annie. It was a bright, brisk morning. A perfect day to be out on the water. But he had work to do at the marina, and running would only postpone the inevitable reckoning he and Annie Payne had coming.

"It's the hair," Yuma said. "You know what I mean?"

Garvin sighed. "No."

"All those blond wisps. Makes her seem vulnerable, you know? And those big blue eyes—"

"Yuma, the woman drives around town with a rottweiler."

"So?"

"She also grew up in Maine. Her father was a fisherman who died when she was a baby. Annie Payne can take care of herself."

Yuma grinned. "Who you trying to convince?"

"Michael, you're being—"

"Sexist," he supplied easily.

"Yeah, I'd say so."

"Well, I'm only half serious. If she were a man, I'd still say she's probably in a heap of trouble, never mind whether or not she can handle it on her own. Am I right? She's in trouble and you want to help?"

Garvin threw down an undershirt-turned-rag. If only all he wanted was to help Annie Payne. But that wasn't the case. He wanted to know what she knew about Sarah Linwood, and he wanted to kiss her again.

He wanted more than just to kiss her again.

"Hell, Yuma, if you're implying I'm being sucked into something because Annie Payne has wispy blond hair, you're even crazier than I thought."

"Okay, my man. If you say so. You don't have an urge to protect this woman, you don't. Won't catch me saying otherwise. What I'm thinking, though, you can't do nothing about."

"One more word, Yuma, and I swear—"

"What? I'm agreeing with you."

"You're goading me."

Yuma shrugged. "You're saying it's sexist because I think Annie Payne's in trouble. It wasn't sexist when you thought I was in trouble."

"You weren't in trouble, Yuma. You *were* trouble."

He laughed, a long ways from the messed-up kid he'd once been. "What about your blonde? She trouble too?"

Garvin grabbed a gallon of sealer, refusing to answer. Michael Yuma was just trying to get under his skin and force him to sort out where he stood on the subject of Annie Payne. Well, he didn't want to sort that one out. He'd have to remember the feel of her mouth on his, the look of shock and desire in her eyes. He'd have to remember the jolt of sheer panic he'd felt when he'd realized how much he wanted her.

But she *was* trouble. She'd connived with Sarah Linwood, she'd lied to him, she'd damned likely lied to Vic Denardo.

What she hadn't explained was why. Why buy Sarah's painting of Haley at the auction? What was in it for Annie Payne newly of San Francisco?

"You growling?" Yuma asked.

"You know, I can still throw you in the drink."

Yuma was unperturbed. "You haven't met Beau yet, have you?"

"Beau?"

"New guy. I hired him yesterday as our part-time outdoor maintenance man. He's six foot four, two eighty. He's on probation, needed a job to keep himself on the straight and narrow."

"So 'we' gave him one."

"After he'd been turned down everywhere."

"And now he likes you," Garvin translated.

"Yep. If I go in the drink, two minutes later, you're in with me. O' course," he went on, dipping a thick brush into the can of sealer, "from the looks of you, a dip in the ice-cold San Francisco Bay would do you no harm."

"Change the subject, Yuma."

"Uh-huh."

That afternoon Garvin gave up on Yuma and the new guy, Beau, and drove out to Union Street and parked within a block of Annie's Gallery. When he arrived in her courtyard, Otto was prancing around, one end of his heavy leash attached to his collar, the other dragging behind him.

"He's restless," Annie said, her back to Garvin as she checked her door, making sure it was locked. "He needs a good walk."

"I know how he feels."

She turned to him, zipping up a black fleece jacket that reminded him of her Maine roots. She wore a short, close-fitting dress in a dark burgundy, and her hair was held back, more or less, with a brightly colored scarf that trailed down her back. Garvin felt a tug of emotion, an empathy for her that he couldn't seem to resist. Annie Payne was trying so damned hard to build a new life for herself, and she'd stumbled into one hell of a mess. But he knew it wouldn't be any less of a mess if he'd just stayed away from her. She'd still have Vic Denardo on her case, thinking she could lead him to Sarah Linwood.

Knowing it.

"I was going to call you when I got home," she said in that blithe, nondefensive way of hers.

"Were you?"

She kicked off her black suede shoes and pulled on exercise socks right over her burgundy tights, then slipped on sneakers. He had on his boatyard clothes, khakis, polo shirt, denim jacket. She ignored his dubious tone. "Yes, I was."

He exhaled sharply, annoyed with himself for not just giving her a chance. Maybe she was trying to make up for lost ground and had decided to be straight with him, even to trust him. "It's quite a walk up to your place."

"Otto and I both could use the exercise."

She threw out a foot and stepped on her dog's leash, stopping him midstride. It was a sign of obedience on his part. If he'd wanted to, he could have dropped her on her behind. She swooped up the leash.

Her smile crept back. "It's a beautiful day but a little on the cool side. I saw the weather report for Maine. I'd be eating soup by the woodstove tonight."

Garvin noticed the wistfulness in her tone. "Homesick?"

"My home no longer exists."

No self-pity, just a crack in her voice that she covered with a quick tug on Otto's leash. She sailed up the walk without so much as a backward glance. Garvin sighed through clenched teeth, even as he felt a surge of warmth for her. Annie Payne wasn't a woman who liked seeing her own vulnerabilities or liked other people seeing them. It made her frustrating to be around, to try to understand, but also intriguing.

He shot forward, catching up with her as she hit Union Street.

"Cynthia Linwood stopped in again today," she said conversationally. No crack to her voice, no discomfort. "She brought an old map of San Francisco for me to frame and invited me to lunch next week."

Garvin smiled. "Cynthia as one of the ladies who lunch. It's an interesting transformation."

"Have you known her a long time?"

"We met just before Haley and I were married. She helped us find our house. After Haley's death, Cynthia stepped in and handled selling the house when I wanted out. She did everything right, so far as I was concerned. She was discreet, knew what to ask, what not to ask."

"But she wasn't seeing John Linwood then," Annie said.

Garvin shook his head. They were moving in the general direction of his car. Maybe her zest for walking would peter out by the time they reached it. "I don't really know when they started seeing each other. I haven't kept up with either of them."

Otto jerked forward to sniff a mailbox. Annie paused, obviously trying to give her dog a little freedom to maneuver. Passersby gave him wide berth.

"She and John seem happy," Garvin went on. "I think people are too willing to dismiss her as a trophy wife. That's not what Cynthia's about."

"A trophy wife? What's that?"

Annie seemed truly mystified. Garvin explained. "Older, wealthy, successful man marries younger, attractive, often but not necessarily successful woman. Usually a first wife is dumped along the way, but that's not the case with John. His first wife—Haley's mother—died about ten years ago. I never knew her. If he and Cynthia can find happiness together, I figure it's none of my business."

"It must be tough to have people dismiss you as a trophy for some man without knowing anything about your relationship." Annie made a face, shuddering. "I guess it happens, though. I'd hate that myself. I'd rather just not get married." She grinned suddenly, casting a smart-assed look up at him. "Not that I'm trophy material."

Oh, Annie. Garvin had all he could manage just to keep himself focused on not tripping over his own damned feet. And not carting her off somewhere private, quiet, free of distractions like rottweilers and Linwoods and too many memories. If there were such a place.

Otto started forward again, Annie after him.

Garvin fell in beside them. "You didn't leave some man heartbroken back in Maine?"

She cut a grin at him, showing the dimple in her cheek. "I might have, but if I did, I don't know about him."

But he couldn't match her light mood, and as they came to his car, he touched her arm, remembering his conversation at the marina with Ethan Conninger. "Annie—about Cynthia Linwood. She has the same questions about you that everyone else does."

Annie cocked her head back, alert, curious. "That you do, you mean."

"I'd just hate for you to think she was trying to take you under her wing, help you get established here in San Francisco, and all along she had another agenda."

Her look turned sharp. "You know something."

He sighed, dug in his pockets for his car keys. "Nothing that should surprise you. Ethan Conninger stopped by the marina on Monday. He said Cynthia was curious about you and had decided to look into why you bought the painting of Haley. He's keeping his eyes open, too."

"I see," Annie said, tight-lipped.

"It doesn't mean she thinks any less of your gallery. Or you."

Annie wrapped Otto's leash around her wrist and drew it taut as a couple with two pugs walked by. "I prefer to take people at face value. They say what they mean, mean what they say. I like *being* that way myself." She threw her head back, exhaled at the sky. "Lord, what a week."

"Annie—"

She faced him, her eyes clear, determined. "If you'll give me a ride, I'll take you to see Sarah Linwood."

Garvin held his breath, said nothing.

"Otto will fit in your backseat. He won't—at least I think he won't tear up the leather." She attempted a grin. "He's not used to leather, so I can't say for sure."

"Annie." His voice was strangled, just a hint of the tension that had him in its grip. "He can tear up the whole damned car for all I care."

"You hear that, Otto? Permission to commit mayhem."

But her humor rang hollow, undermined by the loss of color in her cheeks. Garvin got the doors to his car open, tried not to wince when Otto galumphed into his backseat. Annie settled in front, her knees together, her feet tucked in, hands folded on her lap. Not nervous, just uneasy.

When he climbed in beside her, she smoothed the skirt of her dress and said, "Head toward Twin Peaks."

Her tone was steady, difficult to read. Her eyes were pinned straight ahead. Garvin hesitated. "Annie, if you're not sure—"

"Sarah's sure. That's what counts."

He eased out into rush-hour Union Street traffic. He had a dozen questions he resisted asking. Where had Sarah been living the past five years? What had she been doing? Why was she back in San Francisco? Had she been there all along? And Vic Denardo—

But they were questions that had to wait.

Annie gave him general directions as he headed out Market, traffic heavy but moving. Her tone was crisp, matter-of-fact. She had her own troubles. A business to establish, a new life, her own memories to hold at bay.

"Look, Annie, you can just give me her address. If you don't want to put yourself through this—"

"No. I told her I'd come with you." She glanced sideways at him. "When I bought that painting on Saturday on Sarah's behalf, I had no idea I was thrusting myself into the middle of two unsolved murders. Maybe I should have been more careful, but I wasn't."

"Sarah didn't tell you?"

"And I didn't ask."

"Why—"

"The rest is for her to tell you, Garvin. I will tell you this one thing. She thinks you believe she had Vic Denardo kill her father."

"Jesus," Garvin breathed, keeping his eyes on the road.

"She doesn't think you believe she had your wife killed. They were too fond of each other. She thinks you believe Denardo did that on his own when he realized that Haley—that your wife knew what had happened. That finished any romance he and Sarah had left, and they both took off in separate directions."

"That's the scenario Sarah thinks I've worked out?"

Annie nodded, not looking at him.

"Does she deny it?"

"Yes."

"And you believe her," Garvin said.

Annie turned to him, her expression difficult to read in the shifting shadows of dusk. "You'll see why in a few minutes."

Chapter Eight

Street by street, Garvin followed Annie's snaking directions up to an isolated cul-de-sac of small, tidy houses. His head pounded, his blood pumping hard and fast.

Annie gestured out her window. "She lives in the pink house."

Garvin shifted his gaze to Annie. His chest felt compressed, his breathing labored. "You can wait here, if you like. This isn't your problem. Maybe the less you know the better."

"That might have been true two weeks ago, but not anymore."

She pushed out to the paved circle and waited for him to come around the front of his car. Her scarf had fallen off, and she'd just draped it around her neck. He could see she was tense, ambivalent. Even in the twilight her eyes shone, giving his gut a painful twist. He touched her shoulder. "Annie, I know you're in a hell of a position here."

"It's my own doing. I don't blame you or Sarah. I acted without sufficient information. You'll understand why in a minute."

As she swung away from him, Garvin caught her by the elbow and pulled her back around to him. He didn't release her. In the fading light he could see the strain of the past days taking their toll. Dark smudges under her eyes, pale cheeks, a resolute set to her jaw. He wanted to erase them, see her smile, hear her laugh. She was trying to build a new life in San Francisco and chase a dream. Instead, she had stumbled into the nightmare of two five-year-old unsolved murders.

He curved his arm around her small middle, drawing her close, and he kissed her softly, gently. "Forget Sarah, Annie. I'll take you home."

Her fingers dug into his upper arms, her gaze intent as she shook her head. "No, it's okay. You're here now. Sarah's expecting you."

She slipped away from him and swept across the pavement toward the small pink bungalow.

Garvin stiffened. "Sarah can call me and tell me to come herself. You don't need to be her go-between."

He started back to the driver's side of his car, leaving Annie to make up her own mind about what she wanted to do.

She heaved a sigh behind him. "I'm not doing this just for Sarah's sake. I'm doing it for my own, too."

Garvin kept walking, vaguely wondering what he'd do about Otto. Take him home with him? Could be interesting. He was one big dog. If he decided he was being kidnapped, it could be a rough trip across the Golden Gate.

"Garvin."

Of course, Annie *could* realize he was serious and get back in the car with him and her dog. Whatever her motives were now, however she rationalized her involvement, she had no place in anything that might bring Vic Denardo back onto her doorstep.

She hissed quietly, impatiently, behind him. "God, you're a stubborn man. Sarah doesn't have a phone."

"She can use a pay phone."

"It's not that easy. She's—" Garvin could feel her grinding her teeth. "Damn it, Garvin, Sarah's practically an invalid."

He came to an abrupt halt. Blood pulsated in his ears. He steadied himself. *An invalid.* Sarah Linwood? He turned. Annie was silhouetted against the darkening sky, all of San Francisco glittering at her feet. He could feel how torn she was, how determined to do the right thing, how conflicted about what that was.

"I think she has rheumatoid arthritis. She gets around, but with difficulty. She—" Annie breathed in, added softly, "I wasn't going to tell you anything and let you see for yourself. But she's probably a lot different from the woman you remember."

"Annie—"

"Come see for yourself."

She didn't wait for him to respond and continued on toward the house. Garvin could hear her footsteps echoing. His throat ached with tension. His fists were clenched at his side, every muscle in his body knotted.

He lurched after her, knowing now he had no choice.

The little house was bright against the darkening sky, every light apparently on. Annie knocked and gave a quick, furtive glance back at Garvin. He tucked a few stray hairs behind her ear. His fingers were stiff, cold. "This isn't easy for you either, is it?"

She gave a small, tight shake of the head.

"I've run roughshod over you to get what I want. I know it's too late, but I'm sorry if I've hurt you in any way."

He could see her swallow. "I know."

A voice from within the house instructed them to come in, the door was unlocked.

Annie went in first, then Garvin, his breath held.

A plain, misshapen woman with graying strawberry hair was seated in her small living room.

Her striking blue eyes swept over him, and a sharp arrow of shock struck its mark as he stared back at her.

"Hello, Garvin." Her voice was clear, the words distinct.

"Sarah."

He almost choked on her name. If not for Annie's word, he wouldn't have believed the woman before him was Sarah Linwood. She wore a loud flowered top, baggy, cheap jeans, mismatched socks, cheap sneakers with holes in the toe. Her gnarled hands were unmanicured, her hair unstyled. This wasn't the prim, correct woman he had always known as Sarah Linwood. Even gambling, even in the midst of her affair with Vic Denardo, she had been refined, dignified.

But she regarded him with similar shock, as if she didn't recognize him as the man who'd married her niece.

Two murders, Garvin thought, had changed them both.

Slowly, he took in the canvases scattered about her small home. Still lifes, landscapes, the occasional portrait. His shock deepened as he absorbed the power and mesmerizing quality of her work. Her art was no longer a polite, innocuous, wealthy woman's hobby. No wonder Annie had decided to represent Sarah at Saturday's auction. If Annie's Gallery could introduce Sarah Linwood as a brilliant new artist, it would distinguish hers from all the other struggling new galleries in San Francisco and help it make its mark in the city's competitive art world.

She had drifted into the kitchen, removing herself from his confrontation with his wife's aunt. His throat caught suddenly at the sight of her. She seemed so damned alone.

But Sarah started speaking. "It's been a long time, Garvin. And yet sometimes—sometimes it seems like the blink of an eye when I last held Haley on my lap as a toddler. You're looking well. Different, of course, but well."

He pulled his gaze from Annie, turned to the swollen-jointed woman in the rattan chair. She had aged more than her five years away should have warranted. Yet she looked freer than she ever had before, somehow more whole. It wasn't just the cheap clothes, the simple surroundings. It seemed to radiate from inside her.

"You've changed too," he said.

"Oh, yes. I've been living in the Southwest for most of the past five years. I studied painting, moved around quite a lot. I kept a low profile and lived quietly. It didn't occur to me that I might ever come home."

"Why did you?"

"The house going on the market. It was just a fluke that I even found out. I read about it in a newspaper I was crumpling up for a fire. So, I came back. I found this place, then I found Annie." She seemed to sense his censure and raised her eyes to him. "There's nothing sinister in our arrangement, Garvin. I wanted my portrait of Haley. That's all."

"Why the secrecy?"

Her gaze didn't waver. "I couldn't bring myself to go to the auction."

"You could just have called John—"

"I couldn't do that, either."

"So you hired a woman who didn't know anything about you, anything about the murders." He spoke harshly, more so than he'd intended. "You sent her to that auction never anticipating that the price would go so high that people wouldn't believe she was the legitimate buyer."

"You mean you, Garvin," Sarah said in a steady voice. "You didn't believe her."

"Neither did Vic Denardo."

She inhaled sharply. "We don't know for sure—"

Garvin shook his head. "We know, Sarah."

"I had no idea—these last weeks—" She faltered, running a broad, shaking hand over her face. "I can't expect you to understand. I don't even ask that you do. It was so exciting, thinking about coming home, making my plans. But the reality of being here—" She shook her head. "I just wasn't ready to come forward."

"Sarah—"

"I told the police everything I knew about the murders, Garvin." She spoke in a strong, firm voice; she wasn't being defensive. "Everything. That was my father and my only niece murdered. Can you possibly think I would have held anything back? My God, Haley and I…we…"

"I don't doubt that you loved Haley very much," Garvin said softly.

But she shook off his interruption and breathed in deeply, holding back any emotion. "If I knew anything that could bring her murderer, my father's murderer, to justice, I'd have provided it to the authorities at the time. If I'd thought of anything in the past five years that would help, I'd have given it over to the police."

"She was investigating your finances—"

"Garvin, I would never have withheld a single, solitary bit of useful information or evidence. That's the truth. Believe me or not."

"Why did you run?"

"Because I didn't know what else to do. I blamed myself for putting Father and Haley in danger. I don't know for certain Vic killed Father and Haley. But my relationship with him, the lifestyle I led at the time—they caused pain and dissension in my family and likely led to the deaths. I couldn't stay. I believed my presence would only lead to more heartbreak and violence. At the time, leaving seemed the only proper option." She leaned back in her chair, exhaustion graying her face, bringing out the lines of age and pain. "And I left, Garvin. I didn't run."

Out of the corner of his eye he saw Annie pacing in the kitchen, arms folded on her chest, gait stiff. Garvin had no doubt she was listening to every word and blamed him for Sarah's being upset.

"The past can't be helped, Sarah," he said. "That's not why I'm here."

She leaned forward, ashen-faced. "You're after Vic."

"He seems to have a bone to pick with you. And he seems willing to intimidate Annie—possibly even hurt her—to get to you."

"But he hasn't been back—"

"He will be."

She slumped back in her chair. "I know." She inhaled, choking back a sob, and Garvin could see a hint of the Sarah Linwood of old, who would have hated the idea of crying in front of anyone. "Oh, God. I never intended any of this. How could he think I tried to blame the murders on him? I only want the truth—"

Garvin stood close to her. "Did you set him up, Sarah?"

Her head jerked up. "No."

"What could Haley have learned that would have gotten her killed? Nothing irregular was found in your records—nothing that we didn't already know about your gambling—but I don't believe she wasn't killed for a reason. I think she found something."

"If she did, she never told me, and I don't know what there could be, beyond the evidence of my terrible addiction to gambling."

"Do you think Vic's guilty?"

"I don't know," she croaked, shutting her eyes, tightening her hands into gnarled, imperfect fists. She shook her head as if in great pain. "I don't want to believe it."

"Sarah," Garvin said, steady, "you need to tell me everything you know."

"I have."

Annie shot him a nasty look. By her standards, he would be badgering an infirm woman in her own home. He didn't want to be cruel, but Sarah Linwood's emotional comfort could stand some jostling if it got them all closer to the truth about what had happened five years ago.

"I wish I did know something." Her eyes were open now, leveled on him. Color was creeping back into her cheeks. She'd be fine, Garvin thought. Sarah Linwood could always hold her own. He wondered if she'd come to believe that herself, as her father never had. But Haley had. Haley had always sensed her aunt's strength and resourcefulness. "I wish I could snap my fingers and bring whoever murdered my father and Haley to justice, but I can't."

Annie swung around, clearly agitated. "Otto hasn't been out all afternoon. He needs a walk."

"Then go walk him," Garvin snapped back.

She dropped her hands to her sides in tight fists. "He's getting hungry. If I don't get him home soon, he'll eat out the back of your car."

"I don't care."

"*I* want to go home now, Garvin."

Her back was ramrod straight and her cheeks as pale as chalk, and Garvin doubted she was going to give up anytime soon. She was another one whose strength and resourcefulness were not to be underestimated.

He growled under his breath and shifted back to Sarah. "You have the painting here?"

"It's in my bedroom."

"Cynthia Linwood's suspicious of Annie, possibly Ethan Conninger, as well, and obviously Vic is. I'm not sure John has a clue. If any of them asks Annie to produce the painting she bought for five grand and she can't—"

"As you did," Annie shot across to him.

He ignored her. "It'll only further fuel their suspicions."

"She can tell them she represented me at the auction. I'd asked to remain anonymous, and she complied with my wishes."

Garvin studied her a moment and saw her resolve, but that's all there was. That Linwood determination. He'd seen it in Haley a hundred times. Never mind if she was happy with what she'd made up her mind to do, if she thought it was right, necessary, good. Once resolved, a Linwood did what a Linwood had determined to do, as Haley must have the night she'd returned to the scene of her grandfather's murder.

"Your heart's not in it," he told Sarah.

She gave a short bark of a laugh. "Does that matter? I'm afraid, Garvin. I don't know if I'm ready to—to let my brother, his new wife, my friends see me again. That's the truth. But it makes no difference, and you know it."

"You're right."

Annie groaned, sweeping in from the kitchen. "If you two are donning your hairshirts to protect me and my reputation, you can forget it. I'm not telling anybody about anything. Now." She cast a cold look in Garvin's direction. "I need to see about Otto."

Sarah opened her mouth to speak, but Garvin held up a hand. "Forget it, Sarah. Annie's not going to let up. She's worse than her damned rottweiler when it comes to protecting you." He turned to her, not a happy man. "All right, we can go."

She sniffed and spoke to Sarah as if he weren't there. "Will you be all right?"

"Yes. Thank you, dear, I'll be fine."

Dear, Garvin thought. Hell.

"If you need anything," Annie said, "you have my number. Borrow a neighbor's phone. I'll come as soon as I can. You need time to think."

"Thank you."

"Just rest, Sarah, and don't worry about a thing. Vic Denardo hasn't been back, and Cynthia Linwood has been nothing but nice to me. I've met Ethan Conninger only once, but he was perfectly decent. They might be curious, but I don't think they're going to put a gun to my head and make me show them the painting. So, please don't worry about me."

Sarah smiled, settling back against her chintz cushions. "You're very sweet, Annie."

There was nothing sweet about her, Garvin thought, when she turned to him, tossed her head back, and led the way out.

He gave Sarah a parting glance. "For what it's worth, it's good to see you again."

She almost smiled. "And you."

"But I'll be back."

"I know."

Annie had to hustle to keep up with Garvin's long strides on their way back to his car, but she didn't let him get ahead of her. "You'll do anything to get what you want. Trod over anyone's sensitivities without any evidence, badger an old woman in her own home—"

"Sarah's not that old."

"Physically she is."

Garvin glanced at her, not slackening his pace. "You think I was too hard on her?"

"She's a tormented woman."

"You didn't know her five years ago."

"I know her now."

"Do you?" His voice was calm, deceptively so. "Annie, five years ago she was a compulsive gambler. She'd have sold her own soul for a good poker game. She didn't care about anyone or anything except her addiction."

"Maybe she's changed."

"Maybe she hasn't."

She clamped her mouth shut, standing back impatiently while he unlocked the passenger door. She could just walk home, she thought. It was a long way, but she and Otto needed the exercise.

Garvin pulled open the door, then swung back around at her. "Annie, look, I saw the woman you saw in there. I'm not heartless, but I need to keep an open mind."

"Sarah's not wanted by the police."

"That doesn't mean she told them everything she knows. They attribute her leaving to her family's ostracizing her because of her gambling and her relationship with Denardo, the tragedy she brought down on them. But I don't know. And I'm not sure it matters. If Vic's still out there, he's going to find her."

"She's in a horrible position," Annie said as she climbed in his car.

"We all are."

He shut her door. Otto barely acknowledged her presence and seemed eager neither for food nor a walk, no surprise to Annie. She breathed in, waiting for Garvin to get behind the wheel, not regretting her impulsive decision to drag him off. He'd wanted everything from Sarah now, without hesitation, and wasn't willing to get her story piece by piece or give her a chance to adjust to him.

"It's not as if I wasn't warned," she said. "Even Sarah told me you'd stomp on anyone to get what you want. Those weren't her exact words, but—"

"Is stomping on Sarah worse than badgering her?"

She shot him a fierce look. "Neither's commendable or necessary under the circumstances."

He met her gaze with a composure that would have defeated her. But his eyes glinted, gave away the intensity that lay behind them, despite his mild tone. "A good thing, then, that you intervened before I could whip out the thumbscrews."

Her shoulders sagged, and she sighed. "I suppose I'm being a little sanctimonious, and I've no place judging you after what you've endured. But you still weren't very nice in there."

"No," he said. "I wasn't."

She said nothing more as he negotiated the narrow, twisting streets. There was a turn taken too sharply. A hill too fast. Annie remained unperturbed. She stared out at the glittering skyline, catching glimpses of San Francisco's spectacular scenery. Up close, she noticed the plum trees with their pink and white blossoms, the rows of houses in pale pastels, deep browns, every shade of white. Her mother died never having seen San Francisco. She had lived most of her short life alone. She had her mother and daughter, yes, but not her husband.

"You're right about me, Annie." Garvin's ragged voice broke through her pensiveness. "I'm a cold-hearted son of a bitch. Don't put your faith in me. I can't protect you."

She peered over at him, the details of his face lost in the dark. "I don't recall asking for your protection, and I don't think you're cold-hearted. It'd be so much easier on you if you were."

He hissed under his breath, then said abruptly, "Would you like something to eat? Or won't Otto survive?"

"Oh, I think Otto'll survive."

"I thought as much."

"We should eat," she said. "By all means."

He chose a popular Caribbean restaurant on Haight. It was crowded, noisy, casual—the sort of place where intimacy wasn't an option. They were led to a small table in front of the window, people all around them. The boxy, cinder-block building might once have been a garage or gas station. Now, with its deep, rich island colors, potted trees, and festive music, it pulsated with fun and energy.

Annie frowned over her menu while she waited for the margarita she'd ordered even before they'd sat down. Garvin suggested they share tapas, the restaurant's version of appetizers. She agreed, and they decided on three: fried calamari with a spicy sauce, red potatoes and onions with a couple different sauces, and steamed mussels in a broth of scallions.

When her margarita arrived, Annie took a sip and licked a bit of salt from the rim of her glass, aware of Garvin's eyes on her. He had ordered a beer but hadn't touched it yet. "Maybe I've been too hard on you," she said. "It can't have been easy for you seeing Sarah after all this time."

"It wasn't."

"She's changed a lot?"

He took up his beer and drank. "Yes."

"I met her about two weeks ago. She came to my gallery one day. She wasn't as eccentrically dressed as she usually is, but, still, you can see why she wasn't recognized. Apparently she liked what she saw and called and asked me to come see her, saying she had a business proposition. So off I went. Then when I saw her work—"

"You were hooked."

Annie sipped her margarita; it was strong and tangy, and she only felt a twinge of guilt for leaving Otto alone in Garvin's car. "So much so I didn't ask half the questions I should have when she suggested I represent her at the Linwood auction."

"You didn't wonder why she wanted that particular painting?"

"Of course I did. But it was easy to assume she was just being eccentric, and maybe it was convenient on my part. I'd like to represent her in my gallery. If I'd ever dreamed I'd get caught up in two unsolved murders, stir up so many awful memories for people, I'd probably have turned her down and tried another way to earn her trust."

Their food arrived, effectively changing the mood of the conversation—and the subject. Annie eyed the fried calamari dubiously but took one onto her plate with a dab of sauce. "They're tiny little suckers, aren't they?"

"What about your social life?"

Annie dipped another mussel onto her plate, glad to have a reason not to meet his eyes. "This was small-town Maine, Garvin. It wouldn't have been easy for someone like me, the director of a local museum, well known in town, to shack up with a guy even if I didn't live with my grandmother."

"But you did have men in your life," he persisted.

"I had a romance or two." She spooned some of the rich, oniony mussel broth onto her potatoes. "To be honest, I wasn't much interested in most of the men I knew. They were more like brothers to me."

Garvin leaned over the table, the music loud in the background, people laughing, dishes clattering. He seemed to hear none of it. "I'm not interested in being a brother to you."

"Good," she said lightly, "because I'm not interested in having you for a brother."

He sat back. "Your grandmother—her death must have been difficult for you."

"She was ninety-one. She'd lived her life on her own terms, which isn't to say it didn't have its fair share of tragedies. She was sick for about three months."

"You nursed her."

She nodded, remembering their quiet nights together on the bay, just listening to the tide wash in over the rocks. "It wasn't a sacrifice on my part. She was a wonderful woman, and she was all the family I had left. I could never get that time with her back. It's gone now forever."

"I don't doubt you, Annie." His eyes had taken on a warm intensity. "And then after she died and your cottage was lost, you headed west."

"Yep." She smiled, sitting back. "And here I am."

Garvin ordered strong coffee for them both. Annie wasn't worried about being up all night. She wouldn't sleep, no matter what she drank.

Neither, she suspected, would he.

"Annie," he said at length, "Sarah Linwood's not your grandmother."

"No, she's not. For one thing, Sarah's just in her fifties, and she's a Linwood. Gran seldom left her peninsula and I don't think left Maine more than a dozen times in her entire life. She was a fisherman's daughter and a fisherman's wife, and yes, she was a painter. A wonderful painter. But I'm not looking to replace my grandmother. I know perfectly well loved ones can't be replaced."

Garvin nodded, saying nothing.

"That doesn't mean I can't let new people into my life," Annie went on passionately, more so than she intended. "I know life's pretty much a here-today-gone-tomorrow proposition. But I've learned I can't be afraid of being disloyal to the ones I've lost. Otherwise I'll be lost too."

"Annie—"

"That's the sort of thing you learn from a woman who lives into her nineties. You mourn your losses. You move on. There's simply no other sensible, proper choice."

She stopped. She'd wrung herself out. She shifted in her chair and drank her coffee, welcoming its strong flavor. The margarita. She shouldn't have had alcohol after a day like today, with Garvin MacCrae studying her from across the table.

He didn't back down, not that she'd thought he would. His gaze —incisive, probing, carefully unemotional—remained pinned on her. "You haven't know Sarah for very long, Annie. She's already gotten you into one mess trying to have her cake and eat it too. I just want you to keep your eyes open. I don't want to see you hurt."

"That's my risk to take," she said tartly,

He nodded, sipping his own coffee, studying her over the rim of his cup. "So long as you know it."

They split the check at Annie's insistence. It had nothing to do with money, just with her determination to assert her separateness from him. They weren't in this thing together. Maybe he didn't want to see her hurt, maybe she wasn't holding back anything from him anymore, but she couldn't allow herself the illusion that he wouldn't put his need to learn the truth about his wife's death over anything else.

Once back at her apartment, Garvin double-parked and cast a sideways glance at her. "I'll walk with you to your door."

"That's okay, I don't think Vic Denardo will—"

"I'd feel better if I did this, Annie."

She shrugged. "Sure."

She slid out of the car and opened the back door, grabbing up Otto's leash as he loped out onto the sidewalk. By the time Garvin joined her at the gate, her pulse was racing. Otto pranced down the narrow walk ahead of them, then Annie, aware of Garvin close behind her in the shadows. When they came to her door, she fumbled in her bag for her keys. "I haven't got the hang of all these locks," she said. "I never locked my door in Maine."

But her hands were shaking not because of the locks on her door but because of the man at her side. It was a good thing he was double-parked. She wouldn't have to ask him in, risk having all that was simmering between them explode. She could feel his reluctance to leave, but he needed time to absorb the shock of seeing Sarah Linwood, her paintings, what had happened to her in the past five years.

"Annie," he said.

She glanced at him. He leaned toward her, touched her cheek. He traced her lower lip with one finger, setting her body spinning. She took a breath, abandoning her key in its lock. She started to speak, but he brushed his lips across hers, effectively silencing her. His arm dropped down her back, and he drew her toward him even as she sank against his chest.

Then Otto shook his massive head, sending dog slobber flying. Garvin looked down at him and made a face. He gave Annie a dry smile. "I guess Otto knows I'm double-parked."

"He's a smart dog."

"That he is."

"Good night, Garvin. I'll see you soon."

He kissed her lightly, gently. "Count on it."

Chapter Nine

Annie brought fresh, warm cinnamon streusel muffins for her and Zoe's preopening get-together. She even had a muffin for Otto. Maybe it was just her way of asserting normalcy in her life. *This* was what she'd envisioned, dreamed of, during her long drive west. Muffins, friends, good conversation, a sunlit San Francisco morning. Not two unsolved murders. Not old family animosities. Falling for a man who was sexy and interesting and yet as single-minded as Garvin MacCrae, maybe.

While the coffee brewed, Annie put out her pots of pansies, cyclamen, ivy, lobelia, swept the courtyard, and inspected the impatiens along the border of the brick walk. She'd left the door to her gallery ajar, but Otto waited inside for Zoe and stayed near the muffins. She'd gotten up an hour early and taken him for an extra-long walk, thoroughly entranced by San Francisco at sunrise. Of course, she'd told herself her early rising had nothing to do with last night beyond feeling guilty over leaving Otto cooped up in Garvin's car.

"You must have a green thumb," a man said behind her.

Annie spun around, and the man who'd snuck into her gallery on Sunday—Vic Denardo—grinned at her. "Nice flowers," he said, gesturing to her impatiens. "Healthy looking."

"Thank you," she mumbled.

He had on black jeans and a white turtleneck again, and Annie could suddenly see how Sarah Linwood had fallen for him. He was fit, wiry, and exuded a raw sensuality that was impossible to ignore. Annie brushed off her hands, noticing her visitor sweeping his dark eyes over her. She wore taupe-colored gabardine pants and a pale blue sandwashed silk blouse, with a dab of some perfume Zoe had pressed upon her. It supposedly soothed and energized at the same time.

She cleared her throat, trying not to let her nervousness paralyze her. "Um—is there something I can do for you?"

"Same as before. Tell me where I can find Sarah Linwood."

His flat, dark eyes undermined his conversational tone. Annie pushed back her hair with one hand and told herself he could just be trying to persuade her to talk in the only way he knew how. But he wouldn't actually threaten her—physically or verbally—in such a public setting. Zoe would be arriving soon. Customers. Passersby. And Otto was just inside.

"I'm sorry," she said. "I can't help you."

He shook his head, disbelief compressing his lips. "Bullshit. She's here. She's gotta be. I've figured out that much. I've checked out all the neighborhoods she said she wanted to live in if she weren't a Linwood. No luck." He shrugged. "So here I am."

"I said I'm sorry." Ignoring her shaky knees, Annie started briskly across the courtyard toward her gallery. She glanced back at her visitor. He had to be Vic Denardo. He even had the look of a merchant marine about him. "But that's just not my problem. I really can't help you."

He followed her, no sign of irritation or impatience—or anything—in his dark eyes. "You mean you won't," he said calmly.

She felt a quick stab of fear, but Otto trotted into the gallery's open doorway, his ears back, his brow wrinkled. He gave a low, humming growl as he inspected their visitor. "Otto," Annie warned him, trying to hide her relief. "Be good." Not that there was a chance he'd do anything. She just wanted to pass him off as a rottweiler closer to stereotype.

The gray-haired man backed up a couple of steps. "Nice doggie. I'm not going to hurt the lady."

Otto ventured out to the courtyard and sniffed their visitor, who remained rock-still. Annie just let Otto do his thing. She took a small gulp of air, then blurted, "After the other day when you were here, I wondered—are you Vic Denardo?"

His eyes didn't change. "What if I am?"

"Then you're wanted by the police for questioning."

"You see any police around?"

She rearranged several pots of pansies just to provide an outlet for her nervous energy. Zoe would be there soon. This man, whoever he was, wouldn't accost her in the open, in broad daylight, with Otto "protecting" her. She straightened, aware of

Vic Denardo's eyes still on her. Suddenly she wished Garvin MacCrae would burst down her walk.

"Look," she said, "I don't know why you think I know anything about Sarah Linwood. All I did was buy a portrait she happened to paint."

He smirked. "You do look innocent when you lie through your teeth. How come you've been hanging out with Garvin MacCrae? He want you to take him to Sarah too?"

Annie swallowed, not caring anymore if he saw that she was nervous. Her hands were shaking, even her knees as she considered the implication of his words. "How do you know I've been in contact with Garvin MacCrae? Have you been following me?"

"Nah, not following you. Otherwise I'd know where Sarah's got herself stashed. Just keeping an eye out here and there."

Annie called Otto over to her side, made him sit. She scratched his massive head. He looked like a big, goofy puppy to her, but Vic Denardo—if that was who he was—eased back another step. She returned her gaze to him. "I want you to leave. I have nothing to tell you. If I catch you following me, I'll call the police."

He grinned. "Tough little nugget, aren't you? Okay, kiddo. Have it your way. But you tell Sarah she's got to face me sometime. She knows what she did."

Annie bit down on her lower lip. He'd as much as admitted he was Vic Denardo, the chief suspect in two brutal murders. She would have to tell the police. There was no way around it. It was the only sane course of action. Tell them everything, and let them deal with the Linwoods and Vic Denardo.

And Garvin MacCrae.

"I didn't kill anybody," Vic Denardo said.

"I'm not the one you need to convince."

"You and me, kid, we stepped in the middle of one hell of a mess when we got mixed up with Sarah Linwood."

Annie licked her lips. "I never said I knew her."

He rocked back on his heels, his dark, flat eyes offering a slight glint of humor. "You're consistent, I'll give you that. Okay, sugar, if you didn't buy the painting for Sarah, where is it?"

"The painting's in a safe place. It's not in my gallery or my apartment." She took a breath, hating the position she was in. "Where is really none of your business."

He started to press her further, but Zoe glided into the sunlit courtyard in a whirl of black and ivory. "Morning, Annie. I can smell the coffee already. Youbrought muffins? What kind? No, don't tell me. Let me guess." She closed her eyes, breathed in deep. "Nope. I'll have to go inside. I can only smell flowers and coffee from out here."

Annie managed a faltering smile. She didn't want to drag Zoe Summer into an increasingly messy, even dangerous, situation. "They're cinnamon streusel. I put them up on the desk out of Otto's reach. I'll be there in a second."

Vic Denardo didn't even glance at Zoe, who'd bent down to examine a new hibiscus blossom. He kept his eyes pinned on Annie. "Tell Sarah I'll be seeing her."

Annie said nothing, afraid another stubborn denial—another lie —would make him snap. And if he didn't, she just might.

"Tell her."

Without any warning, he pivoted on his heels and marched up the narrow walk out to Union Street. He would look out of place among the expensive shops, the pretty Victorian and Edwardian buildings, but he didn't seem to give a damn.

He only wanted to find Sarah Linwood.

Zoe stopped in the doorway and glanced back, her brow furrowing in sudden concern. "What was that all about?"

Annie grimaced. "Nothing. Really."

"You sure? You're ashen, Annie. You should see yourself—"

"I'm fine."

"Bullshit," Zoe said softly.

Annie balled her shaking hands into tight fists, adrenaline setting her knees wobbling now that the immediate crisis of Vic Denardo's presence was over. For a brief moment she thought she might even faint.

Zoe touched her arm. "Annie…"

I can't fall apart, she told herself. I can't Bracing herself, she swung around at Zoe. "I need to run an errand. Help yourself to the coffee and muffins. I'll be back."

"When?"

"I don't know, maybe an hour."

"Look, I'm not into prying information out of my friends, but I have a feeling this is about that damned painting you bought at the auction. Annie, for God's sake—you're a wreck." But when Annie started to reassure her, Zoe cut her off with an adamant shake of her head, and with a rush of emotion, Annie realized she had her first real friend in San Francisco. "No, don't explain. Go on and do what you have to do. Take your time. I've got someone in today. I can look after the gallery for a couple of hours."

"Zoe, I wouldn't ask you—"

"I know you wouldn't. Now go on." She managed a grin despite the worry in her eyes. "I'm just trying to get your muffin off you."

Annie tried to smile back but knew she hadn't quite pulled it off. "You're welcome to it. Thanks, Zoe. I owe you. I'll leave Otto here, if it's all right with you, just in case that man comes back. If he does, just sic Otto on him—and call the police, okay?"

"Consider it done," Zoe said dryly, without enthusiasm, a thousand questions in her dark eyes.

Annie had to walk back up to her apartment for her car, but the exercise helped steady her. It was bright and clear and stunningly beautiful driving out over the Golden Gate Bridge, and she found herself fighting tears, wishing for a life that wasn't hers. Her tiny apartment, her struggling gallery, her tenuous hold on San Francisco. She'd tried so hard to make them enough. But now, with the sun glistening on the blue waters of the bay, with a man wanted for questioning in two five-year-old murders harassing her, she couldn't seem to stop herself from wanting more. A husband, children, a sense of belonging—things she'd dared not admit wanting.

"Damn," she mumbled under her breath, maneuvering through the picturesque streets of Marin. She sniffled, brushed tears off her cheeks with her fingertips. She *hated* feeling sorry for herself. It never got her anywhere but right back where she'd started. She was an optimist with a strong pragmatic streak. She didn't wallow, and she didn't whine.

But as she followed the pretty, sun-drenched road out of Sausalito, she couldn't remember ever feeling so alone.

She turned down the narrow, winding road to Garvin's marina, saw boats and men and a couple of women, two scroungy black dogs, a swarm of seagulls. But no Garvin. Annie swung through the parking lot, her hands tight on the steering wheel as she searched for his car. It wasn't there. She had no idea if he was at home or off sailing. She had no idea, really, she thought, how Garvin MacCrae spent his days.

She left the marina, not even sure if she wanted to see him, or why she'd come there instead of immediately calling the police after Vic Denardo had gone. She wasn't thinking straight, and that scared her. Taking deep, cleansing breaths, she headed up to Belvedere. She needed a clear head, and she needed a plan.

She made only one wrong turn before pulling alongside Garvin's front walk. She'd see if he was home. If he was, she'd tell him about her visit from Vic Denardo and her intention of calling the police. If he wasn't, she'd stop back at the marina, tell Michael Yuma, who could then tell Garvin, and head back to San Francisco and make the call.

There, she thought. A plan.

Feeling calmer, she climbed out of her car and started down the walk to Garvin's front door. The air smelled clean and pleasantly cool, cooler than the city. The squirrels were up to their antics in the trees and greenery. Everything was so quiet, so still.

"He's not here."

She spun around, shock nearly collapsing her to her knees.

Vic Denardo sauntered down the walkway. "No doggie with you this time, kiddo?"

She took in a shallow, ragged breath. "Did you follow me?"

"Nope. Beat you here."

"Your car—"

"Out of sight. Pretty smart, huh? If you'd spotted a strange car out front, you might not have stopped. Interesting you should run to Garvin MacCrae after our little talk." He scanned her from head to toe. "You two got a thing going?"

"Mr. Denardo—"

"Has he been on your case too? He thinks Sarah hired me to knock off her old man. Then when Haley figured it out, I knocked her off too, to keep her quiet. Old Thomas was a character, I'll say that. I wouldn't have wanted to be his kid. Haley had his number, though." He squinted at Annie. "You cold? You're shivering."

She tensed her jaw muscles to keep her teeth from chattering. It wasn't the cold, she knew. It was his presence, their isolation. "I'm fine."

"So, have you taken Garvin to Sarah?"

"I hate to keep repeating myself, but—"

"But you can't help me," he said matter-of-factly. "An attractive woman like you, new in town—I'd think you'd fall hook, line, and sinker for a guy like MacCrae. He was a driven bastard when I knew him. Never figured him to give up the money business and take to running a marina. I guess you never know what guilt can do to a person."

Annie narrowed her gaze on him. "Why should he feel guilty?"

Vic Denardo shrugged, and she again noticed that as casual as his demeanor was, his eyes remained flat, unemotional. "A natural reaction. His wife was murdered. He found her." He rocked back on his heels, apparently unconcerned that Annie might jump him or knock him over the head with a rock. "You ever wonder why he was there that night?"

"Where?"

"The Linwood house."

"The newspaper accounts indicated he was looking for his wife when she didn't come home."

"So you've read up on the murders, huh?"

She made herself shrug. "After the rock I unwittingly turned over by buying that painting at the auction, yes, I thought it wise to understand the basic facts of the case."

He nodded, thoughtful. "I wonder if he and Haley would have made it."

"That's certainly none of my business—"

"None of mine, either. Doesn't mean I can't wonder. Haven't you?"

"Look," she said, for lack of anything else to say. She bit her lower lip and glanced at her watch. "I need to get back to my gallery. If you want to hang out here waiting for Garvin, that's your affair."

Her breath held, she started past him. She tried to walk with an air of confidence, as if she had no reason to believe he'd try to stop her.

He didn't touch her, didn't say a word.

She got all the way to her car.

When she had her door open and was climbing behind the wheel, he said softly from the walk, "I didn't kill those two people."

Annie looked back at him. Her throat was so tight, she couldn't swallow. "Then give yourself up for questioning. If you're innocent, you have nothing to lose by talking."

"Sure." He smirked, moving toward her. "You can have a front-row seat at my execution."

She gave a small, curt nod. "I really have to go."

"Tell Sarah I'll be in touch."

"You don't give up, do you?"

His eyes held hers. "Never."

＊　＊　＊

Garvin was waiting for her when Annie returned to her gallery. He wore a thick burgundy cotton sweater and heavy canvas pants, everything about him competent, masculine. An unruly mix of emotions washed over her as he walked out from behind her desk. Relief at having him here, uneasiness, desire, trepidation. She couldn't sort out what she felt, why, and if any of it made sense.

"Michael Yuma caught up with you?" she asked.

He nodded, studying her.

She pushed back her hair, trying not to look as close to the edge as she was. She'd stopped by the marina after her encounter with Vic Denardo at Garvin's house. Michael Yuma had pried what had happened out of her and promised to get hold of his partner on his car phone, but she'd ignored his advice to stay at the marina. She'd had to get back to her gallery. Her work, coffee, Zoe, muffins —even sweeping the courtyard—had all seemed preferable to sitting in a marine supply store, waiting for Garvin MacCrae to show up. She'd needed her world, however fragile it was.

"Where's Zoe?" she asked.

"She went next door. I said I'd watch the place until you got back. I think she's keeping an eye on me."

"She's a smart woman."

Annie realized she was speaking almost in a monotone, as if she were disconnected from herself, not really saying anything. Otto trotted out from the back room, stretched, and she had a vision of him in Maine on the rocks. She could almost see the pale sunrise over the bay, hear the cormorants and the gulls, the tide whooshing in. She could almost smell the balsam branches, the wild blueberries, the cold salt air.

"Annie." Garvin touched her arm. "Sit down. Zoe said she saved you a muffin after all. You look as if you could use a dose of sugar."

"I'm fine—"

"Of course you're fine."

She gave him a sharp look, but there was nothing patronizing in his stance, his expression. He gestured toward one of the tall chairs behind her half-moon desk. She went around and sat, her feet dangling. There were no customers. Probably Garvin had scared them off. Or Otto. He seemed to be more active than usual, maybe because of Garvin, maybe because of Vic Denardo—maybe because of her. He would be able to sense she was agitated. Flopped under the front desk, he didn't bother anyone. Pacing, he could be a deterrent.

Garvin set the cinnamon streusel muffin out on a paper napkin in front of her. "Zoe said she had to hide it from Otto."

Annie managed a smile. "Cinnamon streusel's his favorite."

"She also mentioned Cynthia Linwood stopped by before I got here. Apparently, Otto was still miffed about not getting a muffin and slobbered on her shoes. Cynthia's not your country rottweiler type."

"Poor Zoe." Annie broke off a piece of muffin. "I've barely known her a couple of months, and here she is, dealing with Linwoods and rottweilers and men wanted by the police."

"She seems perfectly capable of handling herself."

"But it's not fair—"

"What does fair have to do with anything?"

Annie nodded, the brown sugar and cinnamon already improving her spirits. Garvin's intensity, however, was almost palpable. And why not? She'd spoken to the man he believed had murdered his wife. After five years, Vic Denardo had resurfaced.

She dusted crumbs from her hands. "Would you like me to tell you everything Vic Denardo said?"

"When you're ready."

"I'm ready now."

Betraying as little emotion as possible, she related the details of her two encounters with the man she now had no doubt was Vic Denardo. Garvin listened without interruption. He stayed on his feet, still, silent. Annie couldn't just talk and pretend he wasn't there. He *was* there. And somehow, some way, she had the feeling that he was always going to be there.

When she finished, he erupted into action, pacing, pounding one fist into the palm of his hand, a mass of coiled energy.

He spun around at her. "Christ, I've been a selfish bastard."

She was taken aback. "What?"

"I've been focused on how I can use your relationship with Sarah to smoke out Denardo, on what *I* want out of this situation. I've hardly considered you at all. The danger you could be in. What you must be feeling."

"I understand. Your wife—"

"Haley *was* my wife, Annie. She's not now."

"But you want her killer brought to justice."

He came around the desk and pulled her to her feet, staring right through her. "Not at the price of getting you hurt." His voice was rough with emotion, not ungentle. "Or scaring you."

"I wasn't really scared. I don't know why, exactly, but I wasn't. Denardo just unnerved me. He does have a certain charisma. I can almost see how Sarah fell for him—not that I trust him, of course." With Garvin holding her, she wasn't even sure she trusted herself. "It's my own fault for going to that auction without more information. I knew something wasn't quite right, but I was greedy—"

"Annie."

She barely heard him. "Once I saw Sarah's work, that's all I could think about."

"Annie." He settled one hand on the back of her neck, threaded his fingers into her hair. "None of it matters. If you want to go back to Maine tonight and visit your friends until this blows over, I'll put you on a plane. I'll find someone to mind your gallery. Whatever it takes."

"No." She shook her head, adamant; at least on this point she was clear. "Thank you, but no. I live here now. I got myself into this mess, and I'm staying. I appreciate your thinking of me—"

"I wasn't just thinking of you. I was thinking of me too. Annie, when Michael called…" He took in a ragged breath, his hand settling along the curve of her neck, his thumb rubbing her jaw. She could just have melted into a hot pool. His voice lowered, deepened even more. "I never thought I'd let something like this happen."

She knew what he meant. She didn't need him to explain. When his wife had died, he'd promised himself he'd never care that much about anyone again, and now he was in danger of breaking that promise. Annie knew because she'd made a similar promise herself when her mother died, then Gran, then when she'd stood on the plot of land where her cottage had been and had looked out to the water that had taken it.

"And so you want to send me away," she said briskly.

"It's better than watching my obsession with finding Vic Denardo get you hurt."

"Garvin, you didn't bring Denardo out of the woodwork. I did. Even if you hadn't followed up on the auction, he still would have. You're not responsible for him looking me up. *I* am, because I made that deal with Sarah. I can't run and hide just because you're worried about feeling bad if something happens to me." She smiled, added a touch of bravado. "Not that I'm not flattered."

"Annie—"

"Nothing's going to happen to me, Garvin."

"You're an optimist."

"I just take each day as it comes."

He ran his thumb along the curve of her jaw, his eyes, deep and mesmerizing, locked with hers. "Will you take me as I come, Annie Payne?"

"I don't see that I have any other choice." But her voice caught, giving away her emotion. His words—his touch—dizzied her, made her spin with too many thoughts, too many conflicting feelings. "I don't trust myself with you, you know. Not right now. I'm thinking I need you, and I'm not used to that."

The intensity in his eyes abated, and he laughed, kissing her lightly, and backed off fast. "You're tough, Annie. I'll say that for you. And I'd probably give you a kiss that'd curl your toes—and mine—except a customer's bound to walk in, and the mood Otto's in, he might make off with my leg." He gave a wry smile. "Or worse. So, did Denardo say what he was doing up at my place?"

She shook her head. "I think he's still trying to figure out how I fit in with you and Sarah."

"Do you want to tell her?"

"I should."

"The police?"

She swallowed. Calling the police was a big step, one she'd been putting off in the hope that the wiry, gray-haired man would turn out not to be Vic Denardo or he just wouldn't show up again. "I probably should tell them too. I can't imagine Denardo's left much of a trail, but they might know something, have other pieces of the puzzle. But then I'd have to tell them about Sarah. They might want to talk to her."

"They can keep her whereabouts confidential."

"You don't have any objections to my going to the police?"

"No, why should I?" He drew back, eyeing her. "Annie, if I get my hands on Vic Denardo, I'm dragging him to the police. That's all. The rest is their responsibility."

"What if he's not the murderer?"

His expression darkened, as if closing off the part of himself that wanted to connect with her, with anyone. He had his mission; he would see to it. Nothing would get in his way. Not Sarah Linwood, not Annie, not himself.

"If Vic Denardo didn't kill Thomas and Haley, then he didn't," he said. "But someone did."

The telephone rang—it might have been a grenade through her window for the jolt it gave her. She fumbled for the receiver, almost dropped it as she put it to her ear.

"It's me, Zoe," the voice on the other end said. "Are you in there kissing Garvin MacCrae?"

Annie almost laughed, her relief was so complete. She glanced over at Garvin, who was watching her intently. She still could feel the warmth of his kiss, his touch. She turned away from him, her cheeks hot. "Not exactly."

"Are you out of your mind?"

"Probably."

"Annie, get rid of him, lock up your shop, and come over here. I've got the perfect potion for you. One sniff and you'll come to your senses. The man has one thing on his mind and one thing only—Vic Denardo. Get it?"

"I get it."

"I'll be over in two seconds with something for you to smell. That'll give you an opportunity to hurry him along his way. Then you and I can have a nice little heart-to-heart about the Linwoods and murders and men who are not suitable for sane women. Honestly." She snorted. "And I thought I could trust Otto to intervene."

She hung up, still muttering.

Annie did likewise and smiled at Garvin, her cheeks still burning as if he'd heard Zoe's every word. "That was Zoe. She's on her way over."

"Ah. She's a smart woman. She knows my reputation. I worked hard to get where I did in finance, Annie. I work hard now. I knew what had to be done, and I did it."

"A man with a mission."

He didn't smile. "I was honest, but I wasn't always nice."

"You know what, MacCrae? That doesn't really worry me. I'm not fragile. I've learned to take people as they come, not as I want them to be. Right now your mission is Vic Denardo, not me. So long as you can keep that straight, we don't have a problem."

He started to speak, but Zoe breezed into the gallery carrying a mortar and pestle filled with a dark yellow-green substance that could have been anything. "I need your nose," she said.

Garvin gave her a tolerant smile. "You can skip the theatrics. I'm leaving." He turned to Annie, his eyes cool, back to business. "What time are you closing up this afternoon?"

"I stay open until six on Fridays."

"Then I'll be back just before six. If Vic Denardo's keeping an eye on you, it's probably not a good idea for you to walk home alone."

Annie saw Zoe's eyebrows go up in alarm. "That's not necessary. If he was going to force me to do anything, he had the perfect opportunity up at your place."

Zoe nearly dropped her mortar and pestle.

Garvin's face became unreadable. "I'll be here, Annie."

"What are you going to do this afternoon?"

"I'll check and see if Denardo left a trail up at my place. Then I'll be at the marina. I have work I need to get done. Have you decided about the police?"

"If she doesn't call them," Zoe said, "I will."

Garvin nodded. "Should they want to talk to me, I'll be at home or at the marina. Otherwise, a few minutes before six."

The dinner for the Haley Linwood Foundation was tonight, Annie remembered. But he was already out the door.

Zoe scraped the yellow-green gunk into the trash can under Annie's desk. "I wouldn't call 911," she said briskly. "I'd look up the number and try to get the homicide detectives who investigated the Linwood murders. Holy shit. My God, Annie. Vic Denardo. I saw him with my own two eyes. And Garvin MacCrae. Do you have any idea what you're mixed up in?"

"I'm getting there."

"Jesus." She flopped onto a chair, spent. "Go ahead. Call the police. I'll wait."

"Zoe—"

"Do it, Annie."

"You don't know the whole story."

"Thank God for small favors." She snatched up the receiver, handed it over. "Call."

Instead of trying to look up the number, Annie just dialed information. Two minutes later, she was connected.

Within an hour, two officers were on her doorstep.

Chapter Ten

Garvin found his way up and around to the little hilltop where Sarah Linwood had her house. He didn't consider why he was there or what he expected to accomplish, just that he had to do something. He'd opted out of going back up to his house to look for traces of Vic Denardo. There would be none.

And staying with Annie Payne hadn't been an option. He needed distance. Waiting for her at her gallery had been torture. He'd been in San Francisco trying to talk himself out of barging in on Sarah Linwood when the call came from Yuma. The arrow of fear had struck hard and deep, the doubts, the questions. What if Denardo had decided to coerce Sarah's whereabouts out of Annie? What if he'd hurt her? Garvin had grown used to worrying about no one but himself. His life was more comfortable for him that way. Easier.

His life was neither comfortable nor easy with Annie in it. Yet he was having trouble imagining returning to the life he'd had before her.

He jerked his car into a parking space, pulled on the brake. Seeing her had been a different kind of torture than waiting. He'd sensed layers of strength and vulnerability and secret desires all mixed up together, motivating and scaring and thrilling Annie Payne, launching her into her new life in San Francisco, into her dangerous deal with a reclusive artist she didn't know. She would take him as he was or not at all. She wouldn't try to soften his hard edges. No. Annie Payne would leave his hard edges up to him to sort out—or she'd tell him to go to hell.

He jumped out of his car and pounded up to Sarah's little pink bungalow, San Francisco sprawling, sparkling, one hundred and eighty degrees around him. He knocked hard on the front door. "It's Garvin MacCrae, Sarah. Open up. We need to talk."

She had her door locked this time, probably for no reason, just as she left it unlocked for no reason. It was a few minutes before she pulled it open, regarding him with a fatalistic attitude he found faintly annoying. The penchant for drama was still there, beneath the weird clothes and artist's discipline. "I was just washing up," she said, and left the door standing open as she gave him her back and withdrew inside.

Biting back a sharp response, Garvin noticed the chill as he entered the house and wondered if Sarah didn't bother with heat or even might have had the windows open. Given her eccentricities, neither would surprise him. But she seemed unaffected by the cold. Using her cane, she returned to her kitchen sink and turned on the faucet. She grabbed a bar of cheap soap and stuck it under the hot, steaming water. She seemed absorbed in the process, almost transfixed by her own hands as she soaped them up.

"I can't seem to get any work done lately," she said without looking around at him. "I suppose it's to be expected."

"You've had a lot on your mind. Your homecoming—"

"That's not what's distracting me." She rinsed her hands one at a time, surgeonlike. "I'm worried about Annie."

"Because of Vic," Garvin said, feeling his own knot of fear.

She nodded, grabbing a towel. She had on a paint-splattered denim smock over brown stretch polyester pants, her socks two different shades of pink, her white Keds scuffed. As far as Garvin knew, Sarah Linwood still had access to the funds in her personal trust. Whether or not she reunited with her family, she wasn't penniless.

She dried off her fingers one by one, almost ritualistically. "I really can't believe Vic killed anyone."

Garvin didn't respond. She settled back against the sink, letting it support her weight. Her brow furrowed in the silence, making her seem plainer, older, but in spite of her bizarre clothes, her obviously troubled state of mind, he could detect vestiges of the woman she'd been. There was a sudden quiet dignity about her, a self-control. The crankiness of only moments ago had vanished.

"That doesn't mean," she went on, "that he's innocent, just that I don't see him killing my father over the relatively small amount of money that was involved. Father could be an ornery old bastard, but Vic knew that going in."

"You don't think he had a motive to kill Thomas?"

"No." She fixed her level gaze on Garvin. "And I didn't supply him with one."

Garvin acknowledged her words with a curt, neutral nod. He ventured deeper into the kitchen area, noting the jars and coffee cans of soaking brushes and other artist's tools neatly lined up on the sink, the paint-stained rags drying on a folding clothes rack. A large wastebasket overflowed with cast-off drawings, a tangible sign of Sarah's frustrating day.

"If my arthritis flares up again," she said, watching him, "I could end up unable to paint."

Surprised at her matter-of-fact tone, Garvin glanced at her. "Does that bother you?"

"Not really. I just think it's ironic. I wonder who I am my entire life—for a long time I didn't even have the courage to wonder. When I try to find out, I bring scandal onto my family, and possibly even murder. Then I develop rheumatoid arthritis. I can't help but wonder if I'd never asked the question, if I'd never tried to become who I am, if any of this ever would have happened."

"Is that what this is?" Garvin could hear the coldness in his voice. He gestured, taking in the small house, the near poverty in which she, a San Francisco Linwood, lived. "Your penance?"

Sarah smiled sadly. "No. No, Garvin, this is all just an extension of who I am. Not who I've become. Who I *am*. It's not that I'm trying to pretend to be poor when I'm not. I see no nobility in poverty, or in wealth, either, for that matter. I just don't care. How I live isn't a statement about anything. It's just how I live."

"Your work—"

"I want other people to see it, react to it. I want that very much, Garvin. I won't pretend I don't." She reached for her cane, leaned up against the sink. "I don't know if you understand how confused and angry I was five years ago. I was in the grip of a gambling addiction I didn't understand—insisted upon denying. I *liked* to gamble. It felt so good. And Vic—" Her features softened. "I was in love for the first time in my life with a man my father couldn't abide."

"You were a grown woman," Garvin said, not without sympathy.

"Yes." Clutching her cane, she moved slowly from the sink. "Yes, I was. But that never seemed to make any difference, did it? I'm not like you, Garvin. You knew Father only tolerated you because you were on your way up and just didn't give a damn what he thought. And because of Haley. He adored Haley."

"She seemed to understand him."

Sarah nodded, still moving slowly, painfully. "Vic used to advise me to get out of San Francisco. 'Hit the road,' he'd say in that way of his. 'Forget the old fart.' But I never asked him to intervene, I never asked him to kill—" She raised her eyes to Garvin, tears shining on her pale, wrinkled cheeks. "He was my father. I loved him."

"Then why did Vic go to him that night? If not on your behalf, if not for money—"

"I think he went to talk sense into Father."

"About you?"

"Vic—in his own way, Vic was trying to help me with my gambling addiction. It's been my worst fear that he went to Father that night to talk to him about ways to help me, and they ended up arguing..." Her voice trailed off.

"And Vic ended up killing him," Garvin finished for her.

She nodded.

"From what he's said to Annie, he seems to think you set him up. Any idea why?"

"No."

"It doesn't mean he's innocent. It could just mean he thinks you set him up to take the fall. You knew in advance he was going to kill your father, you let him do it, and you made sure he would be the police's chief suspect."

"But why would I do that?"

Garvin shrugged. "Guilt. To take the heat off yourself. Maybe no reason."

She sank into a cheap wooden chair at her table and stared out the window. "I didn't put him up to killing my father. I didn't know he would do it. I don't even know that he did do it." She turned to Garvin, her gaze vivid, penetrating. "I don't want to believe that he did."

"If he didn't," Garvin said, "then who did?"

She shut her eyes and slumped back in her chair, and he looked around at her finished canvases, felt their power, that pull of nostalgia and betrayal, hope and despair. They were impossible to ignore, demanding his attention, insisting on a response. Before Vic Denardo, gambling, family murders, and five years on her own, Sarah Linwood had been easy to ignore, had never demanded anyone's attention or insisted on anyone's response. But could she have killed her own father and niece? Could she have arranged to have them killed?

Her jaw set, and she opened her eyes. "What do you want from me, Garvin?"

"There's a dinner tonight," he said.

Sarah paled, swallowed visibly, and nodded for him to go on.

"The foundation established in Haley's name is holding its annual dinner." He moved closer to the table, looming over her, deliberately not sitting down. "I think you should go. It's a small, private affair, but just public and formal enough that people will be on their best behavior. Then everyone will know that Sarah Linwood's back in town. It won't be Annie's secret anymore."

She nodded, grim-faced and so pale Garvin thought she might faint. She ran a trembling hand over her mouth, and a small moan escaped. "Garvin…My God, you don't know what you're asking of me. I should never have come home. Never."

"Sarah, I'm not going to say I can understand what you've been through. I can't. Whatever your role in the murders, or Vic's, whatever I believe or suspect—I'm not going to stand here and judge you, tell you I understand when I don't." He leaned over the table. "But I know this, Sarah. Annie Payne has seen enough of Vic Denardo."

"What time?" Sarah asked, her voice croaking.

"I can pick you up at seven."

"And Annie?"

"Cynthia invited her. Under the circumstances, I think it'd be best if she skipped this one."

"She won't want to, you know."

"No. She won't want to. I'm meeting her at her gallery to make sure she gets home safely. I'll talk to her."

"If I were you, Garvin, I would remember that Annie Payne has no illusions that she's anything but alone in the world. Her life's stripped all of that away." Sarah settled back, calmer. "Perhaps she's luckier than the rest of us."

Garvin thought of her standing in her gallery with her big dog and her eyes wide with fear, determination, anger. She was pragmatic and self-reliant, and she understood on a gut level that life was unpredictable and unruly. But he'd also sensed in her a secret desire to believe in permanence, to find something that would last through the next storm that swept through her life.

"I should have known," Sarah mumbled to herself, "that nothing good could have come from my return home. I should have stayed away—"

"Playing the martyr won't help now, Sarah." His harsh tone surprised him, but he couldn't afford to have her sliding into the swamp of self-pity and regret. It wouldn't do anybody any good, including her.

Her vivid eyes fastened on him without anger. "I could pack up and be out of here before seven o'clock. I'm still a rich woman, you know. I could find someone to get me out of here."

Garvin shrugged. "It's your choice. I'm not going to baby-sit you. But running won't help. Vic'll still need to be convinced Annie doesn't know where you are."

"You always were a hard-hearted bastard, Garvin MacCrae. I wonder if Haley ever knew that about you."

She hadn't, he thought. Not Haley. She saw what she wanted him to be.

"Well, I suppose we often see in others what we need to see." Sarah waved him off, suddenly impatient. "Go on. Let me think. Come back at seven. If I've decided to go, I'll go. If not—well, then, I won't. I know you could force me, but you won't. You're hard-hearted, Garvin, but you're not cruel. You wouldn't force me to see my brother against my will."

He put one hand down on her cheap table and leaned toward her. "Let me make myself clear, Sarah. Annie Payne has Vic Denardo on her case because of you. If I have to stomp on your sensibilities and do something I wouldn't ordinarily do, I will."

"You're in love with her," Sarah said, shocked.

Garvin refused to listen. "Seven o'clock."

He tore open the door and shut it hard behind him, aware of Sarah Linwood staring after him as if she saw through to his heart better than he did. Playing the artist, the observer. Deciding he was in love with Annie Payne.

"Hell," he muttered.

He headed out across the Golden Gate, up to his house, where there was no Vic Denardo, no Annie Payne, nothing but the isolated life he'd crafted for himself in the years since Haley's death. He didn't stay. He drove too fast down to the marina. Michael Yuma had sandwiches, coffee, and commentary about his friend's surly mood, his own mood nicely unaligned with Garvin's.

"Should be a fun afternoon," Yuma said. "Think I'll go find some paint to scrape."

Ten minutes later, Ethan Conninger found his way into the supply store, where Garvin was still nursing a cup of coffee at the counter. Ethan had on one of his conservative money-manager suits. Garvin couldn't imagine being cooped up in an office again. It hadn't seemed confining five and ten years ago, but now—hell, he thought, there were days his own skin seemed confining.

Ethan slid onto the stool next to him. "You're just the man I'm looking for," he said. "Got a minute?"

"About that. There's coffee if you want it. It's fresh."

"No, thanks. Look, I don't want to stir up trouble, but I talked to Cynthia today. She's planning to take Annie Payne to lunch next week. Let her think it's because she's taking her under her wing."

"But that's not the case," Garvin said.

Ethan shook his head. "I'm not saying Cynthia won't want to help her out if she proves legit. It's just the kind of thing she'd do. But right now, I think she's afraid Annie Payne's up to something."

"Like what?"

"Who knows? It's that painting, Garvin. Five thousand dollars—"

Garvin pushed his mug of coffee away. "I know."

Ethan looked uncomfortable. "I have a feeling this thing's not going away anytime soon. Something's not right. I stopped by Annie's Gallery before coming over here. The police were just leaving. I didn't go in. Look, Garvin, I don't want to put you on the spot, but if you know anything—" He blew out a sigh. "I don't know why the hell I don't just mind my own business. Cynthia can take care of herself."

"You think Annie would do something to hurt her?"

"Hell, I don't know. Jesus. I just don't like how this thing smells."

Garvin jumped up, suddenly restless. So Annie had talked to the police. Would they want to question him as well? He raked a hand through his hair and turned back to Ethan. "Vic Denardo's been in touch with Annie."

Ethan took a breath, then muttered, "Holy shit."

"Apparently he thinks she can lead him to Sarah."

"Can she?"

"You're talking to the wrong person, Ethan."

His eyes narrowed behind his glasses. "What's that supposed to mean?"

Garvin deliberately didn't answer.

Ethan stared at him, then heaved another sigh at the ceiling before shifting back to Garvin. "All right. You'll tell me what you can when you can."

"It's decent of you to worry, but none of this is your problem."

"Yeah, it is." He smiled sadly, his dark eyes misting. "I worked for Thomas Linwood, and Haley was a friend. I wish I could have done something to save them. If I'd known Denardo was coming that night, if Haley had told me she was going to the house alone —"

Garvin clapped a hand on his friend's shoulder. "I know. I've played it out a thousand different ways myself. If any of us could have prevented what happened, we would have."

"It sucks, you know, Garvin? You'd think after five years..."

Garvin nodded. "I know. It might help if we can finally get some answers. Then again," he said, heading outside with Ethan, "it might not."

Annie had the flowers in, the courtyard swept, and was starting the framing of Cynthia Linwood's old map of San Francisco when Garvin came into her workroom just before six. He had changed into a black suit that was elegant, masculine, and as right on him as his torn jeans. He seemed equally at ease dressed for a dinner party as for mucking about at his marina.

He swept a brisk, efficient glance over her, quickly dispelling any notion that he might be feeling a little warm-hearted toward her—or at least willing to admit it. "You're ready?"

"Just have to lock up. This isn't necessary, you know. Otto and I can walk home on our own. We've been doing it all week. Last night—"

"Last night was different. Vic Denardo wasn't out in the open."

"He's afraid of Otto."

"Annie, I don't want to argue with you. *I* need to do this, okay?"

"You're overreacting. Don't smother me, Garvin. It won't work." Ignoring the tension twisting her insides into knots, she put away her framing supplies and carefully stored the map. Otto had roused himself from her feet. "And why are you in such a big hurry?"

"I've decided to go to the foundation dinner tonight."

Her expression softened. This explained his curt mood. "I see."

But it was clearly nothing he wanted to discuss. He tilted his head back and gave her a long look as she finished up in her workroom. "Ethan Conninger said the police were here earlier."

"I didn't see him—"

"He didn't want to interrupt."

"It wouldn't have made any difference." She breezed past Garvin into the gallery, determinedly not reacting to him. A visit with the police had sobered her. She grabbed her tapestry bag from behind her desk. "The police weren't uninterested in my story, but there's not a whole lot they can do."

Garvin wandered out from her workroom. His manner was deceptively casual, the evening shadows darkening his eyes.

Annie hoisted her bag onto her shoulder. "I don't have any evidence. I can't give them a license plate number. Frankly, they didn't seem too convinced the man I talked to is Denardo. I guess they've had false reports, people looking for publicity."

"They think this could be a stunt to promote your gallery?"

"They didn't say that. But I'd say they believe it's within the realm of possibility."

"You told them about Sarah?"

She nodded. "They said they'd notify the lead detectives in the case and that they'd probably want to talk to her. In the meantime, I'm to be careful and skeptical. This guy claiming to be Vic Denardo could be a reporter or someone out for the reward or even one of the private detectives John Linwood hired—someone who just got suspicious after I bought the painting." She started toward her workroom for Otto's leash. "For the same reasons you did."

"What do you think?" Garvin asked quietly.

"I think the simplest explanation is probably the correct one. The man who's implied he's Vic Denardo is, in fact, Vic Denardo."

He caught her by the arm. "Annie—"

"I'm all right, Garvin," she said, guessing what was on his mind. "It hasn't been a great day, but I got through it."

"This isn't your problem. Vic Denardo, Sarah—you didn't even know about the murders when you went to that auction."

"I do now."

He released her, his eyes distant, a defense, she knew, against caring too much. "We need to get moving."

She stood back from him and gave him a cool look. Understanding went only so far. Just when did Garvin MacCrae get to call the shots? "Fine."

"Annie—"

"I'm ready whenever you are." Her tone was ice. "I just need to get Otto's leash—"

"I'll do it," he muttered, and stormed past her into her workroom. He snatched Otto's leash off the hook next to her Spiderman poster, returned to the gallery, and ordered Otto to sit. Otto didn't sit. Garvin grabbed him by the collar and snapped on the leash. Otto just watched him with his big brown eyes, as if he didn't understand Garvin's storm trooper mood, either.

"You have to be nice to him," Annie said, "or he won't budge."

Garvin jerked the leash. Otto bowed his neck and sat now that he wasn't supposed to sit.

Garvin looked to Annie as if she were supposed to make her dog mind him.

"Uh-uh," she said. "I'm not intervening. You and Otto have your own relationship."

"He's a dog. We don't have a relationship."

Annie gave an exaggerated sigh. She wasn't going to let him get to her. "I think he was starting to like you. It'd be a pity to lose the ground you've gained with him."

"I don't give a damn if he likes me." Garvin glared at Otto, who stared back at him, calm, resolved. "Come on, Otto. Let's move it."

Annie slung her big tapestry bag onto her shoulder and started for the door. "Otto's going to win, you know. Rottweilers are a very determined breed."

"This isn't a contest," Garvin growled behind her.

She glanced back at him; truly, he was in over his head. "The reason he's going to win is that somewhere deep down in his rottweiler soul, Otto knows you don't want to go to that dinner tonight with dog slobber on your shoes."

"Annie."

"Though I guess it'd be worse having dog slobber on those expensive pants. Otto has no compunctions when it comes to getting his way." She pulled open the door. Dinner or no dinner, she didn't appreciate Garvin's surliness, no matter how understandable the reasons for it. Let Otto teach him a lesson. "I'll be waiting outside."

Neither Garvin's hiss of annoyance nor Otto's look of perplexity deterred her from removing herself to the courtyard. Clouds shifted and churned in the darkening sky. She zipped up her fleece jacket, shivering in the falling temperature. But it wasn't just the cold. By Maine standards, the weather was downright balmy. She'd had a long, confusing day, and Garvin going distant and controlled on her wasn't what she needed from him.

What did she need?

She shook off the question, leaving it unanswered.

Two young men in their twenties headed into Zoe's brightly lit shop, which could stay open until eight, thanks to part-time help. Soon, Annie thought. Soon she'd be able to hire help, keep her gallery open longer hours. She was still so new. There was so much to be done, and here she was, waiting for a man who insisted on going toe-to-toe with a rottweiler.

Otto lunged through the door, a grim-faced Garvin with a tight rein on the leash. "Whoa," he said in an easy, cheerful voice not matched by his expression. "Sit, Otto. There. Good dog."

Annie suppressed a grin. "So Otto won, huh?"

He shot her an unamused look, and her grin erupted. If there was one thing Garvin MacCrae had to learn about her, it was that she didn't give up easily. She went past man and dog and locked up. When she turned back, Garvin was still glaring at her. "You're gloating," he said.

She checked her grin. "Never. But I'll bet having to be nice to Otto, even for purely tactical reasons, has put you in a better mood. It's like skipping."

"Skipping?"

"Supposedly it's a mood elevator."

"I don't skip."

"Of course not. But when push comes to shove, you're kind to rottweilers." Aware of his dark gaze on her, she tucked her keys into her tote. "Here, I can take the leash."

"If you're ready—"

"I've been ready," she said airily. "It's you and Otto—"

"Annie."

She grinned. "All right, I'll stop. You'd better let me take the leash. If Otto realizes you're insincere, you'll never make your dinner on time. Where are you parked?"

"Two blocks up."

"Definitely best I took the leash."

Garvin acquiesced. "He's your dog."

Once he handed over the leash, she expected him to march off to Union Street, leaving her and Otto to pick up his heels. But he didn't. Instead, he drew his brows together, studying her. "You look tired, Annie." His tone had softened, and she wondered if he'd even seen her since he'd walked into her gallery, if he'd been too preoccupied with his own fears and misgivings to really see her. "You work long hours."

She shrugged. "I don't mind. I don't know that many people in San Francisco to hang out with, and I don't have a lot of spare cash for restaurants and movies. I like my apartment, but I wouldn't want to spend hours on end there. And when I'm alone too long—" She sighed. "Well, the long hours don't bother me."

"When you're home alone for too long," he said, starting up the walk together with her and Otto, "it's easy to start thinking about how you're really hanging by your fingernails over the abyss."

The abyss. It held her grief over Gran, her cottage, Maine, the life she'd had, her fears for her future. If she dropped into it, she might fall forever, clawing for handholds, or just giving up, relaxing into a free fall, and taking whatever fate threw at her. Given his own awful experience with loss, Garvin would understand. He would know when she was bluffing, when she was trying to pretend she wasn't scared.

"At least I like what I'm doing," she said.

"That's important."

They turned up Union Street, its shops and restaurants crowded, lit up on the brisk Friday evening. People gave Otto wide berth. Annie did her best to keep up with him. Their sunrise walk seemed only to have made him more energetic, none of yesterday's lethargy in evidence.

When they came to Garvin's car, Otto jumped in back without hesitation. Annie grinned. "I think he likes your leather seats. Either that or you've convinced him you and he are buddies."

Garvin surprised her with a short laugh. "I always make a point of making friends with rottweilers."

Not until they were nearly to her street on Russian Hill did Annie notice that her hands were cold and a bit on the shaky side. She didn't blame her visits from Vic Denardo, her talk with the police, or thoughts of hanging by her fingernails over the abyss. She blamed Garvin MacCrae.

She stole a quick glance at him as he maneuvered his car up her steep, pretty street. Being around him had a way of making her aware of every inch of her body, of *his* body. Her skin felt electrified, sensitized. She couldn't seem to get a decent breath.

"By the way," she said, "I'm going tonight too."

"What?"

"Cynthia Linwood called this afternoon to make sure I knew I was still invited, regardless of what you chose to do."

"Annie—" He sucked in a breath, frowned over at her. "You're not serious."

"I've got an outfit all figured out. If you want to wait while I change, it'll only take me two minutes. Otherwise I can just call a cab."

He was silent. Seething, really, she thought, unperturbed. She was mucking up his plans for her, and he didn't like it.

"It's my choice," she said stubbornly.

He hissed through clenched teeth. "Annie, you know damned well Cynthia Linwood suspects you're in touch with Sarah. I understand she's in a position to help you—"

"I'm not going because of her."

"Annie, damnit—"

She glanced at him in the dim light. "I'm going because of me."

He snatched a parking space half a block up from her building, yanked on the emergency brake, and flopped back in his seat, his grip still tight on the steering wheel.

"Now don't start fretting," Annie told him. "I'm not going off the deep end or anything. I wasn't really paying attention to Linwoods on Saturday at the auction or even Monday night at the Winslow opening. I'd like to know more about them, maybe understand Sarah better." She swallowed, then decided she might as well tell him. "Maybe understand you better too."

He sighed heavily. "Annie, Annie."

"I'm not crazy."

He smiled. "I know you're not." He leaned toward her, brushed the back of his hand along her cheek, sending warm shivers through her. His gaze was mesmerizing. "We'll go together."

Naturally, he refused to wait in the car while she went in to change. Unwilling to let her out of his sight, he followed her back to her apartment. In the apartments above hers lights were on, music was playing. She could hear laughter. It was a taste of other people's Friday nights.

She unlocked her door and shot inside, suddenly aware of her own vulnerability. Maybe rationality had nothing to do with her decision to go tonight. Maybe she just didn't want to be alone. She grabbed her pooper scoop and thrust it and the leash, Otto still on it, at Garvin. "You can give Otto a quick walk while I change."

His eyebrows went up. "I suppose it's too much to hope he doesn't need a walk?"

She smiled. "Way too much."

"Annie—"

"You'd better go."

Otto was tugging on the leash, but Garvin held fast, his gaze locked on her. Then, without any warning, he caught an arm around her waist and gave her a fast, hard, lightning bolt of a kiss. "Just so you don't think I don't know what you're up to," he whispered into her mouth.

He pivoted and retreated down the dark walk with Otto trotting beside him. Reeling, Annie quickly shut the door behind her and literally staggered into her bedroom. She had no illusions that the rush of heat she felt had to do with anything or anyone besides one Garvin MacCrae.

She got out the sweater and skirt she'd worn to the auction. Wardrobe machinations generally bored her, but she'd never attended the annual dinner for a foundation established in honor of a murdered San Francisco heiress. A woman, she thought, who had been married to the man she'd just sent off with her dog.

She pushed the thought aside and concentrated on getting dressed. She thought of outfits swept out to sea. Well, not many of them would do for a San Francisco night out, either.

A silk scarf and dressier earrings gave the outfit a fresh look. She tried fooling with her hair, gave up, and finally settled for giving it a good brushing. Vic Denardo, the police, and Garvin MacCrae had left her a bit pale, so she concentrated on restoring color with her cosmetics.

"Dazzling," she said when she'd finished. She smiled at her reflection, ignoring the twist of pain in her stomach. Nerves. But there was no lipstick on her teeth, no smudges of mascara under her lashes. Also, she thought, no "natural" color in her face. Nor any real confidence she shouldn't just pack up Otto and head east.

She slipped out of the bathroom before her reflection could tell her anything else she didn't want to think about.

Garvin and Otto had returned. The dog had dragged his bowling ball, his favorite toy, from the bedroom and was thumping it around in front of the couch. The man had his eyes on her.

"All my Armani dresses got washed out to sea," Annie said lightly. "Hope this'll do."

"Are you worried it won't?"

She thought a moment, then told him the truth. "Not in the least."

"I didn't think so." He moved toward her and touched the folds of her scarf. "It brings out the blue in your eyes. Annie—"

"No, wait." She felt his emotion, his desire, wished she could understand what was happening between them. "Garvin, I've thought it over. I don't have to go tonight. People are bound to start putting us together. I know we've—well, we've let things get out of hand here a bit." She took a breath, blundered on. "But the Linwoods are your family, and if you'd prefer to deal with them on your own, I understand."

"They were my family, Annie. Now they're people I care about, nothing more."

"But under the circumstances, if you'd rather avoid having to explain me, I can stay here."

He slipped his arms around her waist and drew her close. She could smell his cologne, feel his hard muscle through the soft, expensive fabric of his suit.

"Does it bother you to have people speculate about us?" he asked into her hair.

She just wanted to sink into him, to let him take her weight. "No—well—"

"It does." He eased his palms up her spine, as stiff as a two-by-four, if only as a defense against her own yearnings. "Why?"

He was so direct, she thought for a panicked moment he could see right into her soul. But he waited expectantly, and finally she said, "It's not what other people think. It's what I think. I don't want to give you any misimpression, Garvin. I've never—well, frankly, I've never been good at one-night stands. You know, those torrid love affairs, sex for the sake of sex and no other. Do you know what I mean?"

A glint of humor rose in his eyes. "Theoretically."

She felt her cheeks warm. "I must sound like a prude. I'm not. I'd love to tumble into bed with you." She heard herself and almost choked. "Theoretically, I mean. Oh, geez. Forget I said that. I'm all in a muddle."

"Forgotten."

But the humor had gone out of his eyes, and he enclosed her in his arms and kissed the top of her head, and she let her arms go around him. She leaned against his chest. He felt so strong, so good. She was tempted to explain herself but was afraid she'd only put her foot in her mouth again. She'd always believed in having a solid relationship with someone before getting physically involved. But with Garvin, the physical was so hard to hold back, and her feelings were moving fast too, all mixed up with her fears and desires and that insistent, pragmatic side of her that warned of heartache to come, reminded her of her promise to take life a day at a time. He intrigued her and fascinated her, and he made her think about herself and her life in new ways.

But Garvin MacCrae was also a man haunted by the horrible death of his wife, and if Annie had no business trusting his interest in her, she also had no business encouraging it.

"Let's go," she said, slipping from his arms and starting briskly for the door.

"Annie, there's something I need to tell you."

His tone made her turn.

"We have to pick up Sarah," he said. "She's coming to the dinner tonight."

Stunned, Annie went still. "This was her idea?"

"No."

"Then it was yours." If she needed proof she and Garvin weren't a team, she had it.

"I thought if she came out of hiding, then Vic Denardo would have no reason to keep after you. I saw her this morning and gave her time to think it over. Then I drove back up again this afternoon, and she said she'd be ready."

Annie straightened, the effect of being in his arms lingering in a thousand different ways. She adjusted her scarf, then glanced over at Otto and his bowling ball. Her life. She had to remember what her life here was to be. She turned back to Garvin. "She shouldn't do this on my account. It's too important. I'm not that worried about Vic Denardo."

"I am."

"I've seen him. You haven't."

His gaze hardened. "I know him. You don't."

"Look here, if—"

"Annie, how do you think Sarah would fare if something happened to you because she had you buy a painting for her?"

She stiffened. "Nothing's going to happen to me."

"No. Nothing will."

Then she saw the flash of fear in the back of his eyes, just for a moment before it was overpowered by the sheer force of his will. He knew she'd seen it, and he didn't like it. He pushed past her to the door. Annie hesitated. He'd been powerless to save his wife, she thought. He would avoid opening himself up to such helplessness again.

"Garvin…"

"We have to go." He glanced back at her, his eyes lost in the shadows. "Sarah's waiting."

Chapter Eleven

Sarah Linwood wore a shapeless red-flowered dress and red corduroy jacket and her white Keds to the annual dinner of the Haley Linwood Foundation. Garvin glanced over at her as they headed down the hill from her house. At least her socks matched. Annie, who'd insisted on sitting in the back, had tried to tell him Sarah wasn't being dramatic or rebellious or thumbing her nose at convention, just dressing as she saw fit. Garvin had his doubts.

"Six or seven years ago you'd have worn basic black and pearls to an event like this," he told her.

Sarah gave him a cool look. "You never know, I might wear all that again. Don't mistake my choice of attire as a statement, Garvin, because it isn't."

"Then what is it?"

"It's nothing. I don't like to think about clothes anymore, so I don't. I don't mind if other people do. I'm not a reverse snob. You and Annie, for instance, both look lovely tonight."

Garvin grinned and glanced in the rearview mirror. He'd agree Annie looked lovely, but given her skittish, tight-lipped mood, he thought it prudent not to tell her. "I'm not sure anybody's called me lovely before."

"I didn't call you lovely," Sarah amended. "I said you *looked* lovely. There's a difference. Your personality is anything but lovely. Never has been. I saw that about you from the start, Garvin MacCrae. I'm not saying you're a cretin. You've a certain integrity and courage."

Garvin grinned over at her. "But I'm not a lovely person."

She smiled. "That you're not."

A few minutes later, he pulled up to the lobby of the small, elegant hotel on Nob Hill that was Cynthia's choice for the dinner. The evening weather had turned windy and drizzly with no promise of improvement. Garvin expected Annie's shawl was not sufficient to keep her warm. But when she stepped from the car, she didn't seem the least bit cold. Probably, being a Mainer, she was undeterred by a San Francisco winter.

She slid out of the car on his side and barely looked at him. He leaned into her, smelled the clean fragrance of whatever soap or perfume she used. "Keeping me at arm's length, Annie?"

Her eyes flickered over him. "I wouldn't go to the trouble."

He laughed and turned his keys over to the valet while Annie went around and helped Sarah out of the car. For a woman in her position, Sarah seemed calm, even serene. She'd brushed her graying hair, to little avail; its thin wisps seemed to keep floating into her eyes. In the harsh outdoor lighting, her plain, unmade-up features revealed the hardship of the past years, the ravages of loneliness, grief, and disease. Yet Garvin couldn't shake the feeling that he'd never met anyone who'd appeared as free as Sarah Linwood did at this moment.

Annie, on the other hand, looked sleek, beautiful, and trapped. She'd gotten more than she'd bargained for when she'd agreed to her little deal with Sarah Linwood, but she meant to see it through. She was stubborn like that, Garvin thought, joining them at the hotel entrance. A doorman held the door. Sarah went through first, at her tortured pace.

When they reached the ornate lobby, she gave no indication she thought she might look a bit out of place. She turned to Garvin. "My brother's in good health, isn't he? I wouldn't want him to have a heart attack or anything when he sees me."

"So far as I know, he's in excellent health," Garvin said.

"I assume his wife will be here tonight. I remember her as being rather charming. I knew she had her eye on John. She's protective of him, I'm sure. Selling the house was her idea."

"It's a symbol of the past—"

She stopped suddenly, raised her eyes to him. "You can try to wipe the slate clean, Garvin, but you can never succeed. My brother does have a past."

Even with her disability, she managed to push on ahead. She looked around as if she were taking in every inch of the glittering lobby, as if she'd never seen such opulence before. Yet she'd lived most of her life in one of San Francisco's most opulent mansions. Garvin decided he wasn't going to waste his time trying to make sense of Sarah Linwood.

Annie eased in beside him. She looked tense, uncomfortable. He touched her arm. "You can still change your mind and sit this one out."

"I will if Sarah wants me to. She does have certain rights."

"Rights? So you think I've coerced her into coming tonight?"

"You have."

"She had a choice."

Annie's eyes cooled, more gray than blue, as they narrowed on him. "No, she didn't."

Before he could respond, Sarah dropped back, glancing suspiciously from Annie back to Garvin. She sighed, frowning. "If you two are bickering about me, please stop. You've been my only consolation this past week. Knowing I brought you two together has made it easier for me to tolerate the guilt I feel over the mess I've created. So, please." Her small smile took some of the edge off her words. "Get along."

But Annie was intent upon her own agenda. "Sarah, if you don't want to do this, I'll take you home. We'll call a cab."

Garvin resisted stepping in to argue his case. Annie, he noted, was avoiding his eye.

Sarah shook her head. "I want to see my brother." She leaned on her cane and looked up at Garvin, and if there was a flicker of reluctance in her vivid blue eyes, there was no fear. "Shall we?"

Given her physical condition, they bypassed the open staircase and took the elevator to the small, private dining room on the second floor. They were running late; laugher and the clinking of glasses drifted up the corridor. As Sarah shuffled along, Garvin felt a sudden, unexpected urge to protect her. Whatever lingering doubts he had about her and what she knew about the deaths of her father and niece, she was infirm and maybe a bit off center, and she could very well be walking into the lion's mouth. But she showed no outward signs of nervousness as she moved slowly forward on her cane.

Neither, for that matter, did Annie. Garvin felt a surge of protectiveness toward her, too, never mind that it would only annoy her if she knew. In her mind he was the coercive bastard; she was the self-reliant Mainer. She was in no mood to know he was willing to get bloodied on her behalf.

When they came to the dining room, Annie hung back in front of the open double doors. Garvin narrowed his eyes on her, but she gave a tight shake of her head. "No—you and Sarah go on. I'll wait here until the dust settles. The Linwoods aren't my family."

They weren't his, either. But this wasn't the time to argue, to explain, to finally make her understand that Haley Linwood had been his wife but was no longer.

"If you're sure," he said.

She nodded. "I'm sure."

"This shouldn't take long. John's either going to kick us both out or invite us all to dinner. Either way, people will know Sarah Linwood's back in town." He turned to Sarah, who was staring silently into the dining room. "Are you ready?"

Some of the old dignity asserted itself as she raised her chin, wisps of reddish gray hair in her eyes. "Yes."

They entered the dining room side by side. Glittering chandeliers provided soft lighting for the fifty or so who had gathered for the dinner. They were friends of the Linwoods, wealthy residents of the Bay Area, the executive staff of the foundation, and Sarah's brother and sister-in-law, all the immediate family she had left.

A stunned silence followed their entrance. Garvin put a hand under Sarah's elbow in case she teetered, but she didn't. She held her head high and leaned on her cane in her bag-lady dress and bright red jacket. She would appreciate the drama of it all, Garvin thought with a lack of cynicism that surprised him. Considering the life she'd led for so long, she deserved the attention.

Unless she'd played a direct role in the deaths of her father and niece.

But that was a reckoning for another day. Garvin pushed the thought out of his mind as he heard a shocked, "Sarah." He saw her smile. She looked pleased, relieved, even happy, and she said in a clear, steady voice, "Hello, John."

Her brother emerged from the crush of guests, waiters, tastefully set tables. "Sarah. Good heavens." His voice choked. He moved toward her, half stumbling, his elegant dinner suit a contrast to his younger sister's eccentric attire. If he noticed—and Garvin was certain he did—he would be too mannerly to comment in front of his guests. "Come in, come in. Welcome. My God, Sarah, welcome home."

"Thank you, John." Her voice faltered, but she quickly cleared her throat and smiled. "It's good to be back."

Garvin backed off. Other guests, obviously not knowing what else to do, quickly resumed their chatting and drinking, casting furtive, curious glances at their unexpected fellow diner. Sarah Linwood stuck out. Even if she'd worn a black dress and pearls, she would have drawn attention, if only because she was a Linwood who had left San Francisco five years ago in disgrace. Her brother didn't get too close to her, as if he were afraid his younger sister might have gone crazy in the past five years and come home with lice.

There was shock and confusion, but from his own experience with the Linwoods, Garvin knew there would be no histrionics. Given the setting, John would button up any urge to throw Sarah out on her ear, to scream at her, throw a fit, demand what in hell she thought she was doing—or what she'd done five years ago.

Satisfied that all was calm for the moment, Garvin slipped back out into the hall. Annie hadn't moved from her spot on the Oriental rug. He grabbed her by the hand, noticing it was cold. "Nobody's fainted or thrown anything at anybody."

"That's not why I didn't go in."

"I know it's not. Look, you might as well come in."

She frowned at him, unamused. "Are you enjoying yourself?"

He stared back at her. "Why the hell would I be enjoying myself?"

Her shoulders slumped. "I'm sorry. I guess it annoys me that I should have listened to your advice and stayed home."

She slipped her hand from his and ran it through her hair, the dim light bringing out the flecks of slate in her eyes. She seemed to have a fresh set of misgivings. The Linwood dinner, Garvin realized, was far removed from the world Annie Payne knew. But then, so was San Francisco.

"Do you think Sarah will want to stay for dinner?" she asked.

"Let me put it this way—from what I've seen so far, I don't think she'll want to leave."

Nodding, Annie pressed her lips together. Garvin could feel her tension but knew there was nothing he could do about it. He glanced into the dining room, where John was hovering over Sarah, gesturing toward various guests, probably explaining who was who and trying desperately to adjust to the reality of his sister in a red corduroy jacket and Keds. Cynthia had joined them; she stood at her husband's side, looking uncomfortable and pale. A potential problem there, Garvin thought. Cynthia Linwood wasn't a woman who liked surprises. And her sister-in-law was one hell of a surprise.

He shifted his gaze back to Annie, who showed no sign of relaxing. "If you're worried you'll have to explain your association with Sarah, don't be. People should be able to fill in the blanks without much effort."

"So they should. I don't really care. I only care, Garvin, that you're using her—and me—to get what you want. Tonight has nothing to do with keeping Vic Denardo away from me." She turned to him, her eyes the color of a frozen lake. "It has to do with bringing him to you."

"You know that for a fact?"

She didn't back down. "Yes."

His jaw tightened. "You don't trust me," he said.

"We're not talking about trust. We're talking about your tactics."

He started to argue with her but saw Ethan Conninger coming out into the hall, a drink in one hand. "Jesus, Garvin," he said half under his breath. "A little warning would have been nice. Where the hell did you dig Sarah up?"

"I didn't. She decided to come home." It was the truth, just without the details.

Ethan's eyebrows rose. He glanced at Annie, then back at Garvin. He sipped his drink. "Annie here's known about her all along, I take it?"

Annie's expression didn't suggest she had any doubts about her ability to handle Ethan Conninger's questions. Anyone's questions. As distrustful as she was of Garvin, as annoyed and, in his opinion, thrown by her propensity for ending up in his arms, she was still remarkably self-possessed. She even managed an amiable smile. "I don't know about 'all along.' Sarah and I met a few weeks ago." Ethan started to ask another question, and Annie added, not too sweetly, "I'm afraid anything else is for her to explain."

It was all the answer Ethan was going to get out of her. He seemed to know it. He wasn't hostile, Garvin thought, just as curious and incredulous as everyone else. "I didn't mean to put anybody on the defensive, but—Jesus, she looks like a bag lady."

Garvin shrugged. "She's changed, that's for sure."

Ethan lowered his voice, his expression serious. "What about Vic Denardo?"

"She says she hasn't seen him since she left San Francisco."

"You believe her?"

"I don't know," Garvin admitted. "Right now, I think I do."

"I guess it'll all come out in the wash now that she's back. Jesus. Wait'll this one hits the rumor mill. The gossips're going to have a field day. Well, I should get back in there, be the dutiful money man." He clapped Garvin on the shoulder, managed a grin. "And I thought this was going to be another of those dull charity dinners."

When Ethan retreated into the dining room, Annie touched Garvin's arm, just a brief graze. Her eyes, he saw, had warmed up. "I've been flinging accusations at you," she said, "when you didn't want to come in the first place tonight. The foundation—your wife—"

"Your accusations aren't undeserved, Annie."

She smiled a little. "Did I say they were?" She glanced into the dining room, squared her shoulders. "Well, I might as well get this over with."

Annie Payne, a woman to do what had to be done. Garvin followed her into the dining room, where people were making an obvious effort to carry on with the evening. But he had no illusions that they were unaffected by Sarah's presence. How could they be? She sat at one of the round tables, sticking out like a vase of loud, cheap plastic flowers. And loving every minute of it.

Out of the corner of his eye Garvin saw Cynthia Linwood spot them and excuse herself from her husband and sister-in-law, then charge their way. She had her small hands clenched into tight fists at her side, as if to keep the rest of her from coming unraveled. She ignored Garvin completely and fastened her eyes on Annie. "Well. I see the doubters were right." Her tone was sharp, but at least she kept her voice low. "You didn't have the kind of money for the painting you bought last Saturday. Sarah put you up to it."

Annie remained calm, neither self-righteous nor defensive. "Sarah and I had an agreement. I couldn't break it on my own."

"So you let everyone think what they wanted to think." Without waiting for Annie to answer, Cynthia pivoted around at Garvin. "You could have warned us, Garvin. John—the shock—" She bit back her anger. "Here he is trying to move ahead with his life…" She swallowed, fighting sudden tears, and gave up trying to explain. "Excuse me. There are people I need to greet."

Garvin tried to stop her, but she ignored him. Annie swept a glass of champagne from a waiter's tray. "I suppose we deserved that," she said. "Shall we go see how Sarah's faring?"

"You're taking this in stride."

She shrugged. "In Cynthia Linwood's place, I'd probably have slugged one of us. Maybe both."

"I'll keep that in mind next time I piss you off."

She gave him a small smile. "Do that."

With a quick sip of champagne, she breezed past him. Garvin could see that no matter how much she'd anticipated it, her encounter with Cynthia Linwood had embarrassed her. But Annie Payne was one to brave her way through thick and thin. It wasn't just stubbornness, he realized. It was also determination and no small measure of courage.

He followed her to the table where Sarah had settled, her chin resting on her cane as she listened to her brother. "What doctors have you seen?" John was asking her.

Sarah waved him off. "It doesn't matter."

"It *does* matter. God knows what all this disease has affected."

Her taste in clothes, for one, he seemed to suggest. He was still pale from the shock of seeing his sister after five years, especially, Garvin presumed, in the condition she was in. Sarah hadn't come home subdued and remorseful. She'd come home reclusive and eccentric, a woman no one—even her own brother—would recognize as the one who'd run out on her family at the height of its worst crisis.

She spotted Annie and gestured for her to come closer. "There you are, dear. John, you've met Annie Payne, haven't you? She has a delightful new gallery on Union Street. I'm afraid I lured her into our family whirlwind. She had no idea what she was getting into, absolutely none."

"Yes, I've met Annie." Drawing on his well-bred manners, John managed a quick smile at her. "A pleasure to see you again."

She nodded. "You too."

"We'll get this all sorted out sooner or later." He glanced at Garvin, some of the amiableness dissipating. "Won't we, Garvin?"

"I'm sure," he said.

Sarah peered around her brother at Garvin. "I've been telling John I've spent most of the past five years in the desert southwest. I've ached and ached since I've been back in San Francisco." She chattered on cheerfully, although Garvin had no doubt she wasn't unaware of the current of tension in the room. "Of course, it's so damp this time of year. I never even used to notice the rain."

Her brother inhaled. "Sarah—"

"Did I tell you I went by the house the other day? It was so strange. I can't believe you found a buyer so fast, given its history."

John averted his eyes, obviously uncomfortable with Sarah's easy allusion to the tragedy that had occurred in their family home. Annie seized the moment to scoot off into the crowd with her glass of champagne. Her stiff back and brisk pace suggested she neither wanted nor expected Garvin to follow. But he did.

"Annie, are you okay?" he asked as he came up behind her.

She swung around at him, her hair shimmering in the chandelier light, her eyes hot now, fiery where before they'd been ice. "I'm fine. I have to tell you, this isn't how this sort of thing would go down in my hometown. Someone would stand up and demand to know what the devil Sarah's been up to the last five years, whether she ran off with Vic Denardo, or why she can't buy a decent dress. Why she had to show up at the annual dinner of the foundation set up in her niece's honor. There wouldn't be all this dancing around the real issues." She gulped some of her champagne, her hands shaking. "But that's why you chose tonight, isn't it? Because you knew she wouldn't be attacked."

"That's one reason," he said carefully.

"And me." She drank more champagne, sipping this time. "You were sparing me too. You knew people would control their emotions in such a public setting. And the emotions are running high, aren't they? You can feel them. Even Cynthia—she wanted to rip our heads off for pulling such a fast one on her and her husband. But she held back."

Garvin ached to soothe her, make her smile. "Is it so bad to want to spare you?"

"I want to go home," she said abruptly. Tears sprang to her eyes. "I don't belong here."

"Annie—"

"This isn't anything I need to witness. Staying through dinner —" She shuddered. "I just can't."

"Annie, by midnight everyone in San Francisco will know Sarah Linwood's back in town. It'll be on the evening news. Vic Denardo will hear about it and know he doesn't have to go through you. He'll leave you alone. We just have to get through the evening."

She marched over to a waiter, dropped her glass on his tray, and marched back to him, her spine rigid. "I just can't stay, Garvin. Please understand."

He gave a curt nod, his stomach knotted. He'd warned her about not coming tonight, but he supposed this wasn't the time for an I-told-you-so. "All right."

"I'll call a cab."

"I can drive you—"

She shook her head. "You can't leave Sarah. It wouldn't be right."

Whipping her shawl onto her shoulders, she threaded her way through the crush of people back to the double doors. Garvin hesitated, cursed, and then was on her heels. "Annie, wait," he said. "It won't take long for me to run you up to your apartment."

She kept walking. "It's not necessary, Garvin. Really." Her tone was pragmatic, the independent New Englander doing her thing. "I'll be fine. Just go on back and have dinner and watch everyone stare at Sarah and wonder if she went nuts in the past five years."

They were out in the hall, away from the noise and the prying eyes, and he could sense Annie's ambivalence about tonight and how much she cared about the eccentric painter she'd befriended. It went beyond what Sarah Linwood could do for Annie's Gallery.

"Annie, most of the people in that room have known Sarah for decades. Once the initial shock of seeing her in red corduroy wears off, they'll realize, as I did, that they're not that surprised after all. I wasn't about to ask Sarah to meet John and Cynthia in private. That would have been asking too much. This way—" He broke off, glancing back at the dining room. "Frankly, I think a part of her's having the time of her life being on center stage."

Annie was unmoved. "All the more reason I should go home."

The light from the chandeliers caught her eyes, bringing out the pain in them, the fierceness of a woman determined to carry on with her life no matter what, even falling for a man she believed would steamroller her to get what he wanted. Her skin seemed less pale than it had, and her mouth—her mouth he could have lost himself in for a long time. He couldn't tear his gaze from her.

"You know what I think, Annie?" He spoke in a low voice, tension gripping him. "I think you know you're not in this thing alone and it throws you. Hell, it scares you."

"That's ridiculous. I'm just being practical—"

"Uh-uh. The more I think about it, the more I know it's true. A part of Sarah's reasoning—a part of my reasoning—for being here tonight is to try and keep you from harm. And it rocks you right to your core that we'd go through this even partly for you."

"Horsefeathers." She hunched her shoulders together, clutching her shawl in front of her. "Tonight is about one thing and one thing only—Vic Denardo."

"You're wrong, Annie."

"And you're deluding yourself, Garvin. You said yourself I shouldn't trust you. You said you'd run roughshod over me to get to him. Now I'm going home. As you say, word about Sarah will probably reach Vic Denardo before long. Maybe he's already on his way over here." She cast Garvin a cool, knowing look. "And wouldn't that suit you fine? But if you're still worried about me, don't be. I have good neighbors, I have Otto, and I can call 911."

"And you know where I am," Garvin said, giving up. She had come to think of herself as having no one, needing no one, and to ask otherwise was to open herself up to another loss. Best, in her mind, just to take life one day at a time.

Unfortunately, Garvin thought, he understood all too well that terrible need to stay alone.

"Yes." A little softness crept back into her face. "I know where you are."

He adjusted the folds of her shawl and scarf, all mixed up but somehow working together, making her attractive and sexy and, if not one of the crowd, holding her own. He tucked one finger under her chin. "If it wouldn't complicate an already complicated night, I'd kiss you right about now, and to hell with who might see us."

She laughed. "And I'd probably let you."

"Probably?"

She winked at him, her resilience there, bloodied but unbroken. "You're cocky enough as it is, Garvin MacCrae."

Ethan Conninger gave Annie a ride home. She had found him outside smoking a cigarette and at first refused his offer, but he'd been persuasive, asking her where she lived, saying Russian Hill wasn't that far. If he wanted to, he could get back in time for dinner. Laughing, she'd acquiesced. His easy, irreverent manner was difficult to resist and a welcome counter to the intensity of the evening. He drove an expensive sports car and handled the steep streets with the dexterity of a true native.

"Do you live in the city?" she asked.

He nodded. "I have a condo in the marina. I've thought about moving out of the city, but I don't know. The timing has to be right. Maybe when I have a family."

Annie wondered if he had anyone in mind. He seemed to have attended the dinner alone, which could mean anything from not seeing anyone in particular to not wanting to take her to such an event. "There are so many nice places to live in the Bay Area," Annie said. "But I do like San Francisco."

"Do you think Sarah will stay?"

"I don't know. I don't really know her that well."

"Did you have any idea who she was when you bought the painting for her?"

"None."

Ethan grinned over at her. "Must have been a hell of a surprise when you found out. I don't envy you, Annie. Garvin—well, he figured out the connection between you and Sarah before any of us, didn't he?"

"Apparently. But that's to be expected, I guess. His wife—"

"Yes," Ethan said, turning up her street. "He wants Haley's killer brought to justice."

"Did you know her well?" Annie asked quietly.

"Haley? I don't know. I've always thought I did." He seemed to make a deliberate effort to shake off his sudden seriousness. Annie suspected he wasn't a man who liked to dwell on anything more serious than the shifts in the stock market, which didn't mean he was superficial, just determined to enjoy life. "But hell, I always thought I knew Sarah too. She was educated, sweet-tempered, didn't give anyone any trouble. Then she took up gambling, had an affair with a low-life merchant marine. Now look at her."

Annie was tempted to tell him about Sarah's art, but resisted. That was for Sarah Linwood to reveal. "She's a fascinating woman, I can say that."

He gave her a sympathetic look. "You're caught between a rock and a hard place, aren't you? Sarah sent you off to buy a painting on her behalf without all the facts. You go head-to-head with Garvin and end up paying way too much. He gets suspicious." He grinned. "Am I right so far?"

"Mr. Conninger—"

"Ethan. Please. So Garvin gets suspicious because he thinks you're in touch with Sarah, and he hopes Sarah will lead him to Vic Denardo."

"But she didn't," Annie said, not knowing if she should.

"No, but you did."

She swallowed hard, saying nothing. Ethan Conninger was not to be underestimated. He had worked for the Linwoods for a long time, and he was a perceptive man. He slid up to the curb in front of a fire hydrant near her building. His manner was still easy, even reassuring. There was none of Garvin's intensity. "That's what tonight's all about, right? Vic Denardo figured you could lead him to Sarah too. Which means he probably has a bone to pick with her. I wonder what it is."

"Ethan—"

He peered at her in the darkness, the engine of his car idling softly. "I'm making you nervous. Sorry. I'm just talking out loud. Jesus, I hate thinking about all this stuff myself. I never thought I'd get this close to murder. Well, enough already. Would you like me to walk you to your apartment?"

She shook her head. "This is fine. Thank you for the ride."

"No problem. You're an interesting woman, Annie Payne. I can see why Garvin's attracted to you."

"He's not—"

"Oh, he is." Ethan smiled, amused. "Good night."

She thanked him again and slipped from his car, feeling hot, edgy, even embarrassed. Was what was going on between her and Garvin MacCrae obvious to everyone? Or was Ethan Conninger just more perceptive than most? He and Garvin were friends, she remembered. Maybe that gave him more insight.

Either way, she wished *she* knew what was going on between her and Garvin MacCrae. It had gone beyond simple attraction, at least for her. But from attraction to what? And what was the point?

Halfway down the walk to her apartment, she suddenly felt a tug of guilt for having abandoned him and Sarah tonight. Not very loyal of her, even if they'd managed without her—even if what she'd done had been right. She'd left not for their sake but her own. She'd felt out of place, something of an intruder. Tonight was a Linwood affair. She didn't belong. Perhaps after John and Cynthia Linwood, Ethan Conninger, and their friends and associates came to terms with Sarah's return, she would feel less ill at ease among them.

Something caught her eye. She didn't know quite what it was, except it was something out of the ordinary.

Light.

There was light coming from the wrong place. Her pace slowed. In her rush to get dressed, not to fall into bed with Garvin, had she left a light on she would ordinarily turn off? She frowned, aware of the quickening of her pulse even as she warned herself not to overdramatize and get too far ahead of herself.

Her bedroom window. That was it. She must have left the overhead on. Feeling calmer, she dug out her keys and unlocked her door. Garvin's presence in her life had thrown off all her routines.

"Blame him," she muttered, annoyed with herself, and pushed open the door. Her life was her responsibility, no one else's. If she was off her routines, it was *her* fault.

The moment she crossed the threshold into her apartment, she knew something was wrong. Her heart thudded. She clutched her keys in one hand and went still, barely breathing. She scanned her little main room without moving. Nothing was out of place. But something was wrong.

A breeze. She could feel a light, cool draft wafting in from her bedroom. She hadn't opened any windows before she'd left. She knew she hadn't. The light she could believe, but not an open window. *That* she would remember doing.

Otto. She felt a stab of panic. Where was Otto?

She called him, her voice hoarse with tension and fear.

Nothing.

"Oh, no," she whispered. "No."

Otto had to be all right. He had to be. Her throat tightened, her heart pounded, and a thousand horrible thoughts and possibilities flooded into her mind simultaneously. *Not Otto. Please not Otto.* He was an innocent. He hadn't done anything. He *couldn't* be hurt.

Mobilized out of her frozen state, she ran into her bedroom.

Otto was sprawled out at the foot of her bed, motionless. She leaped to his side, collapsing onto her knees, choking back sobs.

Blood. It was smeared on her beige carpet, matted on the dark fur along his forehead and left ear. Annie moaned, tried to rein in her panic.

"Otto, buddy, it's me."

She placed a palm flat on his abdomen, felt him breathing. He made a soft growling noise in his throat and opened his eyes, then quickly shut them again. Stemming tears and hysteria, Annie leaned over him to examine his wound. He'd taken a nasty gash to the head. He could have knocked something over on himself, couldn't he?

Cold air blew in through her window. Glancing up, she saw that it was open, the screen pushed in, the glass broken.

No, she thought. He hadn't knocked anything over. Someone had broken into her apartment, had dealt with Otto, possibly even had been prepared for him.

"My God," she breathed, shaking all over now.

She scrambled to her feet, still mumbling soothing words to Otto, trying to keep the panic from her voice. He'd hear it. Given his sensitivity, he'd know she was upset, and that would only upset him. She raced to her kitchen, got ice and a cold, wet towel. She was shaking, almost blind with fear, anger, panic. But when she again knelt over her dog, she knew she couldn't manage on her own. He needed a vet, stitches. Ice wouldn't do it.

She had no choice.

Holding the towel and ice to Otto's gashed forehead, she grabbed her cordless phone off the floor by her bed and got the number for the hotel where the Haley Linwood Foundation dinner was being held, dialed, had the front desk fetch Garvin, kept herself focused and under control.

Until she heard his voice and burst into tears.

"Annie, what is it? *Annie.*"

The ice melted into Otto's dark, bloody fur. He still wasn't moving. "Someone broke into my apartment...Otto..." She drew in a breath. "He needs a vet. I can't carry him by myself—"

"I'm on my way."

"But Sarah—"

He'd already hung up.

Chapter Twelve

Garvin gave Sarah two choices: stay and find her own way back or come with him. He didn't explain or give her time to decide. She chose to go with him. He told the Linwoods she was tired and they needed to leave. No one argued with him. John seemed relieved to see his sister depart early and only mumbled a polite, awkward farewell. Cynthia was even less congenial, and they were able to get out of there in short order.

Sarah didn't ask what was wrong until they were on their way to Russian Hill. Garvin gave her a brief explanation. She pursed her lips, inhaling through her nose as she digested his words. "Do you think it was Vic?"

Garvin didn't answer. From the tone of her voice, he knew he didn't need to. Who else could have broken into Annie's apartment and smacked her dog on the head but Vic Denardo? He'd admitted to keeping an eye on her. He'd known she could lead him to Sarah.

But what had he expected to find in Annie's apartment? Directions? Annie herself?

Garvin focused on the task at hand and kept his mind from drifting into the swamp of possibilities, questions, fears. Get to Annie's. Help her with Otto. Everything else had to wait.

When they arrived on Russian Hill, he double-parked in front of Annie's building and left Sarah in the car with the engine running.

Annie must have heard him coming and was waiting in the doorway like a ghost. "I called a vet over on Ninth Avenue. She's waiting for us," she said, leading him into her bedroom.

Semiconscious on the floor, Otto looked even more massive. He managed to growl at Garvin. "Don't worry, he's too weak to bite." Annie knelt down at her big dog's head and stroked his chest. "If you can help me lift him—"

But Garvin had already squatted down and was working his hands, gingerly and carefully, under Otto's middle, his fur hot and damp with blood. He had a foul, musky smell. The big dog gave a low growl as Garvin lifted him. Annie, rising with them, continued to stroke Otto's massive neck and tell him he was a good dog.

Dog paws hanging down in front of him, Garvin grunted under the strain of one hundred and twenty pounds of wounded, cranky rottweiler. "He might be good, but he's not light."

"He doesn't weigh much more than I do."

"You," Garvin said, "would be more fun to carry."

Otto growled. Annie smiled weakly. They were, Garvin thought, a pair.

"Have you called the police yet?" he asked.

She shook her head. "I have to take care of Otto first."

She did have her priorities. She held doors for him and negotiated him through doorways and down the walk alongside her building as he breathed in musky dog odor, felt dog blood seeping into his suit.

When they reached the car, Sarah was still perched in the front seat, waiting nervously. Annie climbed in back first, then helped get Otto in on the seat with her, his head in her lap. In the harsh glare of the streetlights, Garvin could see how pale she was, tears shining high on her cheeks, as if none dared dribble down to her chin until she was ready to give in to her fear.

"Annie—" How could he reassure her? He didn't know if Otto would be all right. "Ninth Avenue. I think I know the place."

Her eyes widened on him. "He can't die, Garvin. I should never —"

"Don't start, Annie," he said gently. "It'll get you nowhere."

Sarah looked around at them both, her face grim and as pale as Annie's. "We should go."

Garvin drove as fast as he dared. At the vet's, he again parked illegally, again left Sarah to fend for herself. Annie had to help him get Otto out of the car, holding up his front half—head, shoulders, and legs—as she slid across the seat. Then Garvin scooped him up and carried him inside. His lower back, his legs, his arms all screamed in protest.

The vet, a strongly built woman in her forties, had him carry Otto to an examining room. "What happened?" she asked briskly.

Annie explained, and Garvin retreated back outside. "I'll drive you home," he told Sarah. "They'll probably know more by the time I get back."

Her vivid eyes fastened on him, determined to see whatever they had to see. "Is there hope?"

He threw the car into reverse, his jaw clenched. "Otto's a big dog. He can probably take a good knock on the head."

"I hope so. Rottweilers were bred to have thick skulls, and with their double layer of fur, it would take a crowbar—"

"Don't, Sarah," Garvin said softly. "Speculating won't get you anywhere."

When they got back up to her house, Garvin insisted on taking a look around for an intruder before he would let Sarah inside. Without protest, she quietly handed him her house keys and remained in the car. The drizzle had turned to a soft rain.

Sarah's house had an eerie feel in the dark, the panorama of lights sweeping out before him not helping. Neither did the canvases, dozens of them. They kept drawing his eye, forcing questions he didn't want to ask. Concentrating on his task, he checked the bedroom, the bathroom, corners. Nothing seemed out of place.

Sarah needed help getting from the car. In spite of her gnarled joints, there was a strength to her that surprised him. But the evening had taken its toll. She moved slowly, with obvious pain, her face gray and perspiration glistening on her upper lip. Once inside, she collapsed into her rattan chair with the chintz cushions.

"If you want, I can stay for a while," Garvin said.

She shook her head. "I'll be fine."

"If you need me—"

"I won't." She focused on him with some effort. "Tell Annie I'm sorry."

"What happened tonight isn't your fault."

She shut her eyes, sank back into her cushions. "Just tell her."

Seeing she wanted to be alone—basically had dismissed him—Garvin nodded and went.

Annie was waiting for him in front of the vet's. She climbed into the front seat almost before he'd come to a stop. Her eyes didn't meet his. "He should be okay," she said. "The vet stitched him up and gave him a shot. She wants to keep him overnight, maybe a little longer." She paused, her lips pressed together. "He was lucky."

Garvin touched her arm. "Annie. Look at me."

It took a few seconds, but when he didn't remove his hand, didn't drive her back to Russian Hill, finally she acquiesced. Her eyes were huge, set against her pale cheeks and the dark smudges under her lashes and at the corners from where her makeup had run. She'd been crying. That was why she hadn't looked at him. She hadn't wanted him to know.

He wiped a tear stain with his thumb. "It's been a hell of a day, Annie. I'm sorry."

"It's not your fault."

His words to Sarah, spoken back to him. Maybe they were all trying to place blame—accept blame—where there was none. Maybe it made them feel a sense of control where they had none.

"I'm okay," she said.

"Why the hell should you be okay? Your apartment was broken into, your dog nearly killed—"

"I don't have any other choice." Her voice was stiff, but not harsh. "I have to be okay. Now I need to call the police. Can we go?"

He leaned over and kissed her gently. "We can go."

Annie agreed to spend the night at Garvin's house. Under the circumstances, it made the most sense. With her bedroom window broken, her apartment wasn't a serious option. Sarah's wasn't an option at all. Without a full explanation, for which Annie was too tired and confused, Zoe's wasn't an option, either. And she didn't even consider a hotel.

She explained all this to Garvin in a clinical fashion as he drove up the winding roads to his house. He listened skeptically, because that was his nature, and with no indication he believed one word she said. But she gave him credit for not telling her she was kidding herself.

Which, of course, she was. She'd agreed to spend the night at his house because she wanted to be with him. It was that simple, and that devastating.

And she suspected he knew the truth.

The minute they arrived at his house, she called the vet from the telephone in the kitchen while Garvin got out a bottle of brandy. The assistant on duty said Otto was sleeping comfortably.

Annie sank into a chair at a round table in the breakfast nook. French doors opened out onto the far end of the deck that spanned the length of the house, the San Francisco skyline lit up across the dark bay. The kitchen was airy and functional, done in a dark wood. Garvin got down two glasses and filled them. He'd pulled off his suit coat and ripped off his tie, but there were stains on his white shirt from where he'd carried Otto.

He brought the brandy to the table, pushed a glass in front of her, and raised his. "To Otto."

Annie's eyes brimmed with tears. "To Otto," she said, and they clinked glasses.

Garvin remained on his feet. The brandy was smooth, just a sip enough to steady the nerves. The house was virtually silent, restful. She tried to let the quiet, the sense of space around her, ease her preoccupation with the events of the day. Images skittered through her mind. Snippets of conversation. Threats. Fears. She kept seeing herself coming upon Otto, thinking he was dead and it was all her fault, and now she was truly alone.

"Crying over a dog." She cleared her throat, sipped more brandy. "Gran would be disgusted."

"Would she be?"

"Gran wasn't one for self-pity, and she had a pragmatic attitude toward animals."

Garvin smiled. "Reminds me of my grandmother on my mother's side. She remembers wringing a chicken's neck in the morning and having him for dinner that evening. She grew up in the country, obviously. But Otto's a pet—"

"He's still a dog."

"You can't form an attachment to a dog?"

"You can, but it's a dog attachment, not a people attachment. Gran wouldn't have me falling apart over a dog getting hit on the head."

"But this is Otto," Garvin said. "He's all you have left of your old life. He's a living, breathing connection to your past."

Annie scowled. "When did you get to be a shrink?"

He was unperturbed. "I've noticed you get gruff whenever I strike a nerve. Drink your brandy."

"I am." She took another sip, having already duly noted it wasn't rotgut brandy. Emotions swirled around her, through her. She made no attempt to sort them out. Having Garvin hovering over her only added to the mix. "I wonder if he saw who hit him."

"Otto?"

"Yes, Otto. He's a very intelligent dog, at least about things like that. If he saw or even smelled who hit him, he'll remember—unless his wound has scrambled his memory."

"Annie, I don't think we need Otto to tell us who hit him."

She shivered, not even the brandy stopping the sudden cool feel of the night air. She set her glass down on the table. Although she hadn't eaten dinner, she wasn't hungry. The vet had made her down a couple of candy bars.

"You think it was Denardo," she said.

It wasn't a question. Garvin had told as much to the police. They'd taken their statements, checked out her apartment, dusted for prints, talked to the upstairs neighbors, who hadn't seen or heard anything, and suggested they would speak to Sarah Linwood first thing in the morning. They weren't resistant to the idea that the break-in was related to the five-year-old Linwood murders, just cautious about signing on. In their view, someone could simply be after a fivethousand-dollar painting whose purchase was highly publicized. Garvin had pointed out the thieves could get a more reliable five grand stealing silver, but the police had an answer for that too. Would-be thieves might not know the painting was worthless, or it could have a certain cachet because of its association with the Linwoods and scandal. They weren't claiming a theory, only that without hard evidence, theoretically anything was possible.

Annie swung up to her feet, feeling just a little dizzy. "If I'm to pick up Otto in the morning before work, I should get to bed. Where's the guest room?"

She could feel Garvin's eyes on her. "Downstairs."

The master bedroom, she'd noted on her first visit, was on the main floor down from the living room, the upper floor of the hillside house. At least downstairs she'd be away from temptation.

"There are two." He leaned against the doorway into the dining room, one long leg bent as he continued to watch her. "Take your pick. The beds in both should be made up."

"Thanks."

"I can walk down with you—"

"*No.*" She gave him what had to be an unconvincing smile. "I can manage."

Just the tiniest glint of humor came into his eyes, tugged at the corners of his mouth. "As you wish."

She went past him into the dining room and out across the thick carpet to the entry, where she'd dropped the grocery bag she'd thrown a few things into before leaving her apartment. Even with moving west, she hadn't yet replaced her luggage; instead, she'd relied on boxes and trash bags. Hugging the bag to her chest, she started for the stairs. She was aware of the silence, the darkness, the space around her. No cottage on the bay was this; no little semilegal San Francisco apartment. Garvin had followed her out into the living room, his eyes on her. Or maybe they weren't, she thought. Maybe she was getting ahead of herself, thinking he wanted to go down to the guest room with her. Amazing what a glass of brandy and a bad day could do to a woman's mind.

But her attempt at humor fell flat, and she looked around at him. "I appreciate your help, Garvin." She said his name easily now, liked the feel of it. "Thank you for carrying Otto."

"You're welcome."

"It's a nasty business, carrying a wounded rottweiler."

He shrugged. "So long as I came away with all body parts, I'm a happy man."

"Well, it was above and beyond the call of duty."

"No, it wasn't."

Her breath caught, and she nodded. "Well, thank you."

He smiled. "Good night, Annie."

She chose the bedroom directly beneath the living room. It had its own door out to a lower deck, and it was big and airy and spotless—but also impersonal. It had a connect-the-dots feel with

179

its queen-size bed cover made up in natural cotton, the handmade cherry dresser and night table, the brown pottery lamps, as if Garvin hadn't put—couldn't put—himself into his surroundings. A large framed photograph of a sailboat at sunrise hung above an unused stone fireplace. She could have been in a hotel room instead of someone's house. Yet Annie welcomed the sterile comfort of the room. She didn't need reminders of where she was and who was on the floor above her.

The adjoining bathroom was done in white with a pedestal sink and a simple bathtub. A wooden rack held a stack of fluffy white towels. Imagining herself wrapped in one, she filled the tub with water as hot as she could possibly stand and dumped in bath crystals from a jar sitting on the edge of the tub. She inhaled their fragrance. Zoe would be able to pinpoint the various scents, but Annie just breathed them in, already relaxing.

She peeled off her dog-smelling clothes and left them in a heap on the floor, to be burned in the morning, she thought. She washed her face with soap and water, feeling her fatigue in her burning, puffy eyes, her throbbing head, the stiffness throughout her body.

Had Vic Denardo broken into her apartment and left Otto for dead?

If not Denardo, who?

Through sheer force of will, she pushed the images and the questions to the back of her mind. Like her heap of clothes, they were something to deal with in the morning.

She stepped into the tub and slowly immersed herself in the steamy, fragrant water. Almond. That was what she was smelling. She breathed deeply, sinking back against the cool porcelain.

The floor above her creaked. She could hear Garvin walking around. In a moment, she heard the water come on, presumably in his own bathroom. Did he know she was in the tub on the floor below? Even with Otto recuperating at the vet's, with a man suspected of two brutal murders having followed her and maybe having beaten up her dog, she could feel her body responding to the simple thought of Garvin MacCrae taking a shower. Warm water slid over her, swirled around her.

So much, she thought, for a calming bath.

Maybe almond was an aphrodisiac. She would have to ask Zoe.

She groaned. Distractions weren't going to work.

The telephone rang, such a surprise she jolted up and then back down again, sliding under the water, almost drowning herself. She came up gulping for air, her heart racing.

Otto. It was the vet calling to tell her he'd taken a turn for the worse.

Without thinking, she leaped from the tub, dripping water, skin pink from the heat. She snatched one of the huge, soft bath sheets and wrapped it around her, opening the door out into the hall.

"Garvin?"

No answer. He'd probably picked up an extension in his bedroom.

She crept to the bottom of the stairs. There was no light on in the first-floor hall, and the air felt even colder just out of her hot bath. But she didn't want Garvin to think she was unavailable to take a call.

"Garvin, I haven't gone to bed yet."

Of course, the call could be for him and have nothing to do with her or Otto. She glanced around, suddenly aware of her situation. Her towel was swept imperfectly around her, water was dripping off her onto the hardwood floor, and she was shivering, preciously close to being stark naked.

Perhaps, she thought, she should retreat back to the bathroom.

"Annie."

She went still, looked up at the top of the stairs. Garvin was silhouetted in the shadows. But she could see he had on a towel much smaller than hers, just wrapped around his waist.

"That was Cynthia." His voice was low, deep, penetrating the silence. "She wanted to know if everything was all right. She apologized for being so unpleasant tonight. I told her you'd had a break-in but didn't go into details."

Annie held her towel close. "I see. Thank you for telling me. I thought—I was worried it was about Otto."

"I know."

The length of stairs might not even have been between them. Annie felt his eyes on her, was aware of her bare shoulders, the water dripping from her hair into her towel. Garvin hadn't moved.

"Annie."

His quiet voice told her: he wouldn't come down unless she made it clear that was what she wanted. A lot had happened today. He wasn't going to take advantage of any vulnerability she might be feeling, any desperate need for closeness.

But she wanted him downstairs with her. Any resistance or any reluctance she'd had was gone. She couldn't even remember why she'd felt it. She was alone, and it was dark, and nothing seemed more right than having him there with her.

"Good night," he said. "Sleep well."

"No—wait."

He turned back, his eyes riveted on her. She could hear the rain lashing against the windows.

She let her towel drop just a little. "I'd like to be with you tonight, Garvin."

His gaze remained on her. "You're sure," he said.

She realized it wasn't a question, more an observation. She nodded. "I'm sure. Trust me. I'm getting cold standing here."

He started down the stairs. "I wouldn't want you to get cold."

As he reached the bottom of the stairs, her gaze drifted to the damp, dark, curling hairs on his chest, his taut abdomen. She studied the line of his jaw, the softness of his mouth. The only light came from her bathroom, making his eyes difficult to read.

He smiled, touching a finger to her lips. "Feeling warmer?"

"As a matter of fact, I am."

Her towel had lowered steadily, not quite exposing her breasts, but his eyes were on hers, as if he were trying to see all the way into her soul. She took a shallow breath, more aware of herself than she ever had been. Every inch of her mind and body seemed open and revealed, not only to him but to herself. She had nothing to hide, not even how much she wanted him.

He trailed his fingertips into her damp hair, snared it up into his palm. "Oh, Annie," he whispered, raw and hoarse, and his mouth came down on hers in a searing kiss, erupting everything that had simmered between them for days into a rolling, uncontrollable boil. Sensations tore through her, her blood sizzled. She clung to him, her towel falling to her waist.

"Tell me this is right," he murmured into her mouth.

"Does it matter?"

"Yes." He drew back an instant, locked eyes with her. "Yes, it matters."

She nodded, her pulse skipping. "I've no doubts."

But he did. She could see them encroaching. A slight darkening of his eyes, a tensed muscle working in his jaw, a tightening of his hold on her—on himself. Wanting her left raw and bare all the emotions—the guilt, the anger, the horror—he'd locked up five years ago. He could have sex with a woman, Annie thought, so long as emotion didn't come into play. So long as he didn't *care.*

"I'm not asking any more of you—or myself—than tonight," she said.

He skimmed a finger down her throat, across the swell of her breasts. "Annie, I'm still going to want you tomorrow. One night isn't going to end it for me. If that's what you're hoping—"

"It's not."

"Good." He caught a lock of damp hair and tucked it behind her ear. "I want you, Annie. Only you."

"That doesn't scare me, you know."

He drew in close, deliberately skimmed his palms over her breasts, down her sides. "Maybe it should," he said, and kissed her again. Her towel sagged to her feet. She didn't know what happened to his except that it was gone. She moaned at the feel of his hard, taut body against hers. His answering moan was low, deep, and without any warning, he scooped her up, her legs a vise around his waist, and carried her into the bedroom. He swept back comforter, blankets, and top sheet with one hand, then fell with her onto the bed, groaning her name in the milky darkness.

Need overcame her, desire pent up from that very first moment she'd spotted him across the crowded Linwood ballroom, all tense and outraged at having a competitor. She couldn't get enough of touching him, stroking him. Nor could he of her. She could feel his desperate need, let it fuel her own as his mouth lingered on hers, slid down her throat, found her breast. She arched, moaning, dazed and hungry with want.

"You're so beautiful," he whispered and with one hand stroked the curve of her hip, slipped his fingertips between her legs. She shut her eyes, buried her head in his chest. One sensation after another stunned and rocked her, and she writhed with pleasure, a tangle of limbs and aching, shimmering desires.

"Garvin." His name came out in a strangled cry. "*Now.*"

He didn't need to be told twice. Fumbling in the drawer to the nightstand, he produced a small foil package. He gave her a wry smile. "The perfect host."

But his voice was hoarse, ragged, and in a few seconds, protection seen to, he eased back onto her, coursed one palm up her side, sending her pulse racing. She was aching and wet and vibrating with the need to feel him inside her. "I'm not fragile," she whispered. "You're not going to hurt me."

She didn't know if he heard her or not, if she'd even spoken aloud, for in that next instant, he settled into that dark, hot spot, then plunged inside, fast and deep and so hard it took her breath away. Pleasure speared through her, spread, tumbled out of control. Her blood sizzled, her head spun. She was in a dark labyrinth, wading through even darker caverns, searching, wanting. She heard soft voices urging her on, other voices warning her back, until finally there was no moving forward, no turning back. She cried out, and light spilled over her.

"*Annie.*"

She wrapped her arms around him in the dark, held herself close to him. "I'm all right. More than all right."

She felt his smile, the feather touch of a kiss on her hair. "I know."

She opened her eyes, looked at him. "You do, don't you?"

He stroked her hair. "Mm."

"What about you? Are you okay?"

"Just fine."

She smiled. "I don't mean *that* way. I mean—" She frowned, thinking, not wanting to spoil the moment with their lovemaking still fresh. "I think deep down you're afraid if you love me, if I love you back, that I'll come to a bad end."

He was silent, and in the darkness and the stillness, Annie was struck by how different her life was. Six months ago she'd been living in her cottage on the coast of Maine, running a maritime museum, enjoying Otto and her friends, and not thinking too much about the future. Now she was in San Francisco in bed with a man she wasn't sure could ever really let himself love again.

She wriggled free of him and sat up, aware of the tangle of sheets around them, the soft sheen across her breasts and stomach that told of their lovemaking. "I'm right," she said stubbornly, but not without sympathy, "and you know it."

His gaze held hers, his expression impossible to read in the shifting shadows. "Was tonight about love, Annie? I don't know. I think it was just about you wanting me and me wanting you back. I think you're just as afraid—maybe more so—of letting anyone else into your life, risking loss."

His words held the ring of truth. Here today, gone tomorrow. That was her philosophy in all things, wasn't it? Why not in love? She shivered, suddenly cold. "I'm still right," she said, finding an edge of top sheet, drawing it up over her breasts.

"Let tonight be what it was, Annie," he said softly.

She noted his use of the past tense, knew he was leaving her bed even before his feet hit the floor. Silhouetted against the shaft of light coming from the bathroom, he looked magnificent. She wasn't sorry. She knew she'd been cast into labyrinths and caverns for a reason. Somewhere, hidden in a deep, dark place within one of those labyrinths, one of those caverns, was the part of Garvin MacCrae that would risk loving again. That would take the chance that another woman he loved wouldn't die on him and leave him feeling responsible.

He was already pounding up the stairs. She heard him curse. A door slammed shut.

She wasn't afraid. Not in the least. Not of him, not of herself. And she had no regrets about their lovemaking. Yes, she'd wanted him, and he'd wanted her. She wouldn't deny it. She felt bad about how awkwardly their night together had ended, but no matter what happened tomorrow, she'd have tonight.

Another door slammed. Water came on.

He was taking a shower, she thought.

"I hope it's a cold one," she muttered, knowing that the night would have brought on more lovemaking, hours of it.

Groaning under her breath, she slipped from her bed. Her ill-fated bath awaited her. The water, of course, was ice-cold, the smell of almonds long dissipated. She drained the tub and filled it again, suddenly energized. In the full-length mirror, her breasts looked heavy and swollen, her skin pink. All from lust, she thought. Pure lust. She gave her reflection a sly smile. There was nothing wrong with wanting Garvin MacCrae, she thought. Nothing at all.

Or with having had him, she added silently.

She pulled on her nightshirt. Everything suddenly seemed so very clear to her. Garvin had stomped upstairs not because he'd had her and once was enough but because he'd had her and once wasn't enough.

She crawled into bed, the sheets still warm from their lovemaking. She stared wide-eyed at the ceiling, wondering if he was up there blaming her fears rather than his own for why he was spending the rest of the night alone in bed. Well, let him. She'd warned him that she was no good at one-night stands. Serious issues existed between them, and they needed to be confronted. Maybe her timing was a little off, and maybe he had good reason to think her own fears had forced her subconsciously to drive him off.

Above her, his shower clanked off. She thought he kicked the door open.

Hugging her comforter around her, she closed her eyes, knowing she would sleep well, not in spite of Garvin MacCrae but because of him. For the first time in a long time, she was thinking not just about today but about tomorrow.

Chapter Thirteen

Annie Payne came to breakfast looking as if she'd passed a perfectly peaceful night. Garvin watched her irritably as she poured herself a bowl of raisin bran. She wore slim black pants with a berry-colored chenille sweater and silver earrings. A touch of blush and mascara, no lipstick yet. She'd already been out for a short walk and called the vet. Otto had had a good night and could go home that morning, although he would need time to recuperate. After she'd hung up, she was downright lighthearted. The snarl of emotions and physical longings left over from last night didn't dampen her mood, at least not that Garvin could see. Otto was on the mend, and Annie was fine.

She dug into her cereal. "I don't think it's a good idea for Otto to rest at the gallery today, but I can't leave him alone at my apartment. I doubt the intruder'll be back—presumably he's finished there—but Otto might not be comfortable there after what happened."

"You're worried about posttraumatic stress?"

"Mm."

Garvin sighed. "He can stay here."

Her eyes lit up. "He can? You're sure you don't mind? He won't be any trouble. He's not incapacitated or anything. The vet says he can go outside to do his business."

"Thank God."

She was oblivious to his mild sarcasm. "This is really nice of you, Garvin. What a relief. I mean, a rottweiler's tough to explain to customers on a good day, but with his head partly shaved and stitches—" She shrugged expansively. "I'm sure he's going to look rather rugged."

"Rugged?"

"You know what I mean. People could get the wrong idea about him and think he was in a fight."

"Maybe he was. We haven't seen what he did to whoever knocked him on the head."

She paled slightly, obviously not wanting to remember such unpleasantness. "There wasn't any trail of blood. You'd think if Otto had managed to fight back, there'd be—well, something left behind."

"An arm or a leg, perhaps?"

"Rottweilers are crushers, not slashers. Dobermans are slashers."

Garvin gave her a dry smile. "Good to know."

Her big eyes fastened on him, as if she'd just realized he was being flip. "I'm serious, Garvin."

"So am I."

"No, you're not. You're miffed because I'm in a good mood and you're not."

"Miffed? Annie, that's not a word I'd associate with me. Pissed, annoyed, irritated. They'll do. But not miffed."

She scowled at him. "All right. So you're *irritated* because I'm in a good mood and you're not."

He leaned over the table toward her. "Why do you suppose that is?"

"Because I have a dog and you don't."

He laughed. He couldn't help himself. He threw back his head and roared, just because he had never, ever, in his life encountered a woman like Annie Payne.

She jumped to her feet. Now she, he thought, was miffed. "This is ridiculous. I'm going to brush my teeth and put on some lipstick. If you can manage it, I'd appreciate a ride to town. If not, I can call a cab or find a bus. Maybe Michael Yuma would give me a ride."

She started to breeze past him, but Garvin caught her by the arm and swung her into him, remembering the feel of her skin against his last night. "Annie," he said into her ear, "I'm not in a bad mood because I don't have a dog and you damned well know it."

She swallowed.

He persisted. "Admit it, Annie."

"Admit what?"

He pulled her lower, settled his palms in the small of her back. Let her wonder at his next move. It was one way of calling her bluff. Dogs. The hell he was irritated because of a damned dog. The hell she *thought* he was irritated because of a damned dog.

"All right, all right." She scooted away from him, clearing her throat self-consciously. "You're not jealous because I have Otto. I don't know what your bad mood's about."

He gave her a dark look.

She pushed her hair back with both hands. "Oh, all right. I do know. You can't stand it that I woke up smiling and you didn't. Well, it's nothing to get mad about. I'm smiling because I knew you'd regret not staying in bed with me last night. And you're grouchy because I'm right. You *do* regret it." She dropped her hands to her side. "There you have it. Simple."

Garvin folded his arms on his chest, still saying nothing.

"And also because of Otto," Annie added quickly. "I'm smiling because he's all right."

"Annie." He kept his arms folded on his chest, his eyes on her. "How do you know I regret what I did last night?"

She returned his gaze, a sly smile at the corners of her mouth. "Don't you?"

"Let's say I do. Why does it put you in a good mood?"

"It doesn't."

He was going to throttle her. It was the only sensible course of action.

"*Knowing* you'd regret last night does. It suggests..." She shrugged, as if she didn't know what it suggested. Or knew and didn't want to tell him. "It suggests a lot of things."

"Name one."

"That I'm cottoning on to you. That I'm unraveling who you are and sorting it out, getting comfortable with the intricacies of your nature. No, comfortable's not the right word. Maybe familiar is better."

He frowned. "Annie, I'm not a damned painting."

She cleared her throat. "This is true."

"So forget about unraveling my intricacies or whatever the hell you've been doing and concentrate on this."

He swept her into his arms and crushed his mouth to hers, feasted on the taste of her, the feel of her, the very scent of her. He would have pulled away if he had felt even the slightest resistance.

But he didn't. Annie settled her arms around him, plundered his mouth as eagerly as he did hers. Probably getting familiar with the intricacies of his nature, he thought.

Well, let her.

Finally, he set her back down on her feet. She ran her fingers through her hair and licked her lips. "Yes," she said. "Something to concentrate on, for sure."

He grinned. "You'll force yourself, will you?"

She regarded him with half-closed eyes. "Don't look so victorious, Garvin MacCrae. You won't have any easier a day than you had a night." She tossed her head back. "Now. I'll be ready in ten minutes. Otto awaits."

It was weird not having Otto with her at the gallery. Annie felt more alone than she would have expected, never mind Gran's many exhortations on animals being no substitute for people. Gran had loved animals, especially the birds she fed and the cormorants and ducks and occasional blue heron that would feed in the bay in front of her cottage, but she'd needed people, too. She had her volunteer work, her friends. Of course, she'd never understood Otto and her granddaughter's attachment to him and would have disdained her missing him when he was in perfectly good hands. It wasn't the dog, she'd say. It's that fellow, Garvin MacCrae. He's got you all in a muddle, and it's easier for you to say it's the dog than him.

She might have been right. Otto was probably having the time of his life in Garvin's big house. Annie trusted Garvin to look after him. After last night, she should be glad all was as well as it was. She *was* glad.

"Just in a muddle," she said under her breath.

Zoe Summer, along with the rest of San Francisco, had heard about Sarah Linwood's return. She wanted details. Annie promised to provide them during the first slow time they had. Given the extra publicity, she had no idea when that would be. Her gallery was packed, even the cash register active. People weren't just looking but buying, mostly low-and medium-priced items, a few frames. There were tons of inquiries.

Two reporters called. One stopped in. They all wanted to talk to Sarah Linwood. Barring that, they'd talk to Annie. She declined. Sarah's whereabouts weren't for anyone but Sarah to divulge, nor were the specifics of the agreement they had made regarding the auctioned portrait of Haley Linwood MacCrae. None of the reporters had yet made the connection between Sarah's appearance at last night's foundation dinner and the police report on the break-in at Annie's apartment. Annie chose not to enlighten them.

Nor did they ask about Garvin MacCrae. She certainly didn't volunteer any information about him. Before he'd dropped her off at her gallery, with Otto slumped in the backseat with his shaved head, he had said he would meet her at closing. They would then head up to see Sarah together and discuss their next move. He was still hoping her open presence in San Francisco would keep Vic Denardo at bay.

It didn't. He called at noon. "The police are looking for me. They think maybe I broke into your place last night and beat up your dog." He didn't sound particularly upset.

"Didn't you?" Annie asked coolly. She was behind her desk, browsers sifting through her gallery.

"Nah. Me and Otto were just starting to get along. I wouldn't hurt him. And why would I break in? You don't have anything I want besides Sarah's address, which I figure you haven't written down anywhere. Am I right?"

"About that, yes. What about the painting?"

"What would I want with a painting? Besides, I know Sarah has it, not you. Look, I didn't break into your place, and I didn't hurt your dog. Believe me or not, it's your choice." He didn't seem to care one way or the other. "Hell, if it'd get you to take me to Sarah, I'd say I did it. How'd Johnny and the new wife receive her?"

"I didn't stay. Mr. Denardo—"

"Conninger? My buddy Ethan was there, wasn't he? We used to sail together. Him, me, Garvin."

"Yes, I know. Mr. Denardo, what's the point of this call?"

"I want to see Sarah. Tell her to name the place, the time. It doesn't matter to me. I'll be there."

Annie inhaled. "She could just name a time and place and have the police meet you instead."

"You're a tough cookie, aren't you, sugar? I'd be watching. You tell her, okay?"

Annie said nothing.

"Okay, sugar?"

She sighed. "I'll tell her."

She slammed down the phone in frustration. A customer, an elderly man, was looking nervously over the counter at her. She smiled. "May I help you?"

An hour later, business was still percolating, and Annie hadn't told the police or Garvin or even Zoe about Vic Denardo's call. She'd almost talked herself into believing the break-in had been a random act, an ordinary urban burglar who'd panicked when he saw a rottweiler, smacked him on the head, probably with whatever he'd used to knock in her window, and got out of there while he had the chance without bothering to steal anything. It didn't *have* to be Vic Denardo's work.

She groaned. Obsessing wasn't going to get her anywhere.

At two o'clock John and Cynthia Linwood walked into her gallery together, a handsome couple despite the disparity in their ages. "Isn't it charming?" Cynthia beamed at her husband, as if showing off a pet project. Last night's chilliness might never have existed. "I just love the feel of the place, its mood. So many galleries are so inaccessible, so snobbish that people are put off or afraid to ask questions for fear of being sneered at. All that attitude. I hate it."

Annie finished ringing up a sale, and Cynthia greeted her with a broad, unselfconscious smile. She wore a close-fitting black suit with pearl earrings and not a strand of her Jacqueline Kennedy hair out of place. John Linwood, also crisply dressed, seemed more awkward, aware of the furtive, knowing looks he was getting from browsers who had recognized him. Either that, Annie thought, or he simply wasn't used to being in a retail establishment.

"I overheard what you said about my gallery," she said. "Thank you."

"I meant every word." Cynthia glanced around, as if to check if anyone was within easy earshot. A young couple with two small children was exclaiming over a series of botanical fern prints. Cynthia sighed at them, then regarded Annie with absolute gravity. "I spoke to Garvin last night. He told me about the break-in at your apartment. I'm very sorry I was so rude to you last night. The shock—well, there's no excuse." She kept her voice low, dignified. "The police have contacted us to find out if we have any reason to believe Vic Denardo's in the area. Of course, we said no. We don't."

"But Sarah," John said in a tortured voice. He averted his eyes, staring down at the toddler with the young couple, who was twirling her jet-black hair around her finger and staring up at him. He gave her a distracted smile, then turned back to Annie. "My sister could be in danger from this man. He...It's possible he..." His eyes shut, and the little girl toddled back to her parents.

"You must know who Vic Denardo is," Cynthia said briskly, her voice still low.

Annie nodded. She could have said more, but didn't. Last night's rules no longer applied, but she still didn't want to act precipitously and blurt out things better left for others to explain. She was the outsider.

Cynthia eyed her, then inhaled, as if guessing Annie was holding back. "Sarah didn't tell us where she's staying. If there's a reason she needs to keep it a secret—"

"I don't know that there is," Annie said. Wasn't half the point of her showing up last night to have her presence in San Francisco and her whereabouts out in the open? But with the break-in, the emergency with Otto, Garvin might have decided to change his plan.

John touched his wife's arm before she could lose patience. She had a prickliness to her that Annie could appreciate, although she didn't doubt Cynthia Linwood's sincerity in her comments about her gallery. She didn't seem the kind of woman to engage in insincere flattery.

"When you see my sister next," her husband said, "please tell her I would be happy to arrange for her security if she should feel any threat from Vic Denardo. I have no idea what their relationship has been since she left San Francisco." He paused, swallowed visibly. "I don't want anything to happen to her."

"I'd be glad to tell her." Annie managed a quick smile. On top of seeing his sister for the first time in five years last night, he had just learned that the chief suspect in the murders of his daughter and father might be back in San Francisco. "I'll probably see her later today. Garvin's meeting me here around six. My dog was injured last night during the break-in. He's recuperating at Garvin's house." She started to say more, then decided that was enough. Let John and Cynthia Linwood figure out her relationship with Garvin MacCrae on their own.

The couple with the two small children departed, promising to return once they'd decided between two different fern prints.

"Please," Cynthia said, "tell Sarah we're concerned for her safety. We'll do everything we can—whatever she wants—" She winced, sighing. "This is so awkward. There's no getting around it. I wish I knew what possessed Garvin to spring this on us the way he did." She broke off with obvious effort, and smiled thinly. "I'm sorry. This hasn't been an easy twenty-four hours. I don't mean to offend anyone."

"It's all right," Annie said, "I understand."

John Linwood drew back his shoulders and took in an audible breath. He'd lost his father and his only child five years ago. He was a handsome man, Annie realized; much better looking than his younger sister, although he didn't have her air of freedom about him, of utter disinterest in who approved of her and who didn't. "I didn't get to spend as much time last night with Sarah as I would have wished," he said. "Please tell her that, Ms. Payne. She's a painter now, isn't she? She said so last night. Is she good?"

Annie nodded. "I think so. I think she's very good."

Her words seemed to please him. "I'm glad for her, then."

"Oh, I don't think she gives a fig if anyone else thinks she's any good, just that her work has meaning for her."

John Linwood's thick gray eyebrows went up, and suddenly he looked very much like his sister, knowing, insightful. "It matters to her, Ms. Payne. Trust me on that one. Sarah wants all the recognition and attention she can get." His words were matter-of-fact, without any apparent harshness or bitterness. He withdrew a business card and, borrowing a pen from her desk, jotted down two additional numbers. "You can dial any of these numbers, day or night, to reach either Cynthia or me. Please feel free to do so."

Annie tucked the card into her hand. "I will."

The Linwoods started to leave, but John hesitated, turning back before reaching the door. His eyes, not as vivid as Sarah's, focused on her with penetrating steadiness. "I want you to know, Ms. Payne, that we appreciate your befriending my sister. She's had a difficult few years. We all have. She's become an eccentric, I can see that. But I don't want her eccentricities or your knowing her to hurt you in any way." His ambivalence about his sister was almost palpable, but he gave Annie a courtly smile. "I hope your dog will be all right."

"Thank you."

Not long after the Linwoods had left, Zoe slipped in with a steaming mug of herbal tea. She was dressed all in black today. She scrutinized Annie. "You look terrible. I'm recommending essential oil of rosemary. Five drops in your tub, a dot on your head, and you'll perk right up."

Annie groaned. "I don't want to perk up, I want to go to bed and sleep for days. This has been the most bizarre week of my life."

"Including the week your cottage was swept out to sea?"

"That wasn't bizarre. That was the result of an act of nature."

"Well, rosemary's the trick. I've got about five minutes for you to tell me everything. My assistant's in, but she'll need my help. We've been incredibly busy—spillover from you and your scandalous goings-on, I take it. You've really been in touch with Sarah Linwood all this time?"

Annie nodded, sinking into her tall chair, numbed.

Zoe made a face, mock insulted. "Shame on you for not telling. Not that I didn't know you were holding back, because I did. I tell my kids I *always* know. So. Sarah Linwood's back in town, she hired you to buy the painting she did of her niece, Vic Denardo's looking for her, Garvin MacCrae's looking for Vic Denardo, and here we are."

"You're not in any danger," Annie told her.

"Did I ask?"

"No, but—"

"Never mind, then. What about the break-in?"

Annie gave her the details of what had happened last night. But not only Zoe Summer's nose was sensitive. She studied Annie, any breeziness gone out of her manner. "Garvin MacCrae," she said knowingly.

"What about him?"

"Don't demur, Annie. It doesn't suit you. Sparks flying between the two of you?"

Annie shifted in her chair. She felt like a squirming twelve-year-old under Zoe's steady scrutiny. "I guess you could say that."

Zoe frowned. "Is this a good thing or a bad thing?"

"To be honest, I don't know. Garvin'd do anything to get his hands on Vic Denardo. I'm not saying he's using me—"

"But he would if he had to."

Annie felt her eyes burn with fatigue. She remembered last night, his passion, his tenderness. But a part of him remained locked up, out of her reach, in some dark, forbidden place.

Zoe sighed, pushing off toward the door. She jabbed a finger at Annie. "Rosemary. It'll do the trick. It won't change Garvin MacCrae, but at least you'll be able to deal with him with a clear head, which you'll need, I'm afraid."

She scooted through the door before Annie could summon the energy to thank her. Essential oil of rosemary. She rummaged through the drawer where she'd tossed various vials Zoe had brought her in thanks for "borrowing" her nose. One was marked rosemary. She unscrewed the cap and sniffed. Smelled minty to her. Well, maybe it would do the trick. Just to be sure, she brewed herself a cup of coffee. Caffeine she trusted.

Thirty minutes later, Garvin called. "Everything's fine," he said. "I just wanted to let you know that Otto's settled in. He seems to be in a tolerable mood. I think he'd love it down at the marina. He and Yuma would get along." He hesitated, a rarity for Garvin MacCrae. "There's just one thing. I don't know if it's the blow he took to the head or just an Otto thing, but does he—has he ever slept in the bathtub?"

Annie grinned in delight. "I should have warned you. Otto loves sleeping in the tub. That was his favorite place back in Maine, especially when he was feeling hot. Gran used to go crazy. I don't have a tub in my apartment. He must be thrilled."

"Then this is a good sign?"

"Absolutely. Oh, and I can bring him his bowling ball. If he's feeling better, he'll want something to play with. It might ease his mind after such a trauma. But if he gets restless, you can give him a two-by-four or something."

"Whatever happened to dog biscuits?"

"They don't last long with Otto. He won't really chew on the two-by-four, just swing it around. And if he does get up and around, watch your refrigerator. He can open most models. He once cleaned mine out, mustard jars and all. Ate my leftover spinach lasagna, a half pound of roast turkey."

Silence.

Annie chewed on the corner of her mouth. "He might not have the energy to get into your fridge. Really, I wouldn't worry."

"A rottweiler swinging around a two-by-four and carrying off the contents of my refrigerator is not high on my list of worries. But you are, Annie. How are you doing?"

She told him straight off about her call from Vic Denardo; but he also wanted to know about her gallery and Zoe and her visit from the Linwoods and how she was managing without Otto there. She told him everything. Maybe even more than she should have.

"Then last night," he said, and was silent a moment. "You're all right after last night?"

"Yes." She realized she had a tight grip on the phone. "You?"

She could feel his smile. "Nope. I can't seem to stop thinking about tonight."

When he'd hung up, Annie was relieved to have the young couple with the two small children return, sooner than they'd expected, with a long, welcome list of questions for her. Yes, her gallery did framing. Yes, she'd be happy to help with the placement of artwork in their home. Yes, she was in touch with artists. And on they went, the perfect reminder, even as she thought about Garvin MacCrae, of why she'd come to San Francisco in the first place.

After a cathartic run and an hour in his weight room, Garvin took a shower in one of the downstairs bathrooms because Otto was still in possession of his upstairs bathroom. He peeked in on him when he went up to get dressed. The big, fierce-looking dog was out cold, sprawled in the tub. Garvin decided it was prudent to let him sleep and returned to his bedroom to pull on a pair of jeans and a thick cotton sweater. He'd actually picked up a two-by-four when he went down to the marina. Yuma, who'd been doing more than his fair share the past week, hadn't asked the questions he plainly had, and Garvin hadn't explained.

He'd also placed a chair in front of his refrigerator, just in case. A clever dog, Otto. Much like his master.

Exercised, dressed, and showered, Garvin felt more in control of himself. He checked around his house to make sure it was reasonably Otto-proof. There was only so much he could do. If the big dog woke up while Garvin was gone and was unsure of his surroundings, he could tear up the place.

"Hell," Garvin muttered, "if he wakes up while I'm here, he could tear up the place. Who's going to stop him?"

He would just have to take his chances. He headed outside.

John Linwood was climbing from his car, parked in the shade along the edge of the road. He was alone, no Cynthia. His hand extended, he walked toward Garvin. "I'm catching you at a bad time," he said as they shook hands.

"No problem. What's up? We can go inside—"

"That's all right, I'll only be a minute. I wanted to talk to you after last night. I—it was a shock to see Sarah. I'm sure you understand. The past five years..." He inhaled deeply, his eyes distant. "She's changed so much."

"So it would seem."

He gave Garvin a sharp look. "You think there's any doubt?"

"Outwardly, no. Sarah's very different. Five years ago she wouldn't have been caught dead in bright red corduroy. But inside —I don't know that she's not the same Sarah she always was, just without the Linwood trimmings and inhibitions." He could see John stiffening, resistant, and shrugged. "Not that I really knew her that well."

John relaxed slightly. "Perhaps none of us did. Look, I just wanted you to know that I—that Cynthia and I both—don't hold a grudge against you for springing Sarah on us last night. You were in an untenable position. I can see that. Now with Annie Payne's apartment getting broken into last night and talk of Vic Denardo —" He sighed, looking worn, older than he was. "She's truly an innocent caught up in this mess, isn't she?"

"She doesn't see it that way. She wants to represent Sarah's art."

"So I've gathered. And you think she's that good too?"

"Yes."

He took a breath, kept his composure. "I see."

"Annie was reluctant to ask Sarah too many questions. She didn't want to spook her. So she doesn't fault anyone for her getting involved."

"Well, she's being more magnanimous than I would have been."

Garvin smiled. "Me too."

John ran a shaking hand through his thinning gray hair, his composure fraying. "Dear God, I'd hoped we wouldn't have to open this chapter in our lives again. I'd hoped we could just move on."

"I know, John, but until Thomas and Haley's murderer is brought to justice—"

"Justice be damned!" He lunged in close, his vivid blue eyes intense, his fists clenched. "Garvin, I don't give a damn anymore about justice. My father and daughter are dead. Justice won't bring them back. Justice won't give me any solace, any closure, that I don't already have. I don't owe their memory justice."

"What about yourself?"

"I owe myself peace." The energy had seeped out of him, and he sagged. "That's all. Peace."

And a new life with Cynthia, Garvin thought. "You deserve it, John. God only knows."

Tears clouded his eyes. He turned away. "I don't want to stir up the past. I don't see the point. If I'd known putting that painting up for auction would lead to this, I'd have burned it myself."

"Sarah was already in town. The painting wasn't what brought her back. It's just what clued me in that she was in San Francisco. I just think Sarah believed it was time to come home."

Her older brother shook his head sadly. "She was wrong."

He covered his eyes with one hand and sank backward, almost as if he were reeling. He wasn't sobbing. But Garvin could feel his pain, an anguish so deep it came from the soul.

He went still, staring at his former father-in-law. Suddenly, his blood literally ran cold.

"John?"

"Dear God…I can't…"

Barely breathing, Garvin took a step toward him. "John."

"*I can't!*"

"Jesus," Garvin whispered. "You think Sarah committed the murders."

John dragged his hand down his face and let it drop to his side. His skin was gray. His eyes were sunken and tortured. His mouth quivered.

Garvin had his answer. It was one thing for him to entertain the possibility that Sarah Linwood had been involved in the murders of her father and niece, quite another for her brother.

"Good God, John. Do you think she actually pulled the trigger?"

"I hope I'm wrong." His voice was a croak, more that of an old man. "You can't know how much I hope I'm wrong."

He knew. He'd had similar suspicions himself. "Do you have any reason—"

He shook his head. "Nothing specific."

Garvin acknowledged John's words with a nod; there was nothing to agree on, nothing to understand. "Do you suppose that's what Vic Denardo believes? If he's innocent—"

"It's possible, I don't know." He cleared his throat, composing himself. "I don't know anything except that this family's suffered enough. *I've* suffered enough."

He'd lost his father and his only child, and, at least in his own mind, he'd lost his only sister: an affair with Vic Denardo, gambling, debts to loan sharks, a five-year disappearance, and now the homecoming of a woman he no longer recognized.

"Does Cynthia know this is what you believe?" Garvin asked quietly.

"No, I can't bring myself to tell her. But I think—I wonder if she hasn't had the same thought."

"What if you're wrong and it's not Sarah?"

"Drop it, Garvin, please. Either way, just tell Sarah to go back where she's been living these past five years. I won't stop her."

"John—"

His head jerked up. "Haley wouldn't want this. She wouldn't want to see either of us tortured this way."

"John, this isn't about Haley. It's about the truth."

"God damn the truth!"

Linwood that he was, he quickly reined in his emotions, dropped the mask of dignity back into place, composed himself as if he hadn't just accused his sister of murder. He squared his shoulders and sniffed. When his gaze again met Garvin's, it was focused and steady. "I'm sorry. Do what you must do, Garvin. I won't stand in your way. You've your own principles and conscience to satisfy. But in this case, I don't know that justice hasn't already been rendered."

Garvin pictured Sarah Linwood hobbling into the private dining room last night in her red corduroy jacket, her face gaunt, her pain so obviously chronic and debilitating. He understood what John was saying, but still shook his head. "Justice isn't about punishment," he said.

John had started back to his car. He turned on the stone walk, his own face gaunt. "I can't handle any more truth, Garvin. I just can't."

A fine mist started to fall. Garvin waited until his father-in-law had left before heading out himself. He felt chilled and uneasy. John Linwood thought his own sister not only capable of murder but capable of murdering members of her own family. Not just hiring Vic Denardo to do it, doing it herself, then cleverly making sure the police believed the killer was her lover.

What a hellish state of affairs. Garvin knew he could do as John asked and probe no further, demand no further answers, ask no further questions. He could turn away from the truth, even run away from it.

John was right about one thing: the truth wouldn't bring Thomas Linwood or Haley Linwood MacCrae back.

In practical terms, Garvin thought, he had only to back off and leave Annie Payne, Sarah Linwood, and Vic Denardo to their own devices. Let them get on with their lives. Ease back into his work, the life he'd had before Saturday's auction.

But Otto was in his bathtub, and Annie Payne awaited him, and Garvin couldn't turn back now.

Late on a winter Saturday afternoon, Union Street was packed, forcing him to wander around for twenty minutes before finding a parking space. He had to walk three blocks to Annie's Gallery. Its fair-haired owner was briskly sweeping the brick courtyard. Even in the gray light, her hair shone, half pulled back, half blowing in her face. Garvin suppressed an image of her last night. He had to or he wouldn't be able to function.

"Almost done?" he asked.

She turned with her broom and smiled. "Almost. Zoe and I have had a ton of people come through here today."

"Maybe you won't have to sweep and tend pots much longer."

"I don't mind. My landlord gave me such a good deal. There are worse things than keeping flowers alive."

She'd already brought them in, he noted. Most of her sweepings seemed to be leaves, twigs, and dirt rather than cigarette butts and litter. She scooped up her pile into a dustpan and returned with it and her broom to her gallery, dispensing with them in the back room. Garvin could see empty spots on the display walls and shelves and assumed she'd had a profitable day.

He started to ask about it when Ethan Conninger burst into the gallery. "Garvin—Jesus, I just heard about the break-in last night." He was dressed casually in twills, a long-sleeved polo shirt, and loafers, but he looked shaken and agitated. "Annie's all right? I'd never have left her if I'd had any idea what she was walking into."

"She's fine," Garvin said.

She emerged from the back room, rubbing a white cream into her hands. "You couldn't have known."

Ethan shook off her words. "I feel awful about leaving you. How's your dog?"

"He's on the mend."

"Well, I hope he got a lick in before he went down. Look—I don't want to keep you two. I just wanted to make an appearance, make sure you were okay. Sarah got home all right last night?"

"She was tired," Garvin said, "but otherwise fine."

"What a weird evening. Jesus. Guess it's not really my problem, though." He raked a hand through his dark hair, pushed his glasses up on his nose. "Well. I just wanted to check in and make sure everything was all right."

Annie smiled. "Thank you. The police didn't find any useful evidence—no fingerprints or eyewitnesses—but Otto's doing well, and right now, that's enough for me. Really, there was nothing you could have done. The damage was already done when we arrived."

"But if whoever broke in had been waiting for you—if we'd arrived any earlier—"

"Moot points," Annie said graciously.

"I suppose." Ethan shifted from Annie to Garvin and then back again. He was jumpy, Garvin thought. Last night hadn't been Ethan Conninger's idea of the good life. Working for the Linwoods was supposed to be low on stress and high on perks. He rubbed the back of his neck. "Do the police really think Vic Denardo's involved?"

"They're keeping their options open," Annie said.

"The bastard. Christ, I think about it and—" He broke off with a heavy sigh and turned to Garvin. "This must be hell for you. If you want to go out on the water sometime to get away, forget all this, give me a yell."

"I will, thanks."

He gave Annie an encouraging wink, and departed. Annie finished closing up. Garvin watched her practiced movements and felt her satisfaction. She was doing what she loved. She wanted her gallery to succeed because she loved running it, arranging the artwork, keeping track of the finances, introducing people to new artists. She would relish even the dusting, the watering of the pots of pansies and cyclamen, the sweeping, and the fertilizing. Seeing her reminded him of his years in school, then in the financial district, when he'd absorbed every detail and nuance he could, loved even the mundane and the arcane aspects of his profession. It wasn't just ego that drove him, but a passion for the work itself.

Annie popped next door to say good-bye to Zoe Summer, then was ready. She pulled out her barrette and let her hair hang loose as they walked out to Union Street, crowded and well-lit early on a dead-of-winter evening. The mist remained unchanged, not developing into a steady rain or even a proper drizzle.

"We can see Sarah first," Annie said, "then Otto."

"Makes sense to me."

Her concentrated expression suggested it didn't matter to her if it didn't. A week ago she'd bought a painting she'd hoped would lead to her presentation of a major new artist. Instead, it had led her into the murky depths of two unsolved murders and into bed with a man she wasn't sure wouldn't run right over her to solve those murders.

Had warned her he would. Had warned himself.

She ducked into a coffee shop for a cappuccino and biscotti to go, and five minutes later they were heading out toward Market Street.

"About last night," Annie said, biting into her biscotti.

"Annie, if you want to forget last night—"

She fixed her gaze on him. "Is that what you want me to do?"

He cast her a brief look. "It's not a question of what I want."

"It's not, is it? Well, I'll have you know I didn't go to bed with you last night out of a sense of charity or confusion. I knew exactly what I was doing. If you've any regrets, they're yours, not mine."

He smiled. He couldn't help himself. "I've no regrets." He did, actually. He should have stayed with her and made love to her through the night. "Do you?"

She gave a tight shake of the head.

"Annie, when that storm took your cottage, what did you do?"

She frowned. "What do you mean what did I do? Garvin, what's this got to do with anything?"

"Did you get hopping, spitting mad? Scream, throw a fit, heave big rocks into the ocean? What?"

"I carried on."

"Ah."

"What's that supposed to mean?"

"Nothing. I'm just not surprised. You're a survivor, Annie. A stiff-upper-lip Mainer. But nature had dealt you a hell of a blow. Weren't you pissed?"

"Of course I was."

"So how did you deal with it?"

She squirmed. Such talk, Garvin could see, made her uncomfortable. She was accustomed to keeping her pain to herself, sharing it with no one. "I tried my best not to take my emotions out on my friends, my insurance agent, or Otto. What happened to my cottage wasn't their fault. So when I felt overwhelmed and self-pitying and furious, I'd—" She stopped, glanced at him. "Are you sure you want to know?"

"Yes."

"All right. I'd sit out on the rocks in front of the clearing where my cottage had been. I'd go out just before sunset, and I'd watch the sun go down, then the moon and the stars rise, and finally, the coming of dawn. There's nothing like watching a Maine sunrise. When the sun was finally full in the sky, I'd go back to town—was staying with friends—and shower and sleep a couple of hours, and then tackle whatever I had to tackle next. There was something about seeing the sun go down and then come up again that gave me the perspective I needed to carry on."

"Beats heaving rocks into the ocean," Garvin said.

"I don't know, I think it does the same thing. You hurl a rock into the ocean, you have to realize you've had no impact, you're at its mercy, and you might just as well accept it and get on with your business."

"No, Annie, it's not the same thing. Heaving a rock isn't a way of making me reconcile myself to the vagaries of nature, it's a way of getting rid of all that anger and frustration that's boiling around inside, expending that energy in some reasonably innocuous way. Today I lifted weights until I thought I'd explode. *That's* the same thing." He gave her a dry look. "Sunsets."

She smiled, unchagrined. "And sunrises."

Garvin looked over at her as she sipped her cappuccino and ate her biscotti, and he imagined her out on a rock on the coast of Maine, wrapped up in a blanket, unworried about night creatures on the prowl as she watched the night come and go, just so she could get a handle on her anger. Instead of coming away depressed with how insignificant she was, how at the mercy of the perils of nature, she'd come away renewed.

It was in that moment he knew that he had fallen in love with Annie Payne.

Chapter Fourteen

They found Sarah at her easel in the corner of windows overlooking San Francisco, with her palette and brushes, her walker beside her. She was working on a still life. Annie noticed the small, teetering table arranged with sprigs of bittersweet, acorn, and butternut squash, parsnips, purple-topped turnips, and yellow onions. Much to Garvin's irritation, Sarah had refused to answer her door. It turned out she'd left it unlocked, and he and Annie just walked in. Sarah didn't acknowledge their presence. Seeing she was deep into her work, Annie touched Garvin's hand to keep him from barking at her.

After two minutes, Garvin glared at her, his patience on its last shred. Annie sighed. She had no idea how long Sarah would ignore them—or even if she was aware they were there. "Sarah," she said quietly, "we need to talk to you."

She dabbed her brush into a vivid splash of purple, not even glancing up from her work.

Annie persisted. "The police have your address. Have they been by?"

"This morning." Her voice was deep and guttural, as if she hadn't said a word in days. "Go. Sit. I'll be done soon."

Impatience flashed in Garvin's eyes, but he kept quiet. "We'll take a walk," Annie said.

Once outside, Garvin swung around at her. "Don't give me a line about temperamental artists. She's stonewalling us because she knows damned well she put you in danger. She does what she wants to do and worries about the consequences when it's too late. That was guilt in there, not temperament."

"Whatever it was, we're not going to get her cooperation by bullying her and not respecting her boundaries."

"Boundaries? The hell—"

"Regardless of her reasons, Sarah needs to work right now."

He cursed under his breath, unappeased, but at least kept walking, following Annie down the stone steps. It was dark, chilly, still misty. She hunched her tapestry bag onto her shoulder, and when they reached the street below, waited for Garvin to join her. She didn't mind the walk. As much as she wanted to talk to Sarah and see Otto, she appreciated the chance to get some air. Even impatient and annoyed, Garvin was a steady presence beside her as they headed up the street. By San Francisco standards, Sarah's was a pleasant, quirky neighborhood of families, professionals, and neighborhood shops.

"One of the things I like about San Francisco," Annie said, "is that so many of its people really love living here. They can get a little cocky about it at times, but basically I think it's a good quality to care about the place you live."

Garvin, she could see, was unwilling to be distracted by chitchat about San Francisco. "I suppose."

"What about you? Do you like San Francisco?"

"It's where I've always lived," he said.

"Your family—it must be nice to have them close."

He shrugged. "I don't see as much of them as I should."

"Why not?"

"They're good people." His tone softened, his mind sliding into the topic. "It hurts them to—well, they've seen me in better days."

When his wife was alive, Annie thought, suddenly struck by how alone he was. Having family nearby didn't in and of itself alleviate that sense of isolation, of removal. It was a choice, an attitude on his part. Although she had no real family left in Maine, Annie knew that her decision to leave had been a choice, the logical outcome of the attitude she'd had at the time. It had been an essential ingredient in redefining herself and moving on with her life. But a cottage swept out to sea and the death of a grandmother from old age and disease had a finality to them that an unsolved murder, by definition, didn't. She could move on. Garvin couldn't.

"Sometimes I find it easier not to inflict myself on the people I care about," he went on, not looking at her.

It wasn't a self-pitying statement, just a declaration of fact. "What about Michael Yuma?" Annie asked.

Garvin gave a short laugh. "Yuma'd make friends with a shark if it suited him. So would you."

"Me?"

"Look at Otto."

"Otto was a drenched, adorable little puppy when I found him."

"How little?"

"Fifteen weeks."

"That's not that little. And he was still a rottweiler. You take everybody—animals, people—as they come, without much of an agenda, without judging. You just dive in and find out who they are, what they're about." He went silent a moment as they headed back up the stone steps to Sarah's house. "That can be dangerous."

Annie shrugged. "I don't know how else to be."

"I know."

Something in his tone made her hesitate. He walked ahead of her, taking the stairs slowly, one at a time, his body stiff, his manner quickening her pulse and tightening her throat. She twisted her hands together, feeling sick at what she was thinking.

"Garvin," she said.

He glanced back at her.

And she knew what she was thinking was on target. "My God," she whispered. "You really think Sarah..." She couldn't go on, couldn't bring herself to articulate the terrible thought. "That's absurd. It's—it's *crazy.*"

He remained calm, but she could tell he knew what she was implying. "Maybe. And it's not what I think, Annie. I'm trying to keep an open mind. I don't want to miss an important fact because I was too blind to see it. This is something that's within the realm of possibility. I have to accept that."

"It's not possible." She spoke with certainty, her shoulders thrown back. The mist dampened her hair, brought out the smells of the lush greenery that encroached on the narrow steps. Garvin didn't move; he was two steps above her, a dark silhouette. She didn't back down. "I'd have seen it in her work. It would be there, Garvin. I know it would. She couldn't have killed her own father and niece and not have it be there."

"Denial's a powerful force."

"Do *you* believe she killed your wife?"

"I can't afford to believe or not believe anything just because I don't want it to be true." His voice was chillingly calm. "I didn't want Haley to be dead but she was. It was there, and I had to believe it."

Annie shivered, hugging herself to ward off the cold, her mind drifting back, far back—before the cottage, before Gran's death. Her mother. Dead. Not wanting to believe. Her father. Too long dead. Never having known him, coming to realize she never would. Trying to come to grips with the reality of him.

"Annie, I'm sorry."

His voice was soft, hoarse, pained. She shook her head. "No. It's all right. You're..." She gulped in the damp air. "You're right. I don't really know Sarah—any of you. I—maybe I need to keep an open mind too."

This time when they entered the house, Sarah was washing her hands in the sink, her brushes soaking in a coffee can, root vegetables covered with a tattered white sheet. She didn't acknowledge Annie or Garvin in any way.

"Vic Denardo called me today," Annie said. "He still wants to see you. You pick the time and the place, and he'll be there."

She turned from the sink, wiping her hands with a frayed dish towel, carefully getting in between her gnarled fingers. When she finished, she tossed the towel into the sink and reached for her walker. She moved slowly, painfully. Every fiber of her being seemed concentrated simply on getting to her chair at the kitchen table. She must have been painting for hours, Annie thought.

Finally, she sank into her chair, sighed with relief, and cast aside her walker. Annie noticed that both she and Garvin had remained on their feet. Sarah didn't invite them to sit. She pushed back her disheveled hair with both hands, more a gesture of self-composure, Annie thought, than an effort to improve her appearance.

"I called the paper this morning," she announced. "I used a pay phone at the market. They sent out a reporter. My whereabouts will be in the morning edition." She paused, fastening her vivid blue eyes on her two guests. "No more secrets."

Annie was shocked—and a little annoyed. "Why didn't you tell us?"

"I just did."

"*Before* you called. You could have—"

"Annie," she said patiently, "the purpose of last night was to let people—Vic Denardo included—know that I had returned to San Francisco and had put you up to buying the painting of Haley. That's all well and good, but Vic—as you saw for yourself today—isn't going to be satisfied until he knows where to find me. Now he will, and not through you."

Garvin, Annie noticed, was taking Sarah's news in stride, as if he'd expected nothing less of her than an interview in the Sunday paper. "What did you say?" Annie asked. "This reporter—"

"I gave him a complete interview." Sarah regarded Annie calmly, but her face was gray, fatigue making the lines more prominent. "He asked about the murders, about my life these past five years. I indicated I'd done some paintings. He assumed it was a hobby, a way of coping, and I let him. I'd covered up all my canvases."

"Why?"

"I didn't want the public to come to my work through a tawdry article in the Sunday papers. If and when my work is shown, it will be at your gallery, Annie. This is the proper forum for any discussion of my paintings." Her eyes clouded. "Unless you change your mind about wanting to represent me."

Only if you're a murderer, Annie thought. She winced. How could she think such a thing? It was ghoulish and disloyal. Of course Sarah Linwood wasn't a murderer. That was just Garvin MacCrae being Garvin MacCrae, keeping his options open, no matter their insanity.

"I won't change my mind," Annie said, with a quick glance in his direction. His face was impassive.

"Talking to the press wasn't a rash decision," Sarah went on. "I've no regrets. If Vic or anyone else wants to find me, I'm here."

"You shouldn't be up here alone." Garvin's voice was even deeper than usual, but his expression was still unchanged.

Sarah shook her head. "That's the only way I will stay up here. Now, if you'll excuse me." She sank back against her chair. "I'd prefer to be alone."

Garvin opened his mouth to speak but apparently changed his mind and tore open the front door without a word. His movements were stiff and icily controlled. From the flash of anger in his eyes, Annie guessed he'd been about to tell Sarah to go to hell. Sarah acted as if she were oblivious to his irritation, but she was too perceptive for that. She wasn't upset, Annie saw, just not unaware.

"Are you sure you don't want us to stay?" Annie asked her.

Sarah smiled. "I'm sure."

"At least lock your doors."

She didn't answer.

Outside, the clouds and fog and mist had gathered around Sarah's hilltop, cutting off much of the view of the sprawling city and bay. Annie suddenly felt isolated and claustrophobic, unable to get a decent breath.

Neither she nor Garvin spoke on the way down the steep, narrow, twisting street to the bottom of Sarah's hill. Not until they reached Market did Annie feel calm enough to speak. She gave him a quick sideways glance. "You look as if you could pick up Sarah's house and heave it into San Francisco Bay."

"I just might," he said through clenched teeth.

"It wouldn't make you feel any better."

"Neither would sitting out on a rock waiting for the sunrise."

Annie settled back, unperturbed. "This is San Francisco. You'd probably be hauled off as a nuisance or a nutcase before dawn."

He didn't relax. He had a vise grip on the wheel. "Sarah's a self-pitying, self-absorbed old crank. *Damn* her for not consulting us. If we hadn't come up here tonight, we'd be reading her interview in the Sunday paper along with the rest of San Francisco."

"It's her way of protecting us."

"The hell it is. She loves the drama. She's always wanted to be the center of attention. Instead of gambling with money, now she's gambling with people's lives—her own life." He gave Annie a quick glance, his eyes dark slits. "She might be a brilliant artist, Annie, but she's a pain in the ass."

After Sarah's performance, Annie couldn't argue. "Do you think she's okay for now?"

He breathed out in a quiet hiss. "Your guess is as good as mine. Either way, there's not much we can do."

Annie nodded. They couldn't protect Sarah from herself. Even if Garvin had his own agenda, he was right about that much. "I suppose not." She stared out her window at the fog and rain. "I want to see Otto."

They stopped at Annie's apartment to pick up her car and Otto's bowling ball and to make sure Vic Denardo hadn't been back. The only change since the previous night was a note from her landlord that had been slipped under her door informing her he'd made arrangements to have her window fixed. It had a whiff of impending eviction about it. A rottweiler, a break-in, two unsolved murders—Garvin couldn't blame the guy.

Annie, plainly in one of her forge-ahead moods, paid no attention, just scowled at the note, tossed it in the trash, and vanished into her bedroom. She reappeared with another paper bag of clothes in case, she said, Otto was in no condition to drive back to the city with her. She made no mention of wanting to stay in Marin for non-Otto reasons. Garvin didn't push for any.

"I'll follow you," she said when they headed back outside.

He shook his head. "I'd rather follow you."

"I'm not sure I can get to your house in the dark. It's hard enough during the day—"

"I'll pull in front of you once we hit Belvedere. Until then, you can lead the way."

She sighed, not liking the arrangement. "Why? You don't think Vic Denardo would follow me and try to run me off the road or anything—"

"Indulge me, Annie."

"All right, I'll indulge you. But I'll warn you, I haven't got all these San Francisco hills down, and I drive a standard, so don't get too close."

He smiled. "I'd never get too close."

When they arrived back at his house, without incident, Annie immediately checked on her dog. He had stirred from the bathtub and was perkier but still not himself. He seemed happy to see his bowling ball. While dog and master visited, Garvin built a fire in the fireplace to take some of the damp chill out of the air, then retreated to the kitchen where he heated up a loaf of garlic bread and some minestrone soup he had in the freezer. He brought it out on a tray. Annie sat on the floor in front of the fire, with her toes practically in the flames. She'd kicked off her ankle boots and pushed up the sleeves of her sweater, its berry color making her seem less pale. But he noticed the dark smudges of fatigue under her eyes, the strain at the corners of her mouth. Otto had curled up —as well as a dog his size could—over in the corner. With his partially shaved head, he looked even fiercer than usual. A hell of a pair, Garvin thought.

The fire cracked and popped. Annie pointed her toes into it. "I've always loved fireplaces," she said. "My cottage had a wood-stove. I guess you can get away with fireplaces in California. Generally speaking, woodstoves are more efficient." She smiled. "But not as romantic."

She took her bowl of soup onto her lap, and Garvin placed the basket of bread between them and sat down next to her. It was a cozy arrangement. He didn't know why he felt so cold, didn't want to delve into the reasons. "San Francisco doesn't feel like home for you yet, does it?"

She shrugged. "I'm not sure it ever will. That doesn't mean I can't be happy here."

"If you could work it, would you have a place in Maine?"

"I don't know. I sold the five acres where my grandparents built the cottage. I could have rebuilt."

"You didn't leave yourself an out?"

She tried some of her soup, her eyes on the fire; but Garvin didn't know what they were really seeing. A similar evening in Maine? Her lost cottage? There was, he thought, so much he didn't know about Annie Payne. He wondered if she could feel her dream of the life she'd lead in San Francisco slipping away.

Finally, she said, "Not an easy out, for sure. I've invested everything I have in my new life out here. If I went back, I'd have to start over."

Garvin tried his soup. It was hot enough, but he tasted nothing. A grating of cheese might have helped, a grinding of pepper. He hadn't bothered with either. "Do you need Sarah for your gallery to succeed?"

"The way I've dreamed of it succeeding, yes, I need her—or someone as good as she is. But I'm pragmatic. I didn't count on finding a Sarah Linwood, especially not right away. I've concentrated on doing what I'm good at, offering what I like, and developing a steady repeat business."

"Do you have a business plan?"

She glanced at him, a glint of humor in her slate blue eyes. "That's the MBA in you talking. I'm just stumbling along, figuring things out as they need to be figured out. That's not very businesslike of me, I know."

"I disagree. The most successful entrepreneurs I know begin with a dream and plan and implement goals and objectives around that dream. Flexibility—a willingness to be responsive, to revise the plan—is critical."

A smile tugged at the corners of her mouth, making the dark circles under her eyes less noticeable. "I see you as a man who runs a working marina. It's hard to think of you as some financial mogul."

"You didn't know me six years ago."

"No, I guess not."

"But a part of me always wanted to run a marina. It was my biggest dream when I was about nine years old. That and playing in the World Series." He could feel the cold gripping him, even with the fire hot in his face. "After Haley's death, I started teaching troubled teenagers how to sail. I met Michael Yuma. His life was a mess in a totally different way from mine. But his energy, his zeal for sailing—they were infectious, they reminded me of that old dream of mine. Pretty soon I was running a marina and he was my righthand man."

"Then running a marina is what you want to do?"

He thought a moment. "Yes, I guess it is. Yuma and I work well together. He handles most of the people end of the business. I prefer working in the boatyard. It's the kind of work I did to put myself through school. I liked it then, and I like it now."

"Do you miss the financial district?"

"No. I enjoyed that life at the time, and it's allowed me to live as I do now. I've no regrets." He looked at Annie. "But I'm not the same man I was. I've changed."

She nodded and said quietly, "I understand."

In that moment, Garvin thought she did, and he didn't feel as cold.

After dinner there was no question, no discussion, about what came next. They went into his bedroom together, and they made love through the night, with the lights out and the curtains drawn, creating their own, impenetrable world, apart from the past, oblivious to the future. As he felt her, tasted her, loved her, Garvin could sense her urgency, her demand—her need not just for physical pleasure, although that was there, but for him. All of him. Nothing held back. In the way she loved him, stroked him, responded to his caresses, he could feel her searching for a way to connect with him beyond the physical. As they came together, as she moaned with passion, he knew he wanted to give that part of him she was looking for, if only he knew what it was.

Toward dawn she came to him. She eased on top of him, slid herself onto him, so that he grew hard inside of her. She rose up, and he caught her breasts in his palms, stared up at her in the silvery light, her hair hanging down, her eyes lost in the shadows.

She smiled and moved her hips, making it impossible for him to think about anything but now, that moment, and her.

Michael Yuma took one look at Garvin and said, "Uh-oh."

Garvin winced. "Sorry. I don't mean to take my mood out on you. Look, you deserve a day off. Go on home."

Yuma grinned. "Think I'm going to let you run this place in the mood you're in? Man, one look at you, people'll duck for cover. You're bad for business, my friend."

Garvin started down the dock. It was a bright, clear, gorgeous Sunday morning, but his night with Annie Payne and the morning paper, with Sarah Linwood plastered on the front page of the city section in all her eccentricity, had taken their toll. His world was damned near spinning out of control. It was something he'd promised himself would never happen again.

Yuma clapped one hand on his shoulder, his dark eyes unusually serious. "Go on, Garvin. Go do what you have to do. I don't have anything pressing at home. I can hang in here another day."

"Look, Michael—"

"I'm keeping up with the talk, and I read the morning paper. You've got a lot on your mind. Now go on. Get out of here."

Garvin hesitated, but he knew Yuma was right. Trying to hold up his end, as preoccupied as he was, wouldn't help anyone. He gave his friend a curt nod. "Thanks, Yuma."

He shrugged off Garvin's gratitude. "Everyone else around here'll be thanking me, too."

As Garvin headed back up to his house, he found himself thinking about being out on the water with Annie Payne. She was the child of Maine seamen, the former director of a New England maritime museum. She would know the water. One day, he thought, then gritted his teeth. It was the first time he'd really considered the future in a long time. Maybe it was a positive sign, maybe it wasn't. But it was there, the thought of sailing with Annie Payne.

She and Otto had taken off in her rusting station wagon. As he picked up Otto's discarded two-by-four from the middle of his living room floor, Garvin understood that come what may between him and Annie Payne, his life up on his hillside had changed forever. The cease-fire he'd had with himself and his past —and his future—was over. He would never feel isolated or removed up here again, or even, he thought, at peace.

On his way out, Vic Denardo emerged from the shadows of a larch and sauntered out to the walkway. Garvin went still, taking in the man who for the past five years he'd believed had killed his wife and her grandfather. He looked remarkably unchanged, a few more lines at the corners of his eyes, an added crease in his forehead, but the lively dark eyes, the irreverent curve of his mouth, were the same. His amiability wasn't feigned. It was natural, even if he had committed premeditated murder.

"I didn't kill anyone," he said, coming toward Garvin.

He could feel the tension in his spine, could feel his hands curling into tight fists. Yet he remembered, too, in spite of everything, that he'd once considered Vic Denardo a friend, a man he could trust in the most elemental and basic of ways. He owed it to Haley, and maybe to himself, to think before he acted, to reserve judgment until all the facts were in. "If you didn't kill Thomas and Haley, Vic, who did?"

Denardo didn't answer.

"Sarah?"

"I don't know. Could be she set me up. She knew I was going to see her old man that night. But I haven't seen her since she took off. I've always figured it was a Linwood thing and I was just a handy outsider to blame it on." His dark eyes fell on Garvin. "For a while I wondered if it was you."

"What changed your mind?"

A grin started, died. "You're a little too eager to cut my balls off."

Garvin didn't smile back, didn't even try. "What do you want?"

"Take me to Sarah." He gazed up at the sky a moment, sucking in a deep breath; then he looked back at Garvin. "I read the piece in the paper. I know I could find her on my own. That's what she wants. But I want to go together, you and me. I was set up once. It's not happening again."

Garvin nodded. "Then let's go."

Chapter Fifteen

The moment Cynthia Linwood burst into her gallery, Annie knew she was in one of her snits. She marched right up to her desk and thumped it with her perfectly manicured nails. Not one hair was out of place. "How could you let Sarah do that interview?"

"It was her idea," Annie said calmly. "I have no control over her."

"You should have stopped her. That woman's determined to bring ruin to what's left of her family just because she didn't live the life she felt she deserved to live. I've no patience with her. She's a rich woman. It's not like she's from the projects."

"If she felt trapped in her life—"

Cynthia sneered, her way, Annie decided, of coping with fear. "She never had to lift a finger to feed herself. So far as I'm concerned, she's ungrateful. Thomas was never as rotten to her as she'd have everyone believe. Her own cowardice and snobbery held her back—and not forever, did it? She managed to do what she wanted to do in the end. Gambling, a sordid affair, now this outrageous high drama of her return home. In fact, Sarah *always* did what she wanted to do."

"You don't like her," Annie said.

Tears sprang to Cynthia's eyes, and some of the anger went out of her. "I don't know her well enough to like or dislike her. I suppose I sound meanspirited—"

"Angry, I'd say."

"I *am* angry. When he saw that article, John—" She took in a sharp breath, her anger bubbling just under the surface, mixing uneasily with her concern for her husband. "Seeing Sarah again has been a terrible strain on him. The article didn't help. She could have called, could have warned us. After he tried to see to her welfare—" She broke off, too agitated to go on.

"I could have warned you too. I'm sorry."

"It's not your fault. Maybe it's not anybody's fault." She dabbed at the corners of her eyes with her fingertips; Annie thought of slipping her a tissue but decided she'd better not.

Cynthia Linwood wasn't a woman who'd want attention called to her tears. "It comes as a surprise to people, but John and I really do love each other. And I'm very protective of him. He's gone through so much. It's been such an ordeal. He's finally come to the point where he can think about the present again, never mind the future. He's been so haunted by the past. I don't know if you can understand."

"I've never lost anyone to murder. Is there something you want me to do?"

Her shoulders slumped. "No, there's nothing. I just came in to yell at you and make myself feel better. We're all just going to have to learn to live with Sarah back in our lives. Have the police had any luck finding whoever broke into your apartment?"

Annie shook her head. Otto stirred under her feet at all the commotion, but he didn't get up, probably just as well, given his appearance.

Cynthia's mouth curved, the result not exactly a smile. "Maybe we'll be lucky this time, and it won't have anything to do with the rest of this mess."

"If I hear anything, I'll let you know."

"Yes. That would be nice." There was a trace of bitterness in her tone.

After Cynthia left, Otto got up and paced, fidgety and uncomfortable. Annie assumed either his head hurt or he'd picked up on her frustration. Before she could decide to call it quits and close up shop early, Zoe sent her part-timer over, as a favor, with instructions for Annie and Otto to go home, put their feet up, and bathe in lavender. Annie was only too glad to comply. Otto seemed likewise delighted, although she doubted lavender would do much for him.

Having come straight to her gallery from Belvedere, she had her car with her and headed straight up to her apartment. The idea was to drop Otto off and let him resume his recovery in peace, but he refused to get out of the car. Annie didn't know if he had bad memories of Friday night or just felt more at home in the back of her station wagon or if he was just being stubborn, but she didn't insist.

It was a bright, still, warm winter Sunday, and San Franciscans were out enjoying it. Pushing back a wave of envy, Annie drove up to Sarah's little cul-de-sac, Otto flopped out in the backseat. With no empty parking space, she turned around to head back down the hill and park on the street below, but as she passed Sarah's house, she saw that the front door was slightly ajar. Even for Sarah Linwood, that was odd.

Annie swung into an illegal space right in front of Sarah's doorstep and jumped out, not bothering with her keys or Otto, not caring if she was overreacting.

She pushed on the door. "Sarah? It's me, Annie."

No answer. She pushed the door open several more inches and peered inside.

"Sarah? Are you all right?"

The door struck Sarah's cane, which was lying on the floor. Annie felt a surge of panic, tried to stifle it, and thrust open the door, praying silently that Sarah had just mislaid her cane and had been in some artistic trance and just hadn't shut her door properly.

Her heart stopped the moment she crossed the threshold.

Sarah was crumpled up on the floor at the base of her easel. Root vegetables were scattered around her, her rickety table knocked on its side.

"*Sarah!*"

Annie lurched to her, dropped to her knees, expected blood, a weak pulse, death; she pushed back the image of Gran lying still, utterly lifeless, in her sterile hospital bed, of her mother, nothing but bones and yellowed skin. *I can't fall apart. I have to keep going.* Words then, words now.

Sarah lay on her side in a heap of cheap flowered smock and elastic-waist polyester pants. Had she simply worked to the point of exhaustion and fallen? Annie leaned over her in an attempt to see her face and check if she was breathing. So far, no blood. "Sarah…"

She moaned.

Alive. At least she was alive.

"Sarah, what happened? Can you talk? Can you move?"

"My head…"

Even as she croaked out the words, Annie saw the swelling at the base of Sarah's head under her left ear. No, she hadn't fallen. "Someone whacked you good," she said, trying to sound optimistic. Had Sarah been knocked unconscious? For how long? "I'll get ice. Then I need to call for help."

No answer, no movement.

Annie staggered to her feet, made it to the refrigerator, dumped out a tray of ice into the sink and collected a half-dozen cubes into one of Sarah's frayed, paint-stained dish towels. She was shaking, trying to keep tears and panic at bay, even as she kept talking. "I'm coming, Sarah. Gosh, this ice is cold. It'll help. You'll be fine." She kept her voice chatty, optimistic. "I know you will. You're too hardheaded to let a whack on the head slow you down for long."

Sarah hadn't moved. Annie placed the towel of ice on the swelling. Moaning, Sarah raised a gnarled hand and held the ice herself. "Thank you," she whispered.

"Just lie still. I'll call—"

"The painting."

Annie went still. "What?"

Wincing in pain, Sarah licked her purplish lips and just managed to speak. "Haley. Check…please. My bedroom."

"That can wait—"

Her free hand shot out and caught Annie's wrist in a vise grip. "Check," she said desperately, in spite of her weakness and pain. "*Please.*"

Not wanting to agitate her further, Annie got to her feet. Her legs were shaking, her stomach twisted into painful knots of fear and tension. The portrait of Haley Linwood MacCrae. The start of it all. Annie had been thinking about it that morning after reading the article on Sarah in the Sunday paper, where in a stark, single sentence, the reporter had stated that the painting had hung in the room where both Thomas Linwood and his granddaughter had been murdered. It wasn't news. It wasn't anything Annie or Garvin or Sarah or almost anyone else in San Francisco didn't know. But Annie had been unable to shake the sentence from her mind. She didn't know why.

She checked under Sarah's simple twin bed, in her near-empty closet. She checked every canvas leaned up against the wall.

The portrait of Haley Linwood was gone.

Annie went out into the main room and checked there, noticing only that Sarah's key chain had been taken apart on her little kitchen table, keys scattered. She returned to Sarah and knelt beside her, the ice still on the base of her neck. "The painting's gone, Sarah. But we can worry about that later, okay? Right now I need to call an ambulance. I don't think you should move until they get here."

"All right," she said weakly, tears dribbling down across the bridge of her nose.

"Sarah…"

"Go. Call. I'll be fine."

Annie had no choice. With no phone, she had to leave Sarah alone. She covered her with a pilled, brightly colored knitted afghan before starting out.

But before she finished the task, Garvin MacCrae and Vic Denardo burst through the door. Annie could see them sizing up the situation even as Garvin grabbed her by the elbows. His eyes were dark pits, focused, determined, any fear buried deep. "What happened?"

"I don't know. I found Sarah like this. She was hit on the head —someone stole the portrait of Haley."

"You're all right?"

Now seeing the spurt of fear in his eyes, she nodded. "I've got to call an ambulance."

"Use the phone in my car. Door's unlocked."

Vic Denardo hung back, staring at the crumpled heap that was Sarah Linwood. "I didn't…I didn't touch her."

Garvin glared back at him. "I'm not flinging accusations."

"It wasn't me. I would never hurt her."

Ignoring him, Garvin headed for Sarah. Annie darted outside and climbed into the front seat of Garvin's car, which was parked directly behind hers, blocking another car in the cul-de-sac. As she dialed, she saw Vic Denardo race outside and assumed he was going to help her. His eyes connected with hers for an instant, then he jumped into her car.

Annie heard the dispatcher come on the line and knew she couldn't go after Denardo, not when Sarah needed an ambulance.

He started the engine, went forward, stalled, started it up again, and screeched out into the street. Annie gave the dispatcher the necessary information, even as she watched her car buck down the steep, curving hill, saw Garvin burst outside and lunge down the hill after Vic Denardo. He gave up after a few yards and stomped up to his car, cursing, kicking a loose pebble.

Annie slid out of his car. "The police and ambulance are on their way."

"That bastard Denardo—damn him, I was just beginning to believe he was innocent."

"I wouldn't worry too much."

"Why the hell not?"

She gave him a faltering smile. "Otto's in the car with him."

Garvin left Annie to wait for the police and ambulance and headed down the hill after Vic Denardo. He hadn't gone ten blocks when he spotted Annie's station wagon rammed up against a telephone pole. Its front end was slightly damaged, and the small crowd that had gathered stood back. As he climbed out of his car, Garvin could see why: Otto was in the front seat with Denardo. He headed over and opened up the driver's door.

"Get this goddamned dog off me," Denardo yelled. Otto had his front paws on his lap and his massive, half-shaved head shoved up against Vic's chest. The big, ugly dog's mouth was open, his tongue wagging, looking fierce enough to scare anybody. Denardo's eyes were wild as he looked around at Garvin. "I hate dogs. Get him off me, goddammit!"

"He might not listen to me."

"Well, *try*, for chrissake!"

"Otto," Garvin said. "Come on, fella. I'll take over now."

The big dog stared up at him with his huge brown eyes. His forehead was wrinkled, giving him a slightly comical look.

"His paws are digging into me," Denardo complained.

"Serves you right. Where the hell'd you think you were going?"

Denardo glanced up at him, his neck stretched back as far as he could get it from Otto's open mouth. "Dog breath. Jesus."

"Vic."

"Okay, okay. Did you see the keys on the table?"

Garvin frowned. "Yes."

"They'd been taken off Sarah's key ring. She couldn't do that, not with her hands."

Vic paused, eyeing Otto. "Go on," Garvin said.

"So Sarah's key to the Linwood house is missing. I remember it, okay? She gave it to me one day to copy, but it's unusual, tough to do."

"Why did she want you to have a copy?"

He licked his lips nervously, Otto showing no sign of backing off. "She wanted me to sneak into her room one night. Thought it'd be—you know, sexy, dangerous, with her father in the same house."

Garvin clenched his fists. "Then that means you could come and go at will. Vic, this isn't helping your cause—"

"I gave it back to her when she got nuts about paying me back the money. Threw it right in her face. Jesus, MacCrae—will you tell the goddamn dog to sit or something?"

"Tell me about the missing key, Vic."

"I didn't take it. I didn't beat the shit out of Sarah. Go ahead, search me. You won't find any key."

"So you're saying whoever assaulted Sarah and stole the painting has it."

He tried stretching his neck back from Otto a fraction more. "Ah-huh."

"Why?"

"Think about it."

Garvin bit off a curse. "This isn't the time for twenty questions, Vic. If you've got something to say—" But he stopped, a thought striking him. He went still. He didn't react. He couldn't. If he did, he wouldn't be able to function. "Whoever stole the painting is trying to set you up again."

"Bastard left the keys out on purpose. Knew I'd see the Linwood key was missing and go to the house."

"But it's been sold—"

"Nah, nah, a buyer's been found, but the paper-work still hasn't been done. It's poetic, you know? Me going back to the scene of the crime. Then I get there, he kills me, blames everything on me. The painting, Sarah, the two murders."

"But you ran instead," Garvin said.

Vic gave a small, tight shake of the head, not enough to spook Otto. "Not this time. I was heading to the Linwood house. I wasn't planning on letting this fuck get away with framing me. Not again."

Garvin inhaled deeply, barely able to think. "Haley…"

"She knew who it was. That's why she went back to the house."

"But why? She knew her grandfather had been brutally murdered—"

Vic's expression softened. "That was Haley, MacCrae. If she knew the killer, understood his motives, she'd think she could reason with him, get him to turn himself in. That's the way she operated. She never did believe people did bad things for bad reasons."

That was true, Garvin thought, remembering the woman who had been his wife. She would have had the courage—and the blindness—to arrange to meet someone she knew was a killer. She would have believed enough in her own goodness, her own invulnerability, to confront a killer with the truth. If the killer was a friend, she would put a positive spin on his motives. *You weren't in your right mind. You were provoked. It was self-defense.* That was Haley Linwood MacCrae, a woman whose optimism was untempered by the harsh realities of life.

Garvin reached inside the car and grabbed Otto's collar. "I'll hold him while you slip out. If you try and steal my car, Denardo, I'll let Otto have you."

Denardo didn't need to be told twice. In a half second he was out of the station wagon and on his feet. Otto twisted out of Garvin's grip and loped after Denardo, not letting him out of his sight. "It's okay, poochie. I ain't going anywhere."

Leaving Annie's station wagon rammed up against the telephone pole and the crowd looking on, mystified, they all got into Garvin's car. Otto in back, Garvin and Vic Denardo up front.

"Christ," Vic said, "I smell like dog slobber."

Garvin didn't reply.

When they got back to Sarah's house, the police and an ambulance had arrived. Two paramedics were wheeling Sarah out on a stretcher.

"She's not here," Vic said.

He meant Annie. Garvin gave a curt nod. If Annie were there, she'd be at Sarah's side.

"She must have seen the keys too," Vic said.

"How the hell would she recognize the key to the Linwood house?"

"How should I know? Maybe Sarah showed it to her. Like I said, it's unusual." He shuddered. "This thing's creepy."

Garvin had already swung the car around and was heading down the hill before the police could recognize them and ask questions. Annie didn't have a car. She would have had to take a cab or rely on public transportation. Either way, she wouldn't have that much of a head start.

"What're you thinking?" Vic asked worriedly beside him.

Garvin kept his eyes on the road. "I'm thinking we're playing right into this bastard's hands. If he touches Annie—"

"He won't. We'll get there in time, MacCrae. She can't be that far ahead of us." Vic settled back in the leather seat but didn't look comfortable. "It could be a woman, you know."

Gripping the wheel so hard his knuckles turned white, Garvin shook his head. He hadn't dug deep enough. Five years ago, when he'd checked into Sarah's finances just as Haley had and had found nothing, he'd assumed there'd been nothing.

He hadn't guessed that somebody knowledgeable and clever— somebody with everything at stake—had been there first, covering up his tracks.

"No. It's a man."

Annie stood at the front gate of the Linwood house on Pacific Heights. She'd fled Sarah's house just as the police were screaming up the hill, leaving Sarah with instructions to have them send someone over to the Linwood house.

Convinced that Vic Denardo would already be there with her car and Otto, Annie had headed to Pacific Heights herself. She could understand Denardo's reasoning. He would think he had no choice. If he didn't get to the Linwood house in time, the real killer would have a chance to plant evidence against Vic and get out before anyone was the wiser.

But if he did get there in time, he ran the risk of playing into the real killer's hands.

The killer wanted Vic Denardo there, Annie thought. That was why he'd deliberately left Sarah's keys on the table. He wanted Vic Denardo to come to him at the Linwood house. He wanted to kill him and finally close the Linwood murder case.

Linwood murderer killed in self-defense after he returns to the scene of the crime.

But the real murderer hadn't counted on Annie recognizing the distinctive key too, remembering it from that afternoon when Sarah had come back from her visit to the house where she'd lived most of her life.

Even as she'd raced down the steps and found a cab, Annie had known she was taking a huge chance. But she couldn't not act. Denardo had a head start on her. By the time she explained everything to the police, convinced them that a simple missing key might mean murder, an innocent man could be killed.

When she arrived at the Linwood house, however, there was no sign of Vic Denardo, Otto, or her car.

"This is nuts," she muttered under her breath.

What if, in the rush of adrenaline, she'd gotten it all wrong? The missing key meant nothing, the missing painting had nothing to do with the murders of Thomas Linwood and Haley Linwood MacCrae.

Chastened, she headed up the front walk and mounted the front steps, glancing back at the street. Still no Denardo, no Otto, no car. No Garvin. No sign of any killer.

Even from the outside, the enormous house felt empty. Annie peered into a panel window. Nobody was there, she thought. She'd just gotten caught up in Sarah's drama. Finding her semiconscious had rattled her.

The front door opened, and Annie jumped back, so startled she almost fell down the steps.

Ethan Conninger gazed out at her from the shadow of the heavy door. "Well. Annie Payne. I wasn't expecting you. I suppose that was naive on my part, given your activities this past week." The easy manner was there, but the handsome dark eyes behind the glasses had a wild look to them. He smiled, opened the door wider. "Do come in."

Annie tried to smile back. "Oh, it's you, Ethan. I thought—I'm looking for Vic Denardo. He stole my car. I think he just assaulted Sarah Linwood."

"Really? Now why would he come here?"

She thought fast and decided to lie, pretend she believed Vic Denardo was the real killer. "He stole Sarah's key—"

"Annie. Don't lie to me. People always think they can lie to me. That I won't notice. That I don't notice anything. Well, sweet cheeks, I do. I notice everything." He opened the door wider. He had on jeans today, a red cashmere sweater, boat shoes. He sniffed. "It's been a hellishly long five years."

"Ethan—"

"Come inside, Annie. We'll wait for Vic Denardo together."

Her stomach churned, and she thought she might be sick.

Ethan Conninger studied her a moment and said matter-of-factly, "Annie, let me be perfectly clear here. I'm at the end of my rope. I've been playing the carefree yuppie for five years while waiting for Vic Denardo and Sarah Linwood to show up, compare notes, and realize what really happened. All week I've done all I could to keep them apart."

"Including breaking into my apartment and beating up my dog."

"Including that, yes. Don't doubt me, Annie Payne, and don't give me any trouble. If I must, I'll shoot you right here on the doorstep and drag your corpse inside."

Annie's nausea worsened, but she struggled to remain coherent. "Ethan, Sarah is telling the police everything. They'll be here any minute—"

"So the bitch lived, did she? Well, it doesn't matter. She didn't see me. I suppose I should have made sure she was dead, but I knew you and my friend Garvin would ride in on your white horses at any moment." He sniffled, sudden tears in his eyes. "Christ, what a mess. If only people had listened to reason."

"I'm willing to listen—"

"It doesn't matter now," he said, rallying. He squared his shoulders and produced a small, lethal-looking black gun.

"Thomas, Haley—they left me no choice. It was them or me. I chose me. There's no turning back the clock. Now, Annie. Do come in."

She could sense his strain, just how close he was to slipping off the edge. She had no reason to doubt him. He would kill her on the Linwood doorstep, and he'd drag her body inside.

In trying to keep Vic Denardo from falling into a trap, she realized, she'd fallen into one herself.

Feeling steadier than she would have ever imagined, she entered the huge house. Her footsteps echoed on the hardwood floor. There was none of the festiveness of last Saturday, no hum of excited buyers, no guards, no discreet auctioneers.

No Garvin MacCrae, she thought.

Ethan made her go in front of him, his gun leveled at her back. He nudged her down the main hall toward the ballroom, having her veer off into an elegant, rectangular room with ornate wood-working, built-in shelves, and an enormous marble fireplace. It was bare except for Sarah Linwood's portrait of her niece at sixteen. It was leaned up against a wall, Haley smiling out at them as if she had nothing to fear.

"She was even more beautiful as she got older," Ethan said.

Annie looked around at him. "I've no doubt she was."

He had tears in his eyes. "She left me no choice. Christ. I couldn't do what she asked. She thought—" He cleared his throat, blinked back tears. "She thought if she was the one who asked me to do the right thing, I would do it. She knew I admired her, respected her. She was the one Linwood I never wanted to hurt."

"She knew you'd killed her grandfather," Annie said.

"Oh, yes. She knew. She'd decided to look into Sarah's finances in order to help her with her gambling problem. She discovered a mistake I'd made."

"How big a mistake?"

"Huge. I lost millions in a scheme I invested in without her grandfather's knowledge. It wasn't easy to do. I suppose in my own way I was as addicted to gambling as Sarah was. I compound-ed the first mistake by trying to cover it up, but with time, I knew I could make up for it. A few more years and no one would have been the wiser."

"You couldn't just 'fess up?" Annie asked, hoping to keep him talking and give the police, Garvin, Vic Denardo—anyone—a chance to get there.

He smiled thinly. "To Thomas Linwood? Not a chance. He wasn't a man to tolerate incompetence in anyone, from the kitchen maid to his own children, and hardly from a trusted financial adviser."

"But Haley—"

"She managed to unravel everything. She was always smarter than Garvin gave her credit for. And so damned sincere. She insisted on telling her grandfather. She wouldn't believe he'd fire me."

"Did he?"

"Of course. There was no reasoning with the man. That's why I didn't tell him about the mistake in the first place. I knew I'd be out the door, discredited." He gave Annie a thin smile. "I like my life."

"So he fired you," Annie said, "and you…" She trailed off, not wanting to complete the thought.

He glanced at the gun in his hand. "I knew what was up the moment he asked me to meet him here. I brought my gun in case he didn't listen to reason and insisted on ruining my reputation, making it impossible for me to work again, as well as throwing me out of a cushy job. But Thomas Linwood—well, he didn't believe a mere bullet could harm him. He certainly didn't believe I, an underling, would shoot him."

"And Haley believed it was an accident?"

Ethan narrowed his eyes on her. "It was an accident."

"He was shot through the heart—"

"Coincidence," he said, as if he believed it.

Annie swallowed, her throat dry and tight.

"Haley had me meet her here, in this room." He looked around, as if picturing that night five years ago. "She never believed I would hurt her. She appealed to my sense of honor. She said she believed me that I'd killed her grandfather in the heat of the moment. She said she knew I couldn't let an innocent man take the blame for something I'd done. She didn't understand that I'd *planned* it that way, in case Thomas met my lowest expectations—which he did. I knew Vic was there that night. Why the hell do you think I brought along a silencer?"

"You're a smart man," Annie said carefully.

"That's right. I am. One *fucking* mistake shouldn't have ruined me, but Thomas would have seen to it that it did. He was that big a bastard." He took a breath, as if making an effort to calm himself. "Haley wanted me to come forward and tell the authorities everything. If I didn't, she said, she would. Jesus! I tried to reason with her. I gave her a chance." The tears, Annie noted, were gone. "Then I did what I had to do."

Annie shuddered and looked around the opulent library, imagining the horror Haley Linwood must have felt when she'd realized that Ethan Conninger would commit cold-blooded murder to keep the life he had.

"She saw everything," he said quietly, almost eerily.

Annie frowned, then saw that he'd turned his attention to Sarah's portrait of Haley.

"I thought she'd been destroyed." He stared at the strawberry-haired girl whose soul Sarah Linwood had seemed to capture on the canvas. "I remember that night afterwards, thinking I should take her with me. But I didn't dare. Then when she turned up at the auction—" He shifted back to Annie. "I knew it was her way of trying to get the truth about me out."

"Ethan, it's a painting—"

"You didn't know Haley."

Annie licked her lips. "No, I didn't."

"She's watching us now, you know." He spoke matter-of-factly, calmly. "I know it sounds weird, but trust me, she's watching us."

"Why would she be watching us?"

"She's waiting for me to do the right thing. That's why I came back here. It's what she would have wanted me to do."

Remaining very still, Annie could feel her knees weakening, her stomach lurching. Ethan Conninger was intelligent, brutal, and guilt-ridden, spooked by the thought of Haley Linwood watching him, judging him, from the canvas of an amateurish painting. But in a way, Annie could understand. In his own way, Ethan was just responding to the power of Sarah's vision. Even before she'd developed her talent, it was there.

"Christ," he breathed, "you can't imagine what I've been through."

She wasn't sure if he was addressing her or the sixteen-year-old Haley in the painting. "No," she said in a low voice, "I don't think anyone can imagine."

His eyes focused on her, suddenly hard, alert, very much in the present and in control. He had the gun leveled at her. "I'm going to give the police their man. That's the right thing to do."

"But you're not it," Annie said.

"You're no dummy, Annie Payne. Trust me, Vic Denardo knows the score. He'll be here. I'll kill him, I'll kill you, and I'll take the credit for stopping a murderer, just not quite in time."

"The way I figure it," Vic Denardo was saying as he and Garvin drove up to Pacific Heights, "Haley must have tried to appeal to reason where there was no reason."

Garvin glanced over at him. "It's a scary thought, Denardo, you and me being on the same wavelength."

"Yeah. Seeing how you been after my ass for five years, it is."

Garvin pulled into an illegal space in front of the Linwood house and leaped out. Otto crawled over the front seat, over Vic, and beat him out the passenger door. Vic cursed about dog hair, dog slobber, dog asses in his face. It was his way, Garvin realized, of keeping fear at bay. "Why the hell couldn't Sarah have picked a woman with a nice little Pekingese or something? No. She goes for the one with the frigging rottweiler. Hey—*hey, come back here!*"

But Otto had already bounded up the walk and over the fence and was charging across the manicured lawn to the Linwood front entrance.

"Jesus," Vic breathed. "He looks like a demon straight out of hell."

Garvin felt a stab of fear. "Yes, he does."

Vic shot him a look. "Annie?"

"He must have picked up her scent. Let's go."

They ran. Halfway up the walk, Vic put a hand on Garvin's arm. "Maybe we shouldn't go in through the front. Bastard could be waiting for us."

Garvin nodded. "All right. We'll go in through the back." He glanced at the older man. "You up for this?"

"I'm an innocent man, MacCrae. All I ever did was fall for an heiress and teach her how to play poker, get her some money when she needed it. I may be five years late, but I'm willing to put it on the line to clear my name." He gave him a weak grin. "And I kinda like this Annie Payne character. You?"

"Yeah," Garvin said, his throat constricted, "me too."

They cut down the narrow yard to the back of the house.

Garvin approached the back door, Denardo on his heels. They'd lost Otto. "I don't have a key."

"I do," Vic said.

"I'm not even going to ask."

Denardo produced a set of keys, and thirty seconds later they were in. Wanting to keep noise to a minimum, Garvin deliberately left the door open. The rear entrance came in at the basement level, lower down on the hill, allowing for the panoramic view from the ballroom. He knew the way to the stairs, but Vic wriggled ahead of him, undaunted by the dark, the potential for wrong turns. Obviously, he'd been this way before. Vic Denardo and Sarah Linwood had carried on their affair right under her father's nose.

They took the stairs up to the main floor carefully, as quickly as they could without sounding like a stampede. The stairs let out in the butler's pantry. Staying close to the wall, they slipped down the hall.

Up ahead, Garvin could hear voices from the library. Neither he nor Vic had a weapon. Garvin didn't care. He would do what he had to do. And maybe he was getting ahead of himself. Maybe Annie wasn't there. Maybe it was just the new owners talking about wallpaper.

He and Vic made as little noise as possible as they stayed close to the wall and came up on the library door.

Garvin recognized Ethan Conninger's voice. His heart sank. If only Haley had come to him, told him the results of her investigation into Sarah's finances, but she'd only dropped hints. She wanted to know the depth of her gambling problem and confront her with the facts. But she'd found something she hadn't been looking for. Preoccupied and troubled, Haley had only said she needed more information before she could tell her husband everything.

She'd never gotten the chance.

"I'm a good shot," Ethan said from the library. "You won't suffer."

"What you are," Annie said, "is a coward who's too scared to face himself in the mirror. You just can't admit it. You want to think of yourself as the carefree playboy type, the urban sophisticate, the ultimate yuppie, but you're just a miserable chickenshit."

Eyebrows raised, Vic looked around at Garvin, who grimaced at her impolitic words. But Annie Payne was a Mainer who'd stood on the edge of the abyss before, and damned if she was going down without a fight.

Garvin shifted forward and peered around the door frame. Ethan had his back to the door, but Garvin could see the gun in his right hand, leveled at Annie. She looked remarkably unafraid for a woman in her position. But that was Annie Payne. An optimist in spite of what she'd seen of life's harsh realities. She wasn't naive or blind, only determined to carry on, no matter what.

"You know," Vic whispered against Garvin's back, "I wouldn't call somebody with a gun a chickenshit."

Garvin glared him into silence.

There was a sound behind them. Vic frowned. "What was that?"

"Hell," Garvin said under his breath, but he was already too late.

Out of nowhere—with no finesse or hesitation— Otto streaked past them in a blur of black fur and muscle. He charged into the library, not growling, not barking, just moving. His rottweiler genes had taken over.

"Holy shit," Vic breathed.

He and Garvin surged into the library together, but Otto was already pouncing on Ethan, sending him sprawling onto the floor, gun flying, Ethan screaming. Otto landed on him with the force of his powerful one-hundred-and-twenty-pound body.

Annie grabbed up the gun even as Garvin got to her, grabbed her, held her. She fell against his chest. She was shaken, he saw, but undaunted.

Otto kept a terrified Ethan pinned under him while Vic sauntered around them both. "I knew this dog'd come in handy," he said proudly. "Right, Otto? You and me, we're pals. You got the fuck. You got 'im."

But Vic's knees were shaking, tears streaming down his cheeks.

"Payback time," Garvin said, holding Annie close, the terror subsiding. He hadn't lost her. "You rescued Otto. Now Otto's rescued Annie."

"I didn't know he had it in him," she said. "He's always been such a sweet dog."

Vic snorted. "Sweet? Yeah, kid, he's sweet all right. He must've remembered our friend Ethan from the other night at your apartment." Vic leaned forward and raised his voice as if somehow Ethan's hearing had been damaged. "When you coldcocked Otto. You knew he'd be there, and you were ready for him. Remember? Big mistake, you rat fuck. Never piss off a rottweiler."

Ethan moaned but didn't move a muscle. "Get him off me!"

A siren sounded outside on the street. Vic looked satisfied. "Sarah must have persuaded the police she wasn't a lunatic. Or someone saw a rottweiler loose in the neighborhood."

Annie sank more of her weight against Garvin, just a little of the tension going out of her body. "It's over," she said hoarsely. She turned her slate eyes up to him. "You have your killer."

"Yes."

He could feel the peace and the horror of knowing the truth settling over him, but at the same time, all he could think about was Annie and how close he'd come to losing her. He glanced at the stunning portrait Sarah had done of his wife. Haley had been a good woman, and the world had lost her too soon. But Annie was his present and his future, even if right now she couldn't trust him to know it.

Chapter Sixteen

The pots of flowers and the courtyard outside Annie's Gallery had never looked so beautiful, so inviting as the evening of her first opening. The invitations had gone out, the publicity was widespread, and she was sure—beyond sure—that Sarah Linwood was about to be declared a major new American artist.

Annie surveyed her gallery. She couldn't have been happier. She'd tied a red bow around Otto's neck for the occasion and had bought a new dress to wear with Gran's crewelwork shawl. Zoe Summer had provided appropriate scents. Vic Denardo had rented a tuxedo. Sarah Linwood had found a new thrift store and purchased a sedate black silk dress she was convinced had once belonged to her. She wore it with a pair of new white Keds and socks that seemed to match.

Cynthia Linwood, who'd promised she wouldn't meddle but wanted everything to be perfect, had helped Annie choose a caterer and hone a guest list. Everyone in San Francisco, she said, wanted to be there. Annie had no reason to doubt her.

An hour before the seven o'clock start of the opening, only Garvin MacCrae was missing. Even Michael Yuma and every employee of the marina, including a huge man named Beau, tattoos on his massive arms, had arrived for an impromptu preopening get-together.

"Think he won't show?" Vic asked, already into the champagne.

"Of course he'll show."

It wasn't just bluster. Annie *knew*. In the weeks since the police had dragged off Ethan Conninger, she had come to know, under-stand, and trust Garvin—to connect with him—in a way she never had with anyone else before, not even Gran. It hadn't been any one thing, any one moment. They'd gone sailing together, they'd spent a weekend driving through wine country, they'd worked on a business plan for her gallery. They'd made love often, everywhere, and they'd taken Otto on long runs on the beach. And each day they were together, Annie found herself backing off from her conviction that for her, life had to be a here-today-gone-tomorrow proposition.

He swept into the gallery just minutes before seven, and before he could spot her, Annie watched him greet John and Cynthia Linwood, kiss Sarah on the cheek, clap a hand on Vic's shoulder. He complimented Otto on his bow, and he thanked Michael Yuma and the guys from the marina for showing up. There was none of the sense of isolation, of holding life at arm's length, that had been there weeks ago at the Linwood auction.

He spotted Annie finally, swept up a glass of champagne, and grinned. Again, as always, Annie was stunned by her reaction to him. It would be that way, she knew, forever. He wore a tuxedo, but that didn't matter. She was just as taken aback by him when he wore torn jeans and threw two-by-fours for Otto down at the marina.

"Sorry I'm late," he said.

"That's okay. I knew you'd be here."

He squeezed her hand. "I'm glad you knew."

She smiled. "Where've you been?"

"Walking the streets."

She raised her eyebrows at him. "Why? Is there something wrong? Garvin, I know tonight can't be easy for you. People are going to think about your connection to the Linwoods. Please don't feel obligated to be here if—"

"Whoa, don't get ahead of yourself, Annie. Tonight will be poignant, yes. But I was walking the streets thinking about tomorrow."

Her heart was racing, and it had nothing to do with the approaching opening. It was knowing this infuriating man. Loving him. "Tomorrow," she said.

He nodded and withdrew something from his pocket. When he held it up, she saw that it was a ring.

"It's nothing fancy," he said, "but it was my great-grandmother's, and I thought—well, I thought you might like it better than a big old diamond."

"Garvin…"

"Marry me, Annie Payne. Tomorrow, the next day, any day you want." He smiled, slipping the ring on her finger as her eyes filled with tears. "I love you, Annie, and I want to be with you."

She sniffled and glanced back at Gran's painting, could see the two of them out on the front porch watching the dawn come and listening to the tide and the gulls, and suddenly she could see her and Garvin and Otto and toddlers. Babies, she thought, so overcome at the thought of her future, she almost couldn't get the words out. "I love you too. Sometimes I think I have since I spotted you bidding against me in that ballroom."

"And you'll marry me?"

She smiled, feeling the weight of the beautiful, simple ring on her finger. "I'll marry you, Garvin MacCrae."

He touched one finger to a tear on her cheek and smiled with such tenderness she wanted to cry. "I'll live with you here in San Francisco or out in Marin or back home in Maine. Wherever you want, Annie."

"Where doesn't matter, Garvin. Here, Maine, Belvedere, some shack in the hills." She took his champagne from his hand, set it down, and, ignoring the first wave of critics and the first stunned oohs and aahs over Sarah Linwood's work, she kissed him lightly and whispered, "Wherever I'm with you I am home."